Jury 25

A MILE OR TWO FROM
MY FIRST LOVE

~~Amanda Cowley~~

Amanda x

Darling Lou –
You are a darling!
twice over –
Big love
Amanda x

YOUCAXTON
PUBLICATIONS

978-1-915972-81-1
Published by YouCaxton Publications 2025

YouCaxton Publications
www.youcaxton.co.uk

For my darling mum,
Patricia Reine (Wren).
Always in my heart.

In memory of
Gladys & Wilfrid Waller
(Florence & Walter Walker).
Forever grateful.

ENDORSEMENTS

Amanda Cowley's first novel is an astonishing look at family life in all its rawness. Taking us on a journey that spans decades the reader has a bird's eye perspective on how misunderstandings happen as events are interpreted by family members. This book will surprise and encourage more understanding of our own family dynamics.

Killy John, Co-Director of Philo Trust
Podcasts 'Heroes of The Faith' with J. John

This is a moving and heart-breaking story of loss, recovery and redemption. The characters are flawed and human and utterly believable and the story weaves past and present into a narrative that will keep you guessing till the end. A profoundly satisfying read.

Maggie Hamand, Creative Writing for Dummies (Amazon)
Resurrection of The Body (Arcadia Books) Virgin & Child
(Barbican Press)

I have known Amanda for more than 25 years and have watched with admiration her remarkable journey of faith alongside her husband, Paul. She is an artist, writer and brave cancer survivor. This book, based on her grandfather's life is tragic but deeply moving.

Pippa Gumbel. NIV Bible in One Year with Commentary
by Nicky and Pippa Gumbel (Hodder & Stoughton)

Amanda has managed to deliver a legacy piece for 'such a time as this'. Through her masterful efforts in memorializing a deeply sincere and honest retelling of her family's prodigal son we have each been given an immense privilege in meeting God's patient goodness page after page. It's the loud found in the quiet, unassuming stories of humanity that I am convinced God loves to elevate and captivate us. Amanda makes us feel known and seen by God, while reminding us that we are each allowed our own personal journey in Christ.

Katherine Warnock, Vice President, Original Content for The Chosen (TV Series)

A gripping tale set across a few continents of how grief, caused by a family tragedy, deeply affects Henry and his daughter, Wren. The pain causes ripples down the generations before eventually faith and hope prevail.

Kate Chorley, retired Commercial Solicitor K. L. Chorley LLB

In many ways, A Mile or Two from My First Love, is a story of regret. However, the beauty in the complexity of the characters, the vulnerability within the friendships and the redemptive power of God at work throughout makes it thoughtful rather than sombre. It's a cautionary tale about how relationships are compromised when we assume to understand how others are thinking or feeling but it also shows how powerful loving curiosity can bring both reconciliation and healing.

Jo Rice, Co-Founder of RESURGO. ICF Professional Certified Coach (PCC)

Amanda's book weaves a tapestry of human emotion and spirituality, presenting a narrative that is both deeply personal to the characters and universally resonant. This novel explores the profound impact that life's events have on the faith of its characters and their individual journeys with God. It is a compelling read that invites reflection on faith, resilience, and the search for meaning in the face of life's uncertainties.

Julia Strachan - World Record Atlantic Rower, Anti Slavery Campaigner and Author of Row for Freedom: Crossing an Ocean in Search of Hope.

PART ONE

We are all visitors to this time, this place.
We are just passing through.
Our purpose here is to observe, to learn,
to grow, to love... and then we return home.

Australian Aboriginal saying

1. HENRY

Wednesday 3 January 1990

A few days ago, I arrived at a care home, on the Sunshine Coast, to spend my last days. It's as good a place as any. But most of the people working here have no understanding of how to treat the elderly.

Everything is disposable, including me.

I hope someone will get to read my memoirs. I seem to have been writing them for decades. To what purpose, I have no idea.

I have been in Australia for the past four years and before that I was living in Spain. I would rather be at home in England but unfortunately the great British weather causes havoc with my arthritis and I end up wheelchair bound. I need the warmth for my legs and Australia's climate is generally good for my old bones. It can be tiresome dealing with extremes; summer heat, flash floods and intense forest fires. The birds and the insects are fascinating unless you have a fear of spiders – the large ones, the size of a fist, appear unnatural but they are safe – the small ones are deceptively nasty.

The food is good. Or rather, it was good when Vivien prepared fresh and interesting delights for us at home. In the care home, if three days are anything to go by, it is far from satisfactory.

The rooms in the care home are monastic, and Room 7 is no exception.

Painted in magnolia, it comprises of; a slim pine wardrobe containing two suits and a few of my favourite shirts, a chest of drawers on which my old typewriter is displayed when not in use, a cabinet next to a bed with an essential notebook and sharpened pencil, a radio, and a small jug of water.

The floor is dull laminate.

The wall facing the bed intimates the presence of a painting with its faint rectangular dust line, a seascape I had removed the day I arrived.

My days are long.

There is only so much you can do with a newspaper. I set aside two hours to read the articles, do the crosswords, then toss it in the bin.

I struggle to get dressed in the morning. Vivien would certainly be losing her temper with me. 'Stop fussing,' she would say, 'please make my life bearable!'

It is quite something to have one's wife only want her life to be 'bearable' when so much intimacy and affection has been enjoyed over so many years together. Twenty years my junior, she is fighting fit and often busy with activities. Scrabble on Tuesdays, Women's Institute on Wednesdays, Bridge on Thursdays. She has the occasional migraine which keeps her in bed for forty-eight hours. I feel inadequate because it wasn't that long ago that I would have taken a flannel and dabbed her brow and made her toast and tea. Not anymore.

I could weep.

I often do.

I miss my daughter, terribly, and I often dream about her. I believe there is something I need to say to her but I'm really not sure what it is. When I ask Vivien what I should do, she is dismissive. She is jealous of Wren, that is obvious.

Where has my life gone?

I was young not long ago and now I am old.

I contemplate letting go of my life and I am scared. The only freedom I can imagine is that I will be released from this body. At present, I feel like the giant in Gulliver's Travels, who after being shipwrecked on the island of Lilliput is pegged to the ground by thousands of tiny people.

The day I arrived, I wrote a short letter to my daughter who is living in Sussex. It was hollow, and I found myself blushing when I handed it to the orderly to post, *foolish old man,* he must have thought.

Opposite the care home is another 60s bleak construction of brown brick, a convent, with an equally uninspiring clock tower. The nuns visit the residents of the care home by rota. Apparently, Sister Constance will visit me on Tuesday. I have been informed she is a 'mature and experienced' nun in her mid-sixties.

Now the glamour and excitement of my life has been extinguished, I have a hope that she will find something in me to rekindle.

2. SISTER CONSTANCE

Wednesday 3 January 1990

This will be my fortieth year of keeping a journal. I started the same year I joined the convent. I am astounded. Where has the time gone? My fellow nuns made a cake for my anniversary. A carrot cake, my favourite.

It is the height of summer.

The sun burns with the intensity of a modern fan oven.

On the way back to my room I am greeted by several of the sisters congratulating me again while my lungs fill with the distinct fragrance of eucalyptus and pine. Overcome by heat, I close the door and remove my habit, letting it slump to the floor. I take off my veil. My hair, now mostly grey and unmanageable, springs out. With no air conditioning I make do with a cold flannel and a small electric fan. I begin to cool down.

Looking around my room I am reminded of the past.

My favourite painting by the Aboriginal artist and activist Mr Tjungurrayi is a maze of ordered colour, a blaze of oranges and reds. I came across him when I went on my walkabout in my twenties from Perth to Balgo in the Northern territories. He is beginning to get some recognition and I am proud to own one. I know, as a nun, I have renounced the material world, but art is beyond the material. It traverses the spiritual and is an expression of God's creation. That's my excuse anyway.

I also love the print of Holman Hunt's *Light of The World* displayed above the dressing table. It was purchased on a trip to London because I had been transfixed by the painting in St Paul's Cathedral: Christ carrying a lamp and knocking on a door overgrown with briars.

On my bedside cabinet, next to my single bed, are two picture frames, the smallest of which contains a faded snapshot of my mother, her dark face rendered almost featureless by the years of touching it before it was framed. Now it is a black hole. One I have fallen through on many nights.

In the larger frame is a copy of *The Sacred Heart of Jesus*, carefully ripped from a magazine. Sometimes in the night, I put it upon my chest not caring that the hard corners of the frame dig into my breasts. The red heart of Jesus, with its crown of thorns and yellow flames of the Holy Spirit bring comfort, enabling me to drift back to sleep with my Saviour sleeping safely in my arms. I am grateful to St. Margaret Mary Alacoque, the seventeenth century French nun, who, after a night of partying had a vision of Christ opening His chest and His heart to her. She was the same age I was when I became a nun, twenty-four. And, like me, it took many more years for her to be accepted after suffering ridicule at the hands of the local people.

She is a sister to me.

Her experience so close to my own, her devotion, far superior.

§

At the care home, we have a new resident, Henry Walker. Apparently, he is a bit surly. I will go and introduce myself to him next week and see if I can be of any help.

3. WREN

Friday 5 January 1990

I shall turn fifty this year. Half a century. A milestone.

Many people never make it to fifty. Some die in their cradle and others in the prime of youth.

I shall not complain about my age.

I will celebrate it.

I have decided to keep a diary this year and write down significant events so I will start by saying that I have just received a short letter from my father who is living on the Sunshine Coast.

I am very impressed with the postal service, considering it was only sent five days ago. He wrote to tell me that he has moved to Beechmont Retirement Home, *a 1960s* contemporary build which he considers 'outdated and lacking in character'.

When they first arrived in Australia, four years ago, Vivien wrote to me several times mentioning his health and how depressed he was becoming. Apparently, nothing satisfies him and most people irritate him. I sensed a frustration in Vivien's correspondence, as if she was living with a creature from the bush – a marsupial – like the Koala, who is lazy by nature and calls for his mate with loud bellowing noises.

I couldn't have cared for him for as long as she has.

He must know by now that I will never fly out to see him. I can't afford the time off work or the money it will cost. It's not as if he is sending me money to help with the cost of the flight which, by the way, is astronomical.

The only interesting snippet of information he gives is that the care home is affiliated with a convent and that he is looking forward to having a visit from a nun. This makes me smile as I can't imagine my father having a fondness for nuns when he has spent years telling me about his dislike of Catholicism. He was a Baptist in his early years and I have always been surprised by his attitude towards other denominations. Even though he is now a non-believer, he seems to have retained an exclusivity for Baptists. I suppose we all do that to some degree. We may stop enjoying football, or think football is a waste of time. But when asked who is your favourite team, one usually recants the team of one's youth. Mine is West Ham United.

Since he describes his prejudice towards Catholicism as having 'waned', I will look forward to any updates on that front. I do hope that as he carries the burden of 'numerous medical conditions on a pilgrimage into the unknown' (his words not mine), someone will have a go at helping him with his depression. As we all know, the mind is inextricably linked to the body and the body to the mind.

I posted a card to him today, a London scene.

I hope he is happy enough.

4. HENRY

Tuesday 9 January 1990

Although my life is restricted to this care home, I cannot complain. Vivien has been a good companion and we have plenty of money in the bank.

Long ago I abandoned hermeneutics and theorising for crossword puzzles and a nightly shot of whisky (although the latter is a pleasure now being denied). In the evenings, to give my strained eyes a much-needed rest, I tune into the shipping broadcasts off the reef, and in a strange way I feel comforted as I drift away on a wave of inane conversations.

Now in my eighty-third year and having read over some of my early memoirs, I find there is an urgency to write more. Maybe, Wren, my darling girl will get to read them. I now have so much to say.

I had a visitor today. Sister Constance! I can't quite believe I have a nun, of all people, prepared to listen to me, although I fear I may have pushed her too far. She was dressed in typical nun attire. A large wooden cross–a holy medallion–hung from her neck on a thin chord. Her rich brown eyes were alluring but absent of flirtation. Physically, she looked strong, her features and light brown complexion indicating part Aboriginal lineage.

When she asked how I was, I replied, 'Well, I'm miserable. How about you? You look miserable dressed like that.'

She smiled at me and said, 'Mr Walker there's no point in being miserable. Life is too short.'

'Particularly at my age?'

'At any age.'

'Why are you here?'

'For you, Mr Walker, if you want me?'

'Is that a proposition?'

'Hardly.'

'It sounds like one.'

'Mr Walker, I am here to offer you a pastoral visit for one hour each week. If you are not interested, I will visit your neighbour.'

Wiping the sweat from my brow with an oversized handkerchief I said, 'He kept me awake for two nights. Snoring loudly! Nasty little man.'

'Mr Walker, what is really upsetting you?'

'Upsetting me? What makes you say that?'

'Well, you said you were miserable, and it is glaringly obvious to me that you have a huge weight upon your shoulders.'

'Pah...' I replied, shaking my head.

'How can I help you with this burden?'

'I'm not sure you can help me, and I find that question rather patronizing.'

'I have no wish to patronize you. My only concern is that you are in a place of peace.'

'There you go again,' I snarled.

'Mr Walker, I have a schedule to adhere to. If you have no wish for my company, then I will let you be. I have no intention of forcing myself or my views upon you.'

'Your views on God and my imminent demise I suppose?'

'I certainly don't know the time of your death and as I said before, I am a nun so I'm not sure what you expect? I'm not dressed as a doctor or a nurse.'

That was true. I paused, the words trapped in my mouth. 'I expect to be able to talk to you without you telling me what I should and should not believe.'

'If you feel that I am telling you anything you don't want to hear, then you must tell me. Until that time, Mr Walker, I would appreciate some respect.'

'Ditto,' I said, directing her to the grey upholstered chair next to mine.

'I'm afraid I cannot stay longer. We will start properly next Tuesday at 3 p.m.'

'If I'm still here,' I said, trying not to appear too desperate. 'I want to tell my story.'

'I look forward to it,' she said.

§

I don't have great expectations, but I may have met my match in this intriguing woman.

Tuesday 9 January 1990

During Matins, Sister Agatha mentioned St Catherine of Siena. She was born during the pandemic of 1348 which killed 50% of Italy's population. She was a mystic, a political peacemaker for the Pope, and a Doctor of the Church, visiting the dying and the outcast. She wrote a vast number of letters and words, but these are the ones which resonate with me, *You, eternal Trinity, are a deep sea. The more I enter you, the more I discover, and the more I discover, the more I seek you.*

In the afternoon, I went to visit Mr Walker in room 7. He was sitting in one of the floral but exceptionally comfortable armchairs with a newspaper splayed across his lap. He was shouting after an orderly to remake his tea. 'Make sure the milk is fresh and not those tiny, long life, plastic containers which are impossible to open with adult fingers... and put it in a jug!'

He was, as reported, surly.

A captain at the helm of his ship.

He beckoned me in as if I was a new recruit. Reluctant to look me in the eye, he resorted to that boyish flirtation common in men his age. I asked if I could call him Henry.

'No... Mr Walker is just fine,' he said.

'Mr Walker it is then,' I replied.

That was a first.

pears to be wrapped in a secret, like a lemon sherbet
to fizz.
oviously burdened by his past.
A troubled man. A caged bird.
Maybe I can open the door just enough.

6. WREN

Tuesday 9 January 1990

My daughter, Amy, has just turned twenty-seven. The shape of her nose and her high forehead reminds me of her father, whereas her older brother, Patrick, is more like my side of the family. He is a Walker in height and stature. It is wonderful to have a son, my honeymoon baby. It is poignant to birth a child of the opposite sex. Having a daughter has its own unique delights, and Amy and I certainly have a special bond.

When Amy says, *it's nothing*, I know it's something. She is like thin parchment, and I can see straight through her. But it is reciprocal. Growing up, she studied my every move. When I put on lipstick without a mirror or nimbly placed large pink curlers into my hair at night, or when I prepared food for our evening meal, she was there, hovering nearby–a hummingbird in flight–absorbing nectar for her own womanhood. When she turned eight years old, she proudly brought her father and me tea and toast in bed. She insisted we all watch Doctor Who but Patrick and Amy spent most of the time crouching behind the sofa, both fearful of the Daleks with their swivelling heads and their mantra, 'We will exterminate. We will exterminate!'

I encouraged her passion to draw, always praising her for the little drawings of horses and birds she copied from books, telling everyone she was a talented artist. I was so proud of her when she achieved an A for A level Art, and she was equally proud of me when I was made Head of English at the local comprehensive. We shared a Babycham and sang out loud, 'I will survive' by Gloria Gaynor.

For the past two years she has been working in the art department of a television company based in Wardour Street, Soho. Their claim to fame being the very successful *Challenge Anneka* with Marmite Anneka Rice. I, for one, like her enthusiasm; how she convinces hundreds of workmen to restore a youth centre in Birmingham or repair an orphanage in Romania in a matter of days. Wearing a shiny blue jumpsuit and giving out free advertising Anneka manages to get them to commit huge amounts of time and money to a good cause. Amy spent most of the autumn running around the countryside on a variety of Anneka's projects. I never miss an episode, avidly looking out for my daughter's contribution, and when complete, I shed a few tears as the team meet the deadline for such worthy causes.

Yesterday, I called Amy to let her know her grandpa had moved to a care home near Brisbane, and she reminded me of when we last saw him in Chelsea in 1986.

7. HENRY

Tuesday 16 January 1990

Generally, I keep myself to myself as I prefer not to mix with the other residents. It is Vivien's visits that break the monotony. She arrives each morning at nine. We complete a crossword together, batting to and fro the questions and answers like a game of tennis. She tells me about her news from the previous evening, and I listen attentively, drawn to her lips as she speaks, remembering how intoxicating I used to find them. Her once white teeth are now a little yellow from smoking and drinking plentiful amounts of coffee.

My legs ache and swell easily, 'Don't grow old.' I told her. 'It's not much fun.'

'I intend not to!' she replied.

I showed her the card I received from Wren this morning: a lithograph of the Albert Bridge by Carel Weight, 1947. A wintery scene with snow on the ground and people bustling along the streets, yellow hues of a sunset dusting the clouds. Vivien smiled. 'How clever she was to find that.'

'Yes, quite extraordinary,' I said. 'It reminds me of when we last met in London four years ago. It's been too long.'

'The biggest shock for me was seeing Amy. She was all grown up. I still think of her at the age of eight but she had blossomed into a young woman. I was envious of her skin. It was as taught and as clear as a perfectly ripe apple.'

'What was she studying again? I don't remember, only that it was a degree I had never heard of.'

'Art and Dance at Roehampton. How marvellous!'

'And wasn't she going out with a soldier? They met in Cyprus if I remember correctly. Wren wasn't pleased about him being in the military.'

'You could have cut the tension with a knife.'

Vivien was right about the tension.

Wren was pretty much as I remembered her, elegant and slim, with a mop of chestnut hair. But I was a little surprised by her attitude towards me. 'She was off-hand... distant.'

'You shouldn't have shouted at her,' said Vivien.

'I didn't shout at her!'

'You asked her if she had the granddaughter clock.'

'She was dismissive. I lost my temper. Couldn't help myself. She can't possibly appreciate its significance.'

'It was fine by the time they left. But I sensed she wouldn't be visiting us in Australia.'

'Maybe I should send her some money?'

Vivien was firm with me. 'Oh no... don't do that.'

'I'd like to see her again. I have a few things I'd like to say to her.'

'You mustn't worry yourself... just let it go now.'

§

I am looking forward to a visit from my nun later today. I will keep her visits secret from Vivien for a while as I want time to process the meetings without her scathing remarks.

8. SISTER CONSTANCE

Tuesday 16 January 1990

I walked with the Kookaburras this morning; they appeared to be laughing at their own jokes. The weather is glorious; the cool breeze brushing my skin, bringing me alive like morning dew on a meadow.

When I went to visit Mr Walker this afternoon, the sun was streaming through the patio doors lighting him up like some divine vision.

'You look a bit hot,' I said, sweat pouring down his face.

'I like being warm,' he said, wiping his brow with a large hankercheif.

I opened the patio doors but there was no breeze. For half an hour we talked about incidentals and then he settled on the subject of his daughter and granddaughter, telling me of their last meeting in London.

Several times he welled up and so I waited for the tears to pass (praying under my breath). Wren, he told me, was distant but he doesn't give a reason.

There is always a reason.

I would love to talk with her and see their relationship from her perspective. I expect she would unearth a tale!

Halfway through the hour I pressed him on his promise to tell me his story. He had mentioned a granddaughter clock, and this intrigued me. My father had given my mother a mantel clock when they were married. The Westminster chimes are logged in my heart reminding me of my youth. They bring back good and bad memories simultaneously.

'Not now,' he said. 'I've changed my mind.'

'Oh,' I said, 'why would you do that?'

'Because it unnerves me.'

'It must be important then.'

I felt as if he was considering something, but he soon became awkward, so I suggested I make us both some tea. He was delighted at this, and we chatted for another twenty minutes until it was time for me to leave.

9. WREN

Tuesday 16 January 1990

Four years ago, on one of my father's visits to the UK, I went with Amy to visit him at a rented flat in London. When we arrived at the Art Deco apartment block in Chelsea, he was sitting by the window, confined to a wheelchair.

Vivien greeted us in her Australian lilt. 'Wren? Ah, Wren!' she said, kissing me on both cheeks. She looked even more amazed to see my daughter, 'Goodness me, Amy, how you have grown. I haven't seen you since you were eight years old and I have missed you so much.'

Amy gave her a big hug, 'I remember my time in Spain with you.'

Vivien exuded good taste. Her green linen outfit mirrored the colour of her eyes, complimented by a Hermes silk scarf tied softly around her neck.

Not having seen my dad for many years I was a little shocked by his appearance. His head was shiny like a buffed plum and his nose was rather bulbous. Thread veins pitted his cheeks, competing with brown spots from the intensity of the Spanish sun.

The room was bathed in cream carpets and opulent wallpaper, interrupted by a blaze red sofa and a large gold mirror set upon the ledge of a marble fireplace.

'You used to live in this block of flats you know,' said Henry.

'I thought it was familiar,' I replied, but the memory of the flat I had shared with my father was sparsely furnished and cold.

'Back in the 1940s. You were four years old. I wanted to revisit the place one last time.'

'It can't have been this flat?' I said.

'No... it was the floor above. Mine wasn't as well furnished as this one is now.'

That figured.

When my father said I looked the same as I did on my wedding day, I laughed. 'That was twenty-six years ago,' I reminded him.

'It's true, Vivien, she has hardly changed since then. Don't you remember?'

'I wasn't at her wedding,' said Vivien.

My father was embarrassed. 'How stupid of me.'

Amy annoyed him by touching his old typewriter. 'Please don't touch it!' He said, 'It is like me, a little fragile.' He then asked her if she had a boyfriend and she told him she was going out with a soldier. This made him laugh but he proceeded to ask her lots of questions.

Vivien interjected, 'Amy, come and help me get the food.'

Sitting with my father in silence, I wrestled with what to say. 'How was the journey from Spain?' I asked.

'Not easy, everything is difficult for me these days.'

Vivien entered the room, her oven gloved hands carrying a hot lasagne, Amy following behind with fresh bread and salad. 'Wren, maybe you could bring your father to the table.'

Due to his size I struggled to manoeuvre the wheelchair. Vivien, meanwhile, laid out the best glasses and cutlery as if we were dining at Harrods.

My father broke the awkward silence, 'Vivien wants to return to Brisbane because the health system is an improvement on the Spanish system.'

Vivien glared at him, 'We both decided on The Sunshine Coast!'

'How lovely,' I smiled.

'We spent thousands of pounds on hospital bills after your father's stroke,' she said. 'I have been running around like a headless chicken trying to organise our move. Endless phone calls, changing pension payments and dealing with property sales and bank transfers.'

Henry scowled at her and turning to me, said, 'You must come and see us in a year or two.'

'Maybe, but Australia is such a long way, and it is so expensive to get there.' I quickly changed the subject. 'You seem to have recovered well from your stroke, Dad, you have a good colour.'

'That's probably down to the drink,' he said, 'but I am struggling to get back on my feet.'

'It will come in time,' assured Vivien.

When Vivien left the room to get the dessert, Henry leant in towards me. 'She's bossy, but she is a good woman.'

'You are lucky to have her,' I said.

He asked me about the whereabouts of the granddaughter clock. 'It is at Craigmore with Florence,' I told him.

'It belongs with you!' He barked.

'It's staying where it is for now,' I replied.

He apologised for his outburst.

On leaving, I noticed he was tearful. Kissing him goodbye, he smelt of port and crackers, slightly musty and it was at that moment I realised I might never see him again.

Once inside the lift, Amy looked at me and smiled a half smile. 'That must have been hard for you?'

'Yes, it was, but he was more engaged than usual. He seemed interested in you and fascinated by your boyfriend.

'He was nice, but a bit grumpy. Vivien has her work cut out for her. I can't imagine he is easy to live with.'

'No... I think not.'

'Are you okay, Mum? You have gone quite pale.'

'It's nothing. I'm fine.'

'You're not fine,' said Amy, taking my hand and holding it tight.

She was right. I was unsettled by the visit.

I was hoping I might be able to compartmentalise my father into a neat space in my brain. But unfortunately, people can rarely be boxed. Thoughts of them seep out. Something they said – their scent – their expression. Slam the door if you will, but their presence stays with you like the chorus of a song which plays itself over and over – circling – repetitive.

10. HENRY

Tuesday 23 January 1990

I have been waking in the night feeling agitated. A combination of my body plaguing me with aches and pains and my mind unable to switch off. The radio becomes annoying and the only purpose I have is to write. In the early hours, I find it's better to use pencil and paper as the typing is aggravating the arthritis in my hands. My eyes are dry, and it takes a while for me to focus properly but once I start writing, I find it hard to stop. It is usually my back which dictates the length of time I can write... or my bladder. I am falling apart.

When I look back at my childhood, I remember racing around everywhere. My legs were turbo-charged. I considered the pace of life was monotonous and adults were as dull as ditchwater, stagnant with no life. My parents were no exception.

I feel less alone when the sun rises. The warmth penetrates the patio doors and rests on my arms and legs.

At 7 a.m. an orderly brings me tea. I can accept this poor excuse for a brew because I am simply desperate and cannot be bothered to make my own. The Kookaburras chatter and the parrots squawk incessantly, acting as an unnecessary alarm clock. I shower and get dressed at a pace my younger self would have baulked at. It is painful to be so handicapped, but it is my own fault. I gave up many years ago, allowing myself to put on too much weight, eating unhealthy food and drinking too much alcohol. I am paying the price now. But hey ho. What can I do? I am resigned. I'm hardly going to start dieting at my age.

I say to myself, you've had a good life. And for a moment I am flummoxed. It's as if a bumble bee has entered my mouth and even though I open it wide it refuses to leave. *A good life?* With all honesty, I'm not sure I can say that.

What happens when tragedy and trauma colours one's happiness? I have certainly had many happy times, but the residue of my sorrow is always there. It came in when I was very small and never left. Other cuts followed. Marks that no amount of food or drink have been able to irradicate. I see some marks on Sister Constance, although she is slim and healthy, I see them in her eyes. I think she sees mine because she recognises them in herself. I may be completely off course, but we shall see. I am looking forward to her visit.

11. SISTER CONSTANCE

Tuesday 23 January 1990

I went to see Mr Walker at the usual time. He was in a better mood and even seemed pleased to see me.

He directed me to his bedside cabinet. I took out what must have been fifty pieces of loose discoloured paper with faint type. 'How old is this?' I asked him.

'I started when I was around twenty-five and stopped in 1939. I didn't start again until recently. No one has ever read it and it seems a shame for me to die and for it not to be shared. I hope my daughter will have it eventually.'

In all my years as a nun, no one has ever given me their memoirs to read. I am looking forward to discovering more about his life.

I placed the paper on the bed, 'I will need my glasses to read this and I have left them in my room,' I said.

'Please take it with you,' he replied.

I removed a tiny bottle of frankincense oil from the pocket within my habit. Proceeding to pour just a few drops into his palm, I massaged it round and round. It was absorbed immediately, his skin, like the outback, thirsty for rain. 'I felt the Lord say to me that you need to return to your first love.'

'First love?' he shuddered; the smell of frankincense, filling the room.

'My goodness, that provoked a response, what made you shiver?'

'A goose walked over my grave.'

'What does it mean to you, your first love?'

'Yet I had not walked above,

a mile, or two, from my first love,

and looking back at that short space,

could see a glimpse of His bright face.'

He took a long deep breath in.

'Henry Vaughan?'

'Yes. The Retreat. I learnt it by heart as a young boy.'

'Beautiful.'

'I can't respect a deathbed conversion, Sister,' he said, looking directly into my eyes.

'It's as good a place as any,' I smiled.

'It's not that simple, Sister.'

'Does it have to be so hard?'

'I can't forgive God for what happened.'

'What did happen? You haven't told me.'

'I have spent many years trying to forget,' he said, lowering his head.

'Has it worked?'

'Has what worked?'

'Have you forgotten?'

'You know I haven't... Why do you think God kills people when they are so young? Is it His plan?' He paused and lifted his head, waiting for the answer.

'Who died?' I said softly.

And there he sat, suspended in time, concerned that in speaking the words, he might betray the memory of someone precious.

'Doris... my sister,' he stammered.

12. WREN

Tuesday 23 January 1990

Today is my wedding anniversary! Thirty years. Unbelievable! I met David back in 1957 when I was seventeen.

The Chamber Music Club in Southend were offering a recital of Bach by a talented trio, composed of three dashing brothers. My cousin, Eve, and I decided to look for ourselves. Sitting in the front row I was hoping to secure the attention of the violinist, instead my eyes were drawn to the young man sitting next to me. At the interval his mother, a stylish woman with mousy hair tied in a loose bun was conducting the air in front of her as she chatted to him. At the end of the concert David Gardner introduced himself to me as we left the hall. At nineteen years old he was striking with fine features and blue eyes, pale skin and fair hair parted on the side.

But he was more than just his good looks, for no one is just their looks.

Realising that we lived about eight miles from each other on the Essex coast, his mother, seeing the mutual attraction, sweetly suggested, 'You should take this young lady to see the grounds of Sutton Hoo in Suffolk'.

'Maybe a cup of coffee first, mother,' said David.

'No, certainly not, she deserves more than a coffee and Sutton Hoo is a splendid first date.'

It was a week later that we arrived by coach at the stately home, in time for morning coffee in the Grand Room. It wasn't long before David took hold of my arm gently and led me out to a bench in the garden. 'I have been watching you for weeks,' he said.

'What do you mean?'

'At the Methodist Chapel on Sunday.'

'Really? I haven't seen you there?'

'I tend to come in late and sit at the back. You and your cousin are always at the front, but I have seen you when you leave to take the children out for Sunday School.'

'Why have you never said hello before?'

'I was taking my time. Deciding who I liked the best, you or Eve.'

'Are you joking?' I was disappointed.

'No, you see I look at it like this. There are many attractive young women about and so I think it is worth taking my time.'

Appreciating his honesty, I stroked his hand with my index finger. He leant forward and, closing his eyes, kissed me. The soft flesh of his lips melding into my mouth. I shivered. Having spent many nights imagining how it might feel to be kissed, I sailed away on the passion of it.

'I noticed your hands. You have such long fingers,' he said, taking hold of my left hand and raising it to his lips.

'You are very charming. Have you had many girlfriends?'

'No, you are the first.'

'Really? Honestly?' I said.

'Yes,' he said, laughing and pulling me in close, 'I've been waiting for you.'

13. HENRY

Wednesday 24 January 1990

Vivien arrived a little late and a little flustered.

'Where have you been,' I said.

'I can't always be at your beck and call. I have things to do you know.'

Sassy, I thought. 'I just miss you when you don't turn up at nine. Every minute is painful.' I meant what I said but she presumed I was being facetious.

I decided not to mention Sister Constance's visit. I thought she might mock the fact that the nun had mentioned my 'first love' and I wasn't in the mood to defend or collude.

For me it was uncanny.

Some would say it was a small miracle.

It made me shiver!

I had asked the nun to take the early part of my memoirs away with her. She would then understand my journey. It means I don't have to tell her everything. I can just sit back and wait for a response.

By mid-morning, the heat has become almost unbearable. I have an air-conditioning unit, but it makes the most awful noise as if it has caught an eclipse of moths in its fan.

14. SISTER CONSTANCE

Sunday 28 January 1990

I have the afternoon off! Praise the Lord. I have a sense of urgency to read Mr Walker's story before I see him again on Tuesday. I have been so busy and unable to read it until now! I imagine I am the first and I feel a certain responsibility.

Henry's parents, Joseph, and Evelyn Walker, lived in Southend-on-Sea, in a semi-detached Victorian house with two bay windows at the front. Mr Walker describes it as, 'Not a house of great character or charm, it was, nevertheless, home to me and my four older siblings, all boys, except for Doris.' It appears they cherished Doris not because she was the only girl but because she was the kindest person in their small world. At thirteen years old she was the eldest which held some kudos with the parents, especially 'Father', of whom they were a little frightened. She was a tall, pretty girl but she wasn't in the least bit proud.

Walter, thirteen months younger, appears to have been the favoured son. He was good at Maths and it was hoped he would go into the family business. It seems Walter and Doris were soul mates, but Doris had a soft spot for her youngest sibling, Henry Walker, who at the time was five years old.

'Come here little man,' she shouted, chasing Henry around the garden, her blonde ringlets bobbing up and down on her chest.

'You can't catch me,' he yelled, racing around the garden in and out of the rose bushes.

Father's manner was harsh. 'Henry, don't run, walk. I told you not to disturb Mother's roses. If you can't behave, you shall go to bed immediately.'

'Please don't worry yourself, Father. He is not doing any harm.' Her blue magnetic eyes drawing him in.

'He looks so silly,' said brother number two, ten years old with a ferocious appetite.

'His buttons are all wrong,' said brother number three, eight years old and as thin as a rake, detesting most food except bread and butter.

Doris lifted Henry onto her lap. 'Come here little man. Let me re-do them for you. You are so clever to get yourself dressed. Now boys, don't be cruel to Henry, it's not so long ago that you both struggled with buttons.'

Henry simply adored Doris. She gave him the attention he needed which was lacking from their mother. Doris tucked him in at night. She peeled his fruit at breakfast. She tickled his belly at any opportunity making him squeal with delight. She was, in Henry's eyes, simply divine.

Then one morning, Doris was curled up and whimpering like a wounded animal. A doctor arrived and diagnosed it as her monthly cycle, but due to his misdiagnosis, appendicitis swelled into peritonitis. A few days later, a different doctor arrived with a nurse, and they busied themselves in the room upstairs while the family crowded around the kitchen range with its red-hot iron openings. Walter was given permission to roast chestnuts, using the iron tongs, whilst brothers two and three, known as "the rascals" by Mother, kept themselves busy by playing with their model train set.

Their father and mother left the room from time to time to go to Doris. When they came back, they either sat in silence or gave the boys tasks. 'Warm this pillow for her,' Walter, said Mother.

Henry sneaked upstairs to see what was happening. He put his ear to his sister's bedroom door, straining to hear the doctor and nurse speaking in whispers. The nurse, carrying a bedpan, opened the door. 'Out of the way,' she commanded, bustling past.

Running to the bedroom Henry fell on his knees beside the bed and raised his hands together in prayer. 'Please God, don't let Doris die. Please God, don't let Doris die.'

But that night, unbeknownst to Henry, as he slept under flower-patterned eiderdowns, death came to Ambleside Drive. Swooping down, it stole Doris, leaving her ringlets damp and flattened to her chest. Father fell to the floor and Mother let out a hollow scream.

In the morning, Henry dressed for school and went downstairs, but it was his father's response which shocked me. 'There will be no school today, Henry. I don't want to hear a word out of you. Go to your room.'

Peering through his father's legs, he saw Mother's slight frame in a heap on the floor. Her hair, usually neatly plaited on top of her head, shrouded her face, while she muttered into her handkerchief next to the fire that had well and truly gone out. Henry bolted upstairs to Walter. 'Doris is dead,' he shouted. 'She's dead!'

'I know little man, I know.' Walter held him in his arms as he wept.

Throughout the day, people came and went from the house. The boys were told to stay in the bedroom. They played dominoes over and over until lunchtime when a neighbour took them to the local park. That night, Henry retreated under the sheets, curled up like a dormouse, listening to his mother wailing in the next room. He surfaced to the sound of his brothers breathing deeply and he whimpered, 'Doris?'

No answer.

Walter sighed.

Turning over, Henry held his well-worn teddy, snuggling him to his mouth and crying himself to sleep.

A coffin arrived and was placed on the extended table in the dining room, a room only used for special occasions, filled with highly polished dark wood furniture. A giant Aspidistra splayed out its viridian green leaves next to Doris who had been placed in the coffin by the undertakers. The curtains shrouded the room in darkness except for a candle which flickered a morsel of light. The next day, a few close neighbours, who had been invited to view Doris, arrived with small posies to place on her body. When they had paid their respects, they retired to the breakfast room with Mother.

Henry was considered too young to view his sister, but he managed to creep into the dimly lit room. Climbing up onto a chair, he lifted the heavy lid of the box. Doris, like a large porcelain doll, held one of the posies, while the others were scattered around her body, decorating her favourite cream dress. As Henry reached out to touch her, the lid fell suddenly with a loud bang. Mother dashed in. 'Henry, what do you think you are doing? Come away from there.' Putting her hands over his eyes, she pushed him out of the room, but he was pleased to have seen his sister dressed for heaven.

A shiny black funeral car followed the hearse, but Henry was left at home to help his aunt lay the table, the table that Doris had just vacated. His aunt sang solemnly of the Promised Land and the pearly gates, while placing plates down one after the other. Trotting behind her, he put a white napkin on top of each plate. Eventually, the family arrived home, followed by the doctor, the minister, friends, relatives, teachers, and schoolgirls; all dressed in black. Blackness and sorrow permeated the house while Mother's face took on an ashen grey overlay, and the little patience Father possessed evaporated.

Then his mother took him to the grave before the flowers wilted. Standing by the mound of earth he imagined Doris in her dress, asleep in her coffin, waiting to get her wings. 'Is she cold, Mother?' he asked.

'What a stupid question,' she replied, pulling him away.

When Walter was left in charge, he wasted no time in gathering his brothers together in the dining room. He stood by the large Aspidistra and read aloud the many letters of condolence. 'We are devastated to hear of Doris's passing and trust that the good Lord has taken her into heaven.' She was such an angel, and we hope you will find some comfort in knowing she is no longer in pain.'

'Read another one,' they all said in unison.

'Doris was such a dear child. We can only imagine that the Lord has a purpose for her in heaven, said Walter. You see boys she is up there with the angels.'

The boys nodded, eagerly wanting a life for their sister that surpassed the grave.

'Will we see her again?' asked brother number two.

'I believe it with all my heart,' said Walter.

Henry rubbed his tummy and cried out. 'I miss her so much it hurts.'

§

Poor Mr Walker, losing his sister, when he was so young. I am learning so much about him–a line at a time–my eyes absorbing the shock and trauma of a young boy now suspended inside an old man's body. His life story is rather like an exceptionally hard jigsaw puzzle. I am only just sifting the edges out from the mass of pieces.

I appreciate how Doris's death would have coloured his opinion of God. Suffering is the biggest hurdle to the Christian faith.

I think of my own losses.

My mother, Tira, a Bush Queen, serving in the Aboriginal Lands Trust before her death ten years ago. Striving for equality and fairness while she was still grieving my father's untimely death thirty years earlier.

He still haunts me.

Years pass but grief is like swimming in a fast-flowing river. You can get up on the bank occasionally, but you must get back in the water as it is the only way homeward.

15. WREN

Sunday 28 January 1990

David cycled the eight miles from his home in Rayleigh to meet me at Craigmore in Westcliff.

In the mid 1930s, my Uncle Walter and Auntie Florence purchased Craigmore, an imposing detached property north of Chalkwell Park. Its narrow front garden was masked from the pavement by a black wooden five-bar gate and an undulating brick wall flanking the gate on either side. It had three reception rooms: the front room, the dining room and the breakfast room, each hosting quite different rituals. The dining room was Walter's favourite place, where he was often discovered, bent over the Times crossword puzzle, flooded in sunlight. Upstairs, there were three good-sized bedrooms and a small office room, where he dealt with tax returns and utility bills. Meanwhile, Florence's domain was the kitchen at the back of the house, with the smell of beef casserole or roast chicken emanating from the open window. Neighbours were always delighted to receive an invitation to join the Walkers for Sunday lunch.

Florence and my mother, Queenie, had been close friends during their school years having studied together for their school certificate examination at fifteen. Florence was much larger in build than Queenie, a less pragmatic woman, not hugely emotional, and I know she thought Queenie a little too religious and demonstrative. Two more different women you could not find, but it was their difference that drew them to companionship.

Sometimes David played his trumpet to the family, captivating us with the opening of Handel's concerto in D minor. Wanting to become a teacher, he had to do extra study to secure a place on a Teacher Training course.

Our weekends were filled with walks and babysitting, and evenings spent listening to *I've Got You Under my Skin* by Frank Sinatra, or Mendelssohn's *Oh, For Wings the Wings of a Dove,* and other romantic pieces. He filled my space, my present and my future. He was everything to me.

I started my nanny training at the prestigious Norland College in Chislehurst. Florence said I looked elegant in my uniform of oatmeal coat, felt hat and white gloves, beige mid-calf dress and white apron, all purchased from Harrods.

I was introduced to the Anglican service by my new best friend, Margaret, the daughter of a Bishop. Having been inspired by the vibrant tones of Billy Graham at the Wembley Arena in 1955 when he preached to 120,000 people, I birthed a simple faith that Christ died for my sins and that I would go to heaven. Because I still hadn't been christened, I was unable to take communion at the morning service and so we went to Evensong.

David was conscripted into the Lifeguards, his uniform only making him more dashing, like Sergeant Troy from *Far from the Madding Crowd.* After six weeks of basic training, he gained a name for himself as a good shot and was asked to play the trumpet in the Army band. But David detested the Army as he felt it betrayed his vocation to teach.

After two years of dating, David said, 'I will have to ask your father's permission'

'What for?' I said.

'To marry you.'

'Don't you think you should ask my uncle Walter?'

'Yes of course, but as you are under twenty-one, I need your father's permission. It's the right thing to do.'

'Maybe you should call him in Geneva.'

'I'd rather go and see him. Why don't we both go?' he said, 'Shall I write to him?'

'No, let me do it. I need to get my aunt and uncle to agree.'

My father, in his early fifties, was living with Vivien, who was in her early thirties and recently widowed. They had met at a drinks party in Geneva and, as he told me several times, were instantly attracted to each other. She was of average height with long brown hair and green eyes. Her best feature was her mouth with its rich pink lips and very white teeth, which protruded slightly.

My father greeted us at Geneva airport.

When we entered the flat, I was to meet Vivien for the first time and she immediately took hold of my hand. 'How strange it must be for you my dear. Your father has told me of your life, and I do not wish to add to the confusion you have gone through, so let us be friends, shall we?'

Unsure of how to respond, I smiled and squeezed her hand. I wasn't convinced by the outpouring. I excused myself and went to the bathroom.

Vivien prepared lunch, which meant David was left alone with my father and rather prematurely launched into his appeal, 'Sir, I would like permission to marry your daughter.'

'Oh? Yes, well I presumed that's why you had come.'

'I love her,' David replied.

'Wren tells me you are a confused Catholic. What does that mean?'

'I was raised a Catholic, but I like the informality of the Methodists... my father says once a Catholic, always a Catholic.'

'Pah! What rubbish! Make up your own mind!' said Henry. 'Doesn't Wren still have to do a placement for a year to qualify at the Norland?'

'Yes, she does.'

'How are you going to provide for her once you are married? You are not expecting her to work as a nanny, are you?'

'I will become a teacher and in a few years' time we hope to have children.'

'Mmmm. Well, she will be a very qualified mother that's for sure!'

Outside the door, I waited with my breath locked under my tongue.

'I would be delighted to give permission,' said my father, and moving towards David grabbed his hand, shaking it firmly. 'Well done, well done. It's wonderful news.'

I sensed my father was delighted that he no longer had to be responsible for me although he hadn't had that role for a very long time.

Before we could marry there was still one thing I would have to do.

16. HENRY

Tuesday 30 January 1990

When Sister Constance visited me this morning, I was sitting in my comfortable chair typing away on my old Remington.

'How devastating for you... to lose your sister like that,' she said, as soon as she walked through the door.

Moving the table away from my legs I gave her a wry smile. I nodded. I suppose it was devastating but until now I had never realised the true impact. Grief was muzzled in those days.

She sat down next to me in her usual spot, 'Do you blame God for the death of your sister?'

'Who else can I blame?' I said, 'God allowed Doris to die, I prayed, and it didn't work.' For many months I held a dull pain in the well of my stomach. I contemplated running away on a regular basis. I packed a small bag... I unpacked it. I sharpened twigs with a pen knife. I took food from the larder, stashing it under my bed for a few hours, only to eat it. Eventually, I sensed that my brothers would not cope with the loss of two siblings in one lifetime and so I remained at home waiting to be rescued.

'Your father is depicted as very distant. Was that how he was?'

'Doris was the only one my father really loved... and maybe... Walter.'

'Do you believe that?'

'I felt it, Sister.'

'Is it possible that what you felt was your father's inability to cope with loss? Imagine if he shut down and could not express his grief to anyone. What would happen to him? He would become frozen in time... and possibly unfeeling to you and your brothers.'

'But isn't that all psycho-babble?' And anyway, he was like that before Doris died. Either way, it confused me and left me feeling inadequate.

'Can you forgive him?'

'I'm not sure. Probably. It's such a long time ago now. I know that my father had a strict Victorian upbringing which, from all accounts, was harsher than my own.'

'Next time you must tell me about your first love.'

I tried to entice her with a delightfully refreshing Assam. I wanted to tell her that I was eight years old when I stood in the hall dressed in my Sunday best.

'I have other people to see, Mr Walker, but we shall meet again next week.'

'I'm sure you have better things to do. It can't be very interesting for you.'

'I am very interested in you, Mr Walker, but we will have to continue this next week. Can you forgive me?'

I sat there contemplating, *not really*, I thought.

'May the Lord bless you and keep you,' she said, as she left the room.

'Yes. And may his face shine upon me too,' I added with a touch of sarcasm.

17. SISTER CONSTANCE

Wednesday 31 January 1990

I think Mr Walker's wife, Vivien, and I are the only interruption to writing his memoirs that he tolerates.

This morning, I sat down for an hour and read the next part of his story before I had to dash over to the refectory and help my sisters prepare supper.

Mr Walker describes himself as 'a tall gangly child with a shot of black hair and my father's full lower lip.' He describes his brothers in dispassionate terms. 'Brother number three at eleven was thin, but not very tall, and brother number two, at thirteen, clutched his ever-expanding waistline. The 'rascals' kicked each other in the shins until Father arrived in the hall and pulled them apart. 'Stop that immediately!' he bawled.

The chapel they attended was a simple red brick building with very little ornamentation and fifteen wooden pews on each side of its narrow aisle. On Sundays, it smelt of linseed oil and beeswax due to the dedication of a few ladies who took turns to polish the pews every Saturday night. Because his father was one of the elders, the family had the privilege of sitting in the front pew. The minister, a short man with a clipped moustache, opened Our Own Hymn Book, by Charles Spurgeon. 'Let us sing out loud to the Glory of God, the hymn on page forty-four, Amidst Us Our Beloved Stands.' At the end of the hymn, the congregation sat down, and the minister took his place at the lectern. 'This morning we will be giving thanks to God for Mrs Whitewell, who as you know, was tragically killed in her bed last week by a bomb dropped from a Zeppelin. Our condolences and prayers go to her husband.' He paused for a moment before adding, 'This war is taking its toll on all of us, but I appeal to you as Christians. We must deplore these revenge attacks on Germans and Austrians living in Southend.' The minister looked out at his congregation suspecting some of them had taken cricket bats and gathered at midnight to smash in shop windows. 'Revenge is not our calling, and I urge you all to remember St Paul's letter to Peter; humble yourselves therefore under the mighty hand of God, that he may exalt you in due time: Casting all your care upon him; for he careth for you.'

After a few minutes, people started to fidget. The minister spoke again with authority. 'Does anyone know what this means? He paused and how it is to be done?'

Henry knew the answer. His heart pounding in his chest. The minister looked directly at him. 'Will you stand and tell us what it means? What is Jesus telling us to do?'

Rising from the pew, Henry gathered some courage, 'Jesus is telling us that when life gets tough, we are not to seek revenge but give him our worries.' He immediately sat down.

'Well done, Henry, you are right. And can you tell us how we cast our burdens on to Jesus?' said the minister.

He stood again, 'We have to pray, sir, and believe.'

The minister looked at Henry's father. 'You have a preacher in the making,' he said, 'let us remember that Jesus tells us, *in the world ye shall have tribulation, but be of good cheer, I have overcome the world.* You may sit down young man.'

The minister continued to preach, but Henry heard nothing more. At the end of the service the minister beckoned Henry forward and handed him a King James Bible, 'Here we are, young man. Read it and treasure it.'

On the walk home, Henry was promoted to the space between Father and Mother, and while the 'rascals' scowled with envy, Walter nodded approval. Gripping the Bible with both hands, Henry held it to his chest, father's outstretched hand resting upon his back. When they arrived home, life reverted to normal as his mother withdrew to the lounge, absorbing herself in her tatting, while his father escaped to his study.

From that moment on, much of Henry's imagination, previously filled with ghosts and dragons, of Kings and knights, became entangled with stories from the Old and New Testaments. David fought Goliath and Henry defeated his demons. He made friends with Moses and Elijah, Samson, Esther and King David, Peter, Paul and doubting Thomas.

But unlike Thomas, Henry, it appears, had no doubts, he had met his first love in the person of Jesus.

18. WREN

Wednesday 31 January 1990

I was twenty years old when I was christened. The vicar, a short man with a kind face, dressed in robes and obviously fond of Florence and Walter, held onto their hands chatting with familiarity. They had, after all, supported his dwindling congregation through the hardship of the war years, and Florence had always managed to spare a few eggs each week to supplement his family's rations.

I was dressed in a simple white frock. My aunt and uncle were by my side and a small gathering gathered around the font. The vicar smiled and held up his hands and said, 'The faith of an Anglican is founded in the scriptures, the traditions of the apostolic church and the early church fathers.'

I renounced the devil and turned to Christ.

Light streamed through the stained-glass window, spotlighting my rite of passage; the smell of incense lingering from the morning service. The vicar, dipping his right thumb into the water made the sign of a cross on my forehead and said, 'For if we have been planted together in the likeness of his death, we shall be also in the likeness of his resurrection.'

Walking out of the church, Florence took my arm and whispered, 'It's a shame your father isn't here.'

'He doesn't approve of such things, you know that. He didn't respond to the invitation. He probably thinks I shouldn't be marrying a Catholic, let alone be getting christened in the Church of England.'

'But he approves of David, doesn't he?'

'Yes. But he doesn't approve of Catholics. In fact, he doesn't approve of the Church full stop!'

We both laughed and the vicar grinned at us, not sure of what was so amusing.

19. HENRY

Tuesday 6 February 1990

Vivien decided not to visit me this morning, she said she had things to do. I wonder if she has met someone else and can't be bothered with me anymore. I wouldn't blame her. She is twenty years younger than me, and I expect she wants more of a life than looking after an old man. At least the nun came to see me. I am growing fond of her. She has a habit of leaning over her knees and placing her head in her hands. I think she sometimes gets frustrated with my negativity.

This afternoon we discussed Jesus.

She started by referring to my memoirs, 'Unlike doubting Thomas, it appears, you had no doubts?'

'I did not need to see the holes in Jesus' hands, feet, and side to believe that he had been raised from the dead. I was love-struck. However, although I no longer wanted to flee my home, I was still haunted by thoughts of Doris, her pale face in the coffin, her body in the soil, her cream dress blackened by decay.'

'Would you say you have a morbid imagination? A fascination with the dark side of life?'

'I don't know Sister; I think I was propelled into the dark side at a young age and only stepped out of it for a time.'

'Your account of your childhood is moving. The lack of paternal and maternal love in the family is apparent and it obviously had a lasting effect, except when you impressed your father. Was he really that different with you after that?'

'A little... but I think it was me who changed.'

'I assume Walter is your favourite brother as he is the only one you name, the other two are mere numbers or *rascals*.'

'Yes. I adored Walter. Do you have siblings?'

'I had twin sisters who in fact were often referred to by mother as *the twins* or as the *Djunkgao* from Aboriginal mythology.'

'How fascinating, do tell,' I said.

'The Djunkgao were sisters associated with floods and ocean currents and considering my siblings were always playing with the hose in the garden, drenching each other despite the chill of winter air, my mother thought it a suitable nickname. When my father found out that the Djunkgao were said to have named all the animals on earth he showed my mother the book of Genesis and she said no more.'

'Do go on.'

'My sisters and I adored our mother's stories of hunting and surviving in the outback. She had been part of a vibrant tribe, but they had been destroyed by alcohol and the white man who believed they were superior because of their skin colour, skin which was to burn and peel in the Australian sun.'

She smiled at me, and I nodded. After all she was right.

'When she was old and dying the *Djunkgao* and I held her hand and she told us that despite some of his strange ways she had loved our father more than her own breath. I am so grateful for my upbringing. My parents played and wrestled, chastised, and adored me and my siblings in equal measure. In that tussle of life, we learnt respect for one another and for our elders.'

'I envy you, Sister,' I said. 'How did your father die?

At that moment her face dropped, and she stood up. 'I must be off now, Mr Walker. I have so much to do.'

'Oh.' I was a little shocked. 'So, I tell you about my sorrow, but you won't tell me about yours?'

'Goodbye Mr Walker, I shall visit you next Tuesday.'

20. SISTER CONSTANCE

Tuesday 6 February 1990

I enjoy writing my journal. Mr Walker and I have that in common. But incessant typing, for me, would destroy the tranquillity of ink pen on paper which is so much more visceral. I am glad, at least, that he is expressing his thoughts by documenting them.

When I met Mr Walker earlier today, I decided not to mince my words, 'Surely, we all hope that God will meet us in our suffering?'

'That's very convenient for you to say, but I have struggled with this for the last fifty years. I remain stoically ambivalent.'

'The experience of God in your youth was profound.'

'It was. I can't deny that. But was it born out of desperation? A child's faith is not developed. Not mature.'

'Truly, I say to you, whoever does not receive the kingdom of God like a child shall not enter it.'

'Mark 10,' he said, with a smile. 'Will I enter the kingdom of God, Sister?'

'I am not your judge, Mr Walker, but I do know that neither the present nor the future will be able to separate us from the love of God. So, your salvation is secure.'

'Romans 8 verse 39,' he said, adding, 'But whoso shall offend one of these little ones who believe in me, it was better for him that a millstone was hanged about his neck, and that he was drowned in the depth of the sea.'

'Matthew 18 verse 6,' I said, smiling at our game of scriptural ping pong. But when I finally left, I wondered what on earth he could have meant.

Mr Walker then unnerved me by asking me how my father died. I must keep my boundaries. I tend to overshare at times.

21. WREN

Tuesday 6 February 1990

On the morning of the wedding, the fire was roaring in the front room at Craigmore, and Florence helped me climb into a full-length velvet ivory dress. She proceeded to fasten the many buttons at the back of my dress while the granddaughter clock chimed eleven times. When the chimes were hushed, she said, 'Would you like to take the clock to your flat after the honeymoon?'

'No, you keep it. I like it in this room, and I can't imagine visiting Craigmore and not hearing the chimes.'

'It will be yours one day.'

'Enough of that!' I said, wincing at her words. 'You aren't going anywhere soon! I won't hear of such talk, especially on my wedding day!' Turning sharply round, I kissed her on the cheek, and she pulled my body into her own.

'When Queenie received the clock from the elders of the chapel, she rang me.'

'What did she say?' I asked, desperate for information.

'She said, "You'll never guess what the elders have given us." But I wasn't in the mood to guess as I had just settled my two boys down for a morning nap and was trying to master a piece on the violin. "It's a huge clock, the same height as me. A granddaughter clock!" Queenie said. "Not tall then", I replied. She thought I was jealous. But I told her that I wouldn't want her clock for all the tea in China. It was just another thing to polish. She told me how the chimes were beautiful, and that they filled the manse. "You are so romantic," I said, but your mother knew I was struggling with Brahms and with her quick wit she said, "Wasn't Brahms one of the leading composers of the Romantic era?"'

Florence roared with laughter, and we let go of each other. 'I loved your mother so very much!' she said.

My father, Henry, flew in from Geneva for the wedding. He wanted to give me away but was politely informed by Florence that I had already asked Walter. A compromise had to be reached. I travelled in the car with Walter to the church and stood with him at the back, while my three bridesmaids, including Eve, fussed around my dress and veil. Walter held my hand and said what I needed to hear, 'You look beautiful, my dear girl. David is lucky to have you. There is no need to be nervous.'

Walking me down the aisle, Walter stood with me until the vicar said, 'Who gives this woman to this man?'

'I do,' said Henry, in his clearest voice. Taking my father's hand, he then passed it to the vicar who, in turn, placed it upon David's hand.

The rest of the service ran like clockwork with several joyful hymns, readings, and witticisms from the vicar. David and I stood on the church steps, having photographs taken, when suddenly my father coughed very loudly, drawing attention to himself.

'Are you all right, Dad?' I asked.

'Yes. It's nothing. Just a cough,' he said, wiping his face and blowing his nose loudly. 'I am so pleased for you, Wren,' he mumbled.

22. HENRY

Tuesday 13 February 1990

This afternoon, Sister Constance asked me to tell her in my own words about my baptism.

I set the scene.

'I was fourteen years old. I can hear my father's voice as if it was yesterday, low, and croaky but also sharp, to the point, "Are you ready to be baptised?" he said. "I've been ready for a long time," I replied. He suggested I read about the baptism of our Lord and handed me his sacred black leather-bound Bible. Lying on my bed, I leafed carefully through the fine cream pages, and I saw—Jesus coming out of the water—the heavens opening—and the voice of God saying "This is my beloved Son, in whom I am well pleased."'

'How beautiful!' said the nun.

'Closing the book, I held it to my chest with reverence. The following morning, I approached Father with an inspired notion. "In the sea?" he baulked. "How ridiculous when we have a perfectly good baptismal pool at the chapel." I insisted that Jesus had been baptised in the Jordan. My father was having none of it, "He was also born in a stable while you were born at home in a comfy bed." But I insisted I would baptised in the sea. He told me that I was to join the other young people on a Sunday in the pool at the chapel." I then bellowed across the room some protestation with the full force of an adolescent. "Do not raise your voice at me young man. It is January. You will perish," he said, hitting the table hard with his fist, the aftershock disturbing the crockery. "Give me my Bible back and get out of my sight!" and that was that. I handed him the book and turned on my heels telling him that I would go and ask the minister myself.'

'How did he take that?' asked Sister Constance.

'Without looking up, he said, "Do as you will."

'When I arrived at the chapel, the minister, as familiar to me as an uncle, was leaning back on his chair in the office, deep in contemplation. I startled him. Announcing my plan to get baptised in the sea, he gave a hearty laugh. "Oh yes, of course but it will have to take place in April, as the sea is at its coldest until then." Patting me on the back he added, "Does your father approve?" I said he didn't and he so kindly said, "Oh well, parents usually disapprove of something. Let it be this," and with a little tenderness, he added, "Don't worry. I will bring him round. He is a good man. Try not to defy him too much."

'Three months later, when the sun had warmed the sea just sufficiently that the minister was hopeful that I wouldn't catch my death, he asked me into his office and told me I would be baptised in the sea the following Sunday. I was delighted. Forty people joined in the procession, all dressed in their Sunday best. At the insistence of the minister, I wore a white surplus over my father's old suit.'

Sister Constance laughed and clapped her hands together, 'Goodness, Mr Walker, you certainly know how to get your own way.'

'Clouds gathered above the party, grey and menacing. Father, the minister, and I, removed our shoes and waded into the sea. Salty water, seeping up my legs and pressing in, accentuated my already tall frame, making me gasp. Father, on my left, held a fixed expression. If he was chilled, he wasn't letting anyone know it. On my right, the minister wore an encouraging smile, holding on to me to steady himself against the waves. Shivering, he wasted no time. "Henry Walker, are you prepared to turn from the devil toward Christ?" my answer was sure and bold, "I turn to Christ!" Standing unevenly on fractured shells and sea worn pebbles, the minister lifted his arms to ask the congregation to support me and welcome me into the tradition. I was baptised in the name of the Father, Son and Holy Spirit and before I was submerged under the stony cold water in the English Channel, I took a huge breath in. The Minister and Father tipped me backwards while holding tightly onto my suit in case the strong waves swept me away. Liberated from the clutches of the devil, I shot up out of the water, punching the air with my fist. Weeping with delight, my ears burned, the wet robe weighing me down while my spirit soared over the ocean like a bird. I was proud and bursting with hope. Walking up onto the beach, the congregation surrounded me, laying their hands upon my shoulders, back and head. The minister said, "Come Holy Spirit. Come and fill Henry up for thy work and thy purpose." I shuddered, almost expecting a dove to swoop down from heaven and land on my head. Mother, presuming I was cold, placed a towel on my back. But if anything, I was as warm as toast and a little euphoric especially when everyone began waving their hankies and singing *Be Thou My Vision*.'

Sister Constance once again clapped her hands together. 'What a storyteller you are Mr Walker,' she said.

We talked for a while, and I must say, I was happy to have her approval!

23. SISTER CONSTANCE

Tuesday 13 February 1990

What a storyteller he is!

On my Tuesday visit with Mr Walker, he rested his head back and ended his Baptism story by looking towards heaven and singing: 'Be thou my vision, O Lord of my heart, naught be all else to me, save that thou art. Thou my best thought, by day or by night, waking or sleeping, thy presence my light.'

I clapped. I was impressed. It reminded me of my childhood. The elders sitting round the fire telling fascinating stories of their initiation rites.

'What a lovely voice you have,' I said. 'Your baptism really made an impact, but did you not feel good enough just being you?'

'Not really... maybe after my baptism I did for a while until life destroyed my faith. And now I think it was just the fantasies of a foolish boy, and... you don't know the half of it, Sister.'

I was not immune to the struggles of a man battling with his past – *You don't know the half of it* – was a familiar statement.

I had been with Mr Walker long over the elected hour and I was aware that Mother Superior had asked us to return to the convent earlier for an extended dusting session. The warm weather had brought with it a layer of sand from the desert, and she was concerned it would affect our lungs, but I was born with a protective layer of red earth from the bush thousands of miles away.

As a nun you may suspect my first love to have been Jesus. But my father was a Catholic who converted my mother the day they met at an open-air festival in Mowamjam, and so I was raised in a household where Jesus was given the status of a family member. He was ever present.

My first giddy experience of love happened when I was 17 years old. We met at a dance. He was tall and thin, with skin as white as an alabaster jar. I was a novelty to him, a dark-skinned girl with broad features.

He wanted to drown in my eyes.

What a poet.

But he wasn't strong enough to withstand the abuse of his friends taunting him, and his mother scolding him. 'Why make your life harder than it need be?' she said on numerous occasions.

I was unsure of how to rebuff his sexual advances. I liked the kissing... and the gifts of flowers. But I was nervous of such intense intimacy. It just felt wrong to me. I was torn between my love for God and my love for a man.

I was grateful that I didn't have to decide. He met another girl who was willing. I considered a vow of celibacy. But for a couple of years, I didn't need to worry because no one showed the slightest interest. As far as men were concerned my timing was always off. The ones I liked never liked me, and the ones that liked me, I wasn't interested in. And then the event that changed my life happened and I was never the same after that.

Sometimes I am jealous of lovers holding hands in the park. Or couples who come to discuss their marriage problems. I have often wondered if it is better to have problems in a marriage than not be married at all. But then I was too wounded to get married. Too damaged and unable to heal my view of men. I do believe, as Saint Paul states in Corinthians, that some people are better off single and that being single can be a huge blessing.

24. WREN

Tuesday 13 February 1990

I fell pregnant on our honeymoon! I was twenty-one. Morning sickness hit like a storm, and I was sick ten times a day for the next thirty-five weeks. It didn't matter what remedies I took to assuage the sickness; it always defeated me. Sometimes I went by train to Westcliff and Florence met me. Strolling through the park arm in arm, I had to stop several times, heaving into a plastic bag before sipping water or nibbling on a cracker. 'Poor you,' she would say, 'it's worrying seeing you like this, I was hardly sick with my three boys. There is nothing of you.' She invited me back to Craigmore for soup and a bed.

It was true, I was becoming so thin, I hardly looked pregnant. I loved staying at Craigmore, in my familiar room with its green eiderdown and hearing kind words from my uncle Walter before bed. The birth was straight forward, although the labour was long and exhausting. Our son, Patrick, was large and chubby and handsome like his dad. He cried a lot too, but we both adored him.

David and I enjoyed our life together, finding everything fresh and new: trips to concerts and the theatre, poetry readings, and our mutual love of books. Of course, we struggled in the early years like most young couples. David was only just out of university and was trying to get a job as an art teacher. We bought a dog and named her PatChoo. She was a mongrel. Her left ear sticking up while the other hung down like a pirate's patch over her right eye. We moved into a small flat in North London, equipped with a few pieces of furniture and some kitchen essentials. I enjoyed being a mother and as my father had predicted, was highly qualified.

Eventually, David secured his first job as an art teacher travelling the short distance to the local Senior School. Our flat was on the High Street, over a hairdressing salon. On Saturday mornings the smell of peroxide wafted up through the cracks in the floorboards. Hoping to overpower one smell with another, David announced, 'It's bacon and egg time!' and produced a lavish breakfast every weekend.

With a gift of £3,000 from my grandmother, David and I moved into a three bedroomed, semi-detached house on Champion Road, in Upminster, Essex, only thirty minutes on the train to Westcliff. It was just in time for the birth of our second child who came along within fifteen months. I was unfortunately just as sick as the first time and Florence and Walter were just as helpful. In late December, I was ten days overdue but I insisted that David go to work that morning as he would be breaking up from school soon. 'Stop fussing, I'll be okay!' I re-assured him.

The pain started shortly after David left the house. I rang the school and gave a message to the receptionist. My waters broke and as I reached down between my legs, I felt a small foot. Holding onto those tiny toes I said hello to my baby, but then the panic set in and I called the midwife who came immediately. When Florence got the call, she dropped everything, and arrived an hour later.

Upon examination, the midwife said, 'I can't feel the baby's head. I will call for the doctor.'

'What does that mean?' I said, sweating profusely.

Florence answered, 'Don't worry dear. The baby will have a head, it is probably too far back and too low down to feel it.' The mid-wife nodded in agreement.

Crouching on all fours, I started the deep breathing exercises I had learnt at the antenatal clinic. 'Giving birth is a natural thing. I'm supposed to enjoy it,' I said, grunting through each contraction.

Florence looked bemused. 'You carry on, dear. Do what works for you, although I'm not sure that any one can say they enjoy giving birth.'

David crashed through the door into the bedroom. 'I'm here, my darling. Got the message, but the receptionist waited until I had completed a double lesson before telling me you'd called.'

'Hold my hand, David. I'm scared,' I said.

'Nothing to be worried about. You've done it before.'

When the doctor arrived, he seemed to spend an age with his stethoscope, skimming across my ballooning tummy. 'I can't feel the head either. Mrs Gardner, I want you to get straight to hospital. No home birth for you.'

At the hospital I was rushed to a private room and examined. After a few inhalations of gas and air, I vomited and pushed the instrument away.

A young male doctor, who must have only been a few years older than David, entered the room with several others. 'Did you have a fall at some point in your pregnancy?'

Weary with pain, I said, 'About a month ago I slipped on the post office steps.'

'That's when the baby must have done a somersault in your tummy.'

'What does that mean?' said David.

'Well, as your wife can testify, you are having a footling!'

My legs were raised in stirrups. Scared and powerless, I surrendered my body, battling with contractions and trying not to push the baby out before I was told to.

Eventually, my newborn footling, with black hair, and almond eyes was placed on my tummy, before being tightly swaddled and whisked away for forty-eight hours observation.

David was so proud. And kissing me, full on the lips, reassured me that he would make the home ready. On Christmas Eve, I held Amy in my arms as I travelled back with David to Champion Road. The next day, Florence and Walter arrived with my son, Patrick. David prepared Duck a l'orange with all the trimmings, while I sat up in bed breastfeeding. Florence leant over and whispered in my ear, 'A son is a son 'til he takes a wife, but a daughter is a daughter all of her life.'

As the children grew up, I needed to earn some money. As a qualified Norland Nanny, I could have secured a great live-in job but as a married woman it was going to be harder. I decided to become a teaching assistant in the nearby primary school. The children were adorable, and they ignited a desire in me to become a teacher.

My father knew very little of my married life, learning a few facts from Walter or from the occasional card I sent him. He didn't know what my joys or fears were as some fathers do. He started with good intentions, a letter, and a cheque, but he soon went quiet again. Little was I to know that one day he would be of great help to me and David.

25. HENRY

Tuesday 20 February

When Sister Constance arrived at her usual time, the small table in front of the chairs was laid for tea. I had ordered sandwiches and shortbread biscuits.

She appeared to be delighted. I remember how to treat a woman and sister Constance is really the only person I can spoil, apart from Vivien. When the nun said sorry that she had not had time to read my memoirs, I was disappointed. She had been on a Catholic Conference for a few days and so asked me to tell her what happened after my baptism. I scoffed, but within a few minutes I decided to tell her, 'A month after I was baptised in the sea on the Essex coast, I met Queenie at the school gate of Southend High School for Girls.'

'Queenie is an unusual name,' she said.

'Her real name was Elsie, but her father called her Queenie. Freddy, her brother, was my best friend and we both attended Southend High School for Boys.

'What was Freddy like?'

'Freddy was short and stocky, nimble on his feet and quick with his fists, joviality inscribed throughout his body like red lettering inside sugary rock.'

She laughed, 'What a wonderful simile!'

'I liked his sister immediately but was unnerved by her beauty, I found it hard to speak to her.'

'So how did you ever get to know her?'

'One afternoon, when Freddy was given a detention, Queenie suggested that we extend our walk back home by going via the seafront at Westcliff. The promenade was virtually empty, as vast grey clouds blown in from the east blew us around like paper bags. "The weather reminds me of my baptism last month," I said. Queenie stopped in her tracks; "You were baptised? Why didn't you invite me?" I explained that I hadn't known her then and it wasn't something I had wanted Freddy to know about. She asked why. "Because he will tease me," I replied. She agreed that Freddy teased everyone but told me not to be ashamed of my faith.'

'It can put people off,' said Sister Constance.

'That's exactly what I said to her! But she said it made her like me more. She told me how when she was nine years old, she was praying on her knees when she saw Jesus standing at the foot of her bed. That amazed me. "What was he like?" I asked. "He was... gentle, but at the same time... powerful," she said. No one believed her, except her father because he said children often see Jesus because they have a simple faith and don't over complicate things. But it is what she said next that made me shiver.'

'What was that?' said the nun.

'That she hadn't felt the same since and that it was as if heaven came down and touched earth.'

'You shivered because you knew exactly what she meant,' said Sister Constance.

'I then did the oddest thing! I punched her on the shoulder!'

'What on earth for?' said the nun.

'I don't know. I was a fourteen-year-old boy. I didn't have any skills.'

'What did she do?' she said, placing her head in her hands (as she often does).

'Queenie flinched. "Ouch. What was that for?" she said, followed by, "Only joking". She then punched me on my upper arm and began to sprint off along the dull slabs of the promenade. When I caught up with her our hands brushed lightly together. Queenie took hold of my little finger and I shuddered. Lunging forward to kiss her, I accidentally hit her nose with my chin. Immediately she pulled away, laughing. I was mortified, having to fight back my instinct to run. Suddenly, Queenie dropped her satchel, and taking hold of my blazer, pulled me down, kissing me tenderly on the lips. I wanted to melt into her—be absorbed by her—she was truly delicious.'

'So... you met her at a young age and how long were you together?' said the nun.

'I'll get to that,' I said.

'Did your parents like her?' she asked.

'Not really, is the simple answer... I think they thought she was a bad influence on me. While in fact she was the most positive influence of my life.'

'You shared a deep faith.'

'I remember a time when we were eighteen and Queenie wanted to attend the Avenue Baptist Church because there was a gifted speaker there who was drawing in a thousand people on a Sunday.'

'That's impressive,' said Sister Constance.

'My mother's response was, "Just because he has a congregation of over a thousand every Sunday doesn't mean he is biblically rigorous." She believed he was simplifying the message to get the numbers. Shrugging my shoulders, I tried to remain aloof saying it was something we had chosen to do together because Reverend Tinsley was a gifted preacher. I asked them to come along one Sunday to see for themselves. My mother laughed. "We shall stick to our own chapel, thank you. It may only have sixty in the congregation, but there is such a thing as integrity you know." My father said that preachers who attracted thousands of people often diminished as quickly as they rose. I was incensed. I reminded them both of Bunyan and Spurgeon, Oswald Chambers and William Booth? "Booth was a Methodist," said my mother, who wanted to end the conversation.'

Sister Constance was surprised, 'Were they really that prejudiced?'

'Oh yes.'

'How did you answer that?'

I said "Does it really matter? He was still a Christian." And then I mentioned that John Wesley had been an Anglican but was also one of the greatest evangelists of his time. Their silence shouted their opinion on that matter!'

'What were Queenie's parents like?' said the nun, who reached for a small purple frosted cake.

'Bert, and Betty, continually surprised me with their broad-minded views. Both, short in stature but huge in grace. Betty always immaculately turned out with an air of glamour, her clothing, her jewellery, both simple but charming. While Bert, a striking man with a tanned face and a shot of wavy brown hair flecked with white, was full of wit and faith. What impressed me most was how they engaged in earnest discussion with Freddy and Queenie without it becoming unpleasant.'

'Unlike your parents?'

'Yes exactly! One Sunday lunch Queenie, annoyed with her mother said, "It is not acceptable that women can only vote if they are over thirty, married to a man with property or have a degree." She talked about how Emmeline Pankhurst had formed the Women's Social and Political Union because all women needed to have a voice. After all, they educate most of the pupils in schools, including the boys. Her mother responded with, "Yes dear, but setting fire to Lloyd George's country home and getting oneself killed under King George's horse, is rather extreme. I think there are better ways to get the laws in this land changed."'

'Queenie was a suffragette?'

'Not really, but she was a political person, believing that passively fighting the law had not made any difference and it is only when women behave like men that they are heard. She was looking forward to getting the vote. I admired her strength immensely.'

'Did you both know what you wanted for your future?' asked Sister Constance.

'Queenie always wanted to become a primary school teacher whereas I was far less sure of my purpose. My father was set on me joining his firm Roland Walker & Co. but I had other ideas I just wasn't sure exactly what they were.'

'Did Queenie become a teacher?'

'She trained at Homerton College in Cambridge under the auspicious Mary Miller Allen, a Glaswegian, whose exacting standards were renowned throughout the university. I remember Queenie telling me that on her first morning in the Great Hall Ms Miller said, "If you remember anything of your two years here at Homerton, remember the college motto, respice finem which means to – consider the outcome or to look to the end of your life – regard your death." Queenie had barely lived, surely it was unnecessary to make her dwell upon her death.'

'What did you do while she was studying?'

'I pined for her every day,' I said.

26. SISTER CONSTANCE

Tuesday 20 February

I spent an intense hour with Mr Walker this afternoon. He touched on his relationship with Queenie. He talks about her with such passion. His voice changes and he is animated and recalls situations in wonderful detail.

I have had my own struggles with voting in my country. But I had no idea that in the year I was born, 1925, women in the UK couldn't vote unless they had a degree or owned property.

There have been, and continue to be, injustices everywhere and considering the First Peoples have been roaming the land for over 75,000 years they were not able to vote, male and female, in all territories until 1965. My mother's tribe denied a voice until then.

Where's the justice in that?

I didn't vote until I was forty years old. So incensed were my fellow nuns that they refused to vote until I was permitted.

Respice Finem – look to the end.

Some words and phrases are like shooting stars. They flash into your consciousness lighting up a path you have trodden for many years. I never did learn Latin, but a scripture like *Respice Finem* is embedded in my psyche. 'Teach us to number our days that we may apply our heart unto wisdom.' This quote from Psalm 90 swung on a painted board above our front door. It was my father's motto. As a teenager it troubled me. Rather like Mr Walker's concern for Queenie dwelling on death. I believed if I dwelt on my death, I would be robbed of my life.

But when I was nineteen years old, I considered the weight of *Respice Finem* and as I have grown older and age has veiled my youth, I believe it is an inspired piece of advice and it goes to the very heart of my existence, placing all things into perspective.

Mr Walker pined for Queenie as he mentioned before but as he reflected on his past, he came alive. When Queenie organized a trip to 'The Orchard' in Grantchester Henry borrowed two bikes from the college and they cycled the few miles down country lanes to the pavilion where he bought tea and scones. Finding a private leafy enclave, they sat for a few hours on green deckchairs.

'Queenie was always the romantic. She told me stories about Rupert Brooke, Augustus John, and Virginia Wolf all having visited The Orchard for tea. I remember one time when I started to take my clothes off.'

'Mr Walker! Do I need to hear this?' I said.

'We were shielded from the foliage of a large ash and an apple tree. When I removed my white cotton shirt, Queenie asked me what I was doing? I said, it was so hot, and nobody could see us. "I mustn't get caught with you half naked," she laughed. "I expect Augustus John took his shirt off. He was quite a rebel," I protested.'

'You obviously felt constrained?' I said.

'Yes, constrained by everything.'

Mr Walker leant forward, a glint in his eye, '"I have had an idea," Queenie said, rather pleased with herself. Why don't you tell your father that you want to become a Baptist minister? Then you can study theology and English at university." She added. "I fancy being married to a missionary. Maybe we could go to Africa?"'

'Now, here we have it!' I said, 'so, did you?'

'Did I what?' he snorted, 'become a minister? Yes... yes I did!'

I was dumbfounded. Mr Walker had been a priest. 'You kept that quiet for six weeks!'

'Ah well... I couldn't tell you everything all in one go.'

'You remind me of my grandfather... he would take an age to tell a story! So, go on...'

'It was such a brilliant idea and my father agreed immediately. I was the only son he allowed to go to university.'

'Where did you go?'

'Manchester... to study Theology and English.'

'What happened to your relationship when you went to Manchester?'

'I went to see Queenie's father and asked for her hand in marriage. Bert was delighted. He had never doubted my love for his daughter and now I was to become a minister he was more than happy to give his seal of approval. Bert was determined to keep my plan a secret from Queenie. The following Saturday morning I drove Queenie to Cuckfield in Sussex to see the work of Charles Eamer Kemp who has adorned churches throughout England with stained glass, furnishings, and paintings. It is where I got down on one knee and asked Queenie to marry me.'

'Oh, how wonderful. And she said yes?'

'Of course!'

'Did you enjoy your studies?' I asked.

'The best thing about Manchester was meeting Ralph, a fellow student who was the same height as me, but some say more handsome, his face dotted in auburn freckles. Over a game of chess, we discussed politics and the international situation, but Ralph was often distracted, his blue eyes searching out the prettiest women at the university, who invariably returned his attentions. I became his advisor on matters of love and was frequently getting him out of scrapes with various admirers. But after three years, Ralph decided against going into the Church and instead secured a position as a journalist for The Dartmouth Chronicle. It was

Ralph, who in our last term, gave me his Remington typewriter. "Write it down, Henry," he said to me. "But I have nothing to say old man," I replied. "Everyone has a story," he told me.'

27. WREN

Tuesday 20 February 1990

I have been teaching for the past twenty-eight years.
It is beginning to really get me down.

Working my way through the ranks, from teaching assistant to Head of an English department, I am now bored with the red tape. The love I once had for literature has almost evaporated. I enjoy the children... well most of them. But it's hard to impart the excitement I had for the Brontës when they have withered on the moors of excessive grading and box ticking. Maybe when I retire, I will get the desire back, like a parcel, lost in the post and finally delivered.

Sifting through the black and white photographs of my mother and father my eyes are drawn to one taken in Cuckfield in May 1926. The day of their engagement. Sitting on a hillock at the back of Holy Trinity, a church of over nine hundred years old, my mother wears a plain dress and a small felt hat while my father is casual for the times but is still wearing a shirt and tie. They are close and they both look happy. When I visited the church in Cuckfield a few years ago, the sun was bright in early May, and the chestnut candles scented the air. The doors creaked as I pushed them open. Inside it was cool with a strong damp odour fusing with the history of worshipping generations. The ceiling is breathtaking, deceptive, as each section is painted to look as if it is puffed out like a pillow, while in fact it is a flat surface. I imagine my parents holding hands in a pew and then walking out to the graveyard, stretching itself out towards the spectacular backdrop of the South Downs. I see him carrying a picnic basket to a small hillock, settling down on a tartan rug, rising onto one knee and taking her hand. The event was frozen in time by a passerby who was offered my father's box camera.

Although my father wanted to marry my mother immediately, she was insistent they wait until he finished his degree and secured a job. Having graduated from Homerton in Cambridge she was offered a teaching position near to his accommodation. Before they both moved to Manchester, they attended Walter and Florence's wedding. At university, my father studied the sermons of Alexander McClaren, who drew crowds in the hundreds at Union Chapel, Fallowfield, during the latter part of the nineteenth century. Sometimes he read McClaren's sermons out loud to Queenie when he visited her in her lodgings, both smoking Woodbines.

Once they had secured the Burrowbridge Chapel, Queenie began to organise their wedding, choosing to get married in December at the Avenue Baptist Church in Westcliff in 1934.

I hold a photograph of their wedding day in my hands.

My father and Queenie are standing on the chapel steps, framed by the high arch of the entrance. On the left of frame, the snow has dusted the branches of a tree covering the path and the steps of the church in a light coat of what appears to be feathers. Henry stands tall and solid leaning ever so slightly into Queenie who is looking directly at the camera. Queenie, wearing a dark coat and small dark felt hat links Henry's right arm with her white gloved left-hand. In her right hand, she carries the other glove. Her foot dangles off the step and she is looking to her left, smiling, maybe at her mother or her father or maybe at her brother, Freddy, who is likely pulling a face.

She appears relaxed and confident.

I am grateful.

28. HENRY

Tuesday 27 February 1990

Last week, when the nun left my room, I chuckled. She was so interested that I had been a Baptist minister. Really quite tickled by it.

I immediately wrote a few pages of an event I had not previously documented. I feel inspired to write and she, at least, genuinely seems fascinated.

When she arrived today, I handed her some pages. 'Please read them before we start our session,' I said.

She sat entranced.

I eagerly awaited her response.

Memoirs 1934/5
When I graduated from university, I quickly became frustrated. Despite many interviews to secure a position of minister within a chapel I was unsuccessful. 'We just have to be patient,' said my darling, Queenie.

It was in the October when 'patience' was finally rewarded. Queenie and I arrived in an overheated Austin outside Burrowbridge Chapel near Bridgwater on the Somerset Levels. The chapel was a red brick construction with 'Ebenezer Chapel 1836' carved into a stone plaque over the porch. Its graveyard at the front bid welcome to the worshippers who passed through the wrought iron gates each Sunday morning. The hipped slate roof, boxed eaves and two arched windows assigned a certain humility, that of a home rather than a church. But its dark pews, seating over one hundred on a Holy Day, wedding, or funeral, dispelled the intimacy of a home, as much, if not more than the granite gravestones.

A group of six elders, including the previous minister, Reverend Wilson, gave us a tour of the building with its substantial Sunday school room at the rear and stables underneath.

But Queenie was more excited by the living accommodation; a detached manse, situated adjacent to the chapel, with a wooden gate opening onto a neat front garden and doused in the aroma of honeysuckle. Travelling through the two rooms at the front of the house she eyed the fireplaces and surveyed the amount of work needed. 'I could make this lovely for us,' she whispered.

The elders took up their positions behind a trestle table in the Sunday school room and began with an hour-long rigorous interview. Questions were raised, such as, 'How much involvement do you believe the church elders should have in making decisions?' And, 'Do you believe in the gifts of the Holy Spirit?' And, 'Would Queenie be involved in the running of the Sunday school?' And, most importantly, 'When are you planning to get married?'

That evening, we ate beef pie with Mr and Mrs Conley, the local butcher, and his wife. Mrs Conley talked incessantly about nothing much at all. At precisely 9.30 p.m. she showed Queenie to her bedroom and then me to mine. In the black of night, we sneaked out onto the landing, careful not to wake our hosts. Giggling like teenagers we stole a kiss before retiring to our own rooms to sleep.

The next morning, I stood in the pulpit and preached a sermon as part of the interview process. For thirty-five minutes I spoke on the ravages of hell and judgment. 'Surely,' I said, 'don't let us get caught up in any Universalist concepts which profess Christ will redeem all people from hell. This makes no sense. Man will be judged on his time on earth, and it would be wrong if people just got away with heinous acts. Judgment is about God being fair.'

The stillness and blank looks at the end of the sermon made me realise that I may have been a little zealous suspecting it was the wrong morning and possibly the wrong century to have expressed my convictions. Queenie, a little dismayed at my postulating, said, 'Was it your intention to scare them half to death?'

Receiving some nods and approval from the elders, it appeared it was their opinion that mattered.

Joining in with *Amazing Grace,* Queenie's silvery voice, a pleasant tone with a striking vibrato, could be heard above the throng. The day came to an end and I drove Queenie home, praying for a favourable outcome.

Having convinced the elders of my passion, I secured the position of Baptist Minister and was able to marry my sweetheart.

I was hugely excited at the prospect of giving my first official address.

I sat upright at my trusty Remington, as if playing a piano, and I completed my sermon. I then read it to Queenie to make sure it was of the right temper, as it was not my wish to scare the congregation but rather to teach them the Biblical truths of justice and mercy.

She set about improving our living accommodation and several days later was washing down two wooden chairs festooned with cobwebs when the elders arrived with the gift of a granddaughter clock.

It was mid-January and I remember there were widespread gales and heavy rain. On opening the front door, the wind blasted through the hall, chilling Queenie's slim ankles. She told me how three of the elders and Mrs Conley stood in a line as if waiting for a decoration. Mr Conley, wearing a flat cap over his tousled hair, stepped forward. 'On behalf of the elders and the congregation of the Burrowbridge Chapel we would like to present you with a gift.'

He held the clock upright and at arm's length, as if he was introducing a child to a teacher on its first day of school; a velvet cream ribbon tied in a neat bow around its neck.

'My goodness,' said Queenie. 'Please, do come in.' Turning on her heels, she ran through the hall to the kitchen removing her pinny as she crossed the garden, calling out, 'Henry, come quickly, Henry.'

I heard her voice and when she arrived at the office I was already standing, alarmed that she was calling on me to extinguish a fire or catch a mouse in the scullery.

'Darling. Come and see what we have been given.' Her voice cried out excitedly as a child on Christmas morning, younger than her twenty-eight years.

Following Queenie back to the manse, my height dictated a stoop in order to avoid hitting my head on the door frame. The clock stood facing us in the hall, the elders frowning, disgruntled by Queenie's excitement.

The granddaughter clock, shorter than a grandfather clock, stood at five feet, the same height as Queenie. Its wooden case, a veneer covered plywood, was enhanced with tiny flower heads on beading either side. The long body of the clock settled on what looks like a separate plinth of the same making, but it wasn't separate at all. The head of the clock, similarly, divided by beading, sat on top. Its silver-plated face sported black painted numbers and two ornate hands and was interrupted by three keyholes set at four, six and eight o'clock.

Pulling the length of ribbon, Queenie's small hands filled with velvet.

Mrs Conley passed Queenie a brass key and pointed to the three keyholes. 'The left one is for winding the strike, the middle one winds the clock, and the one on the right is for the quarter chime... but for now, it is fully wound, we just need to start the chimes.' Opening the small door at the back of the clock, she lightly flicked the pendulum with her forefinger. It beat out a rhythm like a metronome set for a fugue. Opening the glass door on the face, she set the time to three o'clock. Westminster chimes reverberated modestly from the clock filling the small home.

'Oh, the chimes remind me of Big Ben!' said Queenie. 'Thank you! Thank you all so much! This is a most generous gift.'

I nodded in agreement, 'It is a fine year for a clock to be given as it is the hundredth anniversary of the fire at Westminster.'

All eyes were fixed on me.

'But why does that make it a fine year to receive a clock?' asked Queenie.

Patting the clock on its head, I began. 'A fire started under the Lords Chamber, quickly taking hold. The Palace of Westminster soon became engulfed in flames, burning through the night, and thousands of people gathered on Westminster Bridge and in the streets.' The small group regarded me with approval. 'Turner produced some spectacular paintings as a visual record of the dramatic event!' I was in full flow. 'Ten years later there was a call for a *King of Clocks* to be built, the biggest clock the world has ever seen. Big Ben was the name given to the largest bell ever made. So, you see, what a year to present a clock!' Everyone applauded my fine speech.

'I haven't offered anyone any tea. What was I thinking?' said Queenie.

Mrs Conley followed Queenie into the kitchen. 'I'll help you, my dear.' Taking the kettle from the Rayburn, she filled it at the tap and placed it back on to the round hot plate, talking all the while.

The elders, meanwhile, challenged me on how I proposed to raise money to repair the chapel roof.

On entering the room, Queenie was a little flustered. Placing the tray down, she handed out cups of tea. Mrs Conley followed behind her, offering the sugar bowl and tongs. Taking centre stage, she announced, 'Mrs Walker wants to change the Sunday school implying there is something wrong with it. I've told her I think it is fine as it is.'

Queenie laughed spontaneously at the attack. 'That is not what I said, Mrs Conley. I asked you what you would like me to achieve with the Sunday school? It is a totally different thing.'

'It is virtually the same thing,' said Mrs Conley, her cheeks burning red.

I interjected, 'I am sure we have plenty of time to talk and deliberate upon the Sunday school, but for now, let us enjoy the chiming of this auspicious clock.' And as if on cue, the clock chimed quarter past the hour.

Like a naughty child who has been caught bullying in the playground, Mrs Conley sulked in the corner of the room, her face bearing a deep scowl, as if under a curse. The guests remained for another fifteen minutes until the butcher and his wife were the first to leave, nurturing their offense.

After supper, I sat by the fire, my long legs stretched out in front of me, smoke rising in a straight line from my cigarette. Hypnotised by the crackling of wood and the tick-tocking of the clock, I raised my eyes to look at Queenie as she walked in from the kitchen. 'You look radiant, my darling.'

'Thank you,' she said, and moving towards me she sat on my lap, disturbing my slicked back hair with her delicate fingers

'I was proud of you this afternoon when you stood up to that battle-axe. What did she say to you in the kitchen?'

'She asked me how experienced I was working with children. I told her that I was a qualified primary school teacher and had worked since I graduated nearly four years ago. I made some suggestions about developing the Sunday school.'

'There is something mean-spirited about her.'

'She's not that bad. I will get her on my side.'

'I'm not so sure.'

Queenie gently cupped my face in her hands. 'You were wonderful today, Henry.'

'In what way?'

'I had no idea you knew so much about the fire at Westminster and Big Ben. You are such a marvellous storyteller.'

'There's a lot about me you don't know!'

'It would seem that way,' she whispered.

The truth is, there was very little about me that my wife didn't know.

29. SISTER CONSTANCE

Tuesday 27 February 1990

Mr Walker writes beautifully about his wife but I wonder what happened to her.

Although we have had a few discussions on all sorts of subjects he struggles to talk about his loss of faith. Maybe because it is like a forgotten language, the words caught between his brain and his mouth.

'I enjoyed reading about your wife and the gift of the clock,' I said at today's meeting.

'You were obviously surprised about me becoming a minister,' he grinned.

'Well... yes... I was,' I replied.

'We often underestimate what old people have done in their youth.'

I nodded, 'You are so right, Mr Walker,' I said, 'We all experience prejudice at some point in our lives. Each underestimating the other.'

'It seems a lifetime ago now.'

'I'm sure it does... but it was obviously a big part of you.'

'A part of me I shut down...'

'I prayed for you last night,' I said.

'That was a waste of time,' he replied.

'Prayer is hardly a waste of my time. I brought you a Bible.' I handed him the hardback.

'I hope it's the King James.'

'No, it's a Good News.'

He passed it back, 'I can't read this. It's for children.'

'Well, don't read it then,' I said, placing it on the Formica table in front of him. I then took hold of his right hand and gave it a squeeze. 'I enjoy your memoirs, Mr Walker. Queenie is fascinating and you were obviously very much in love with her.'

'I never stopped loving her.'

'What happened?'

'I would prefer to let you read my memoirs. It makes it easier for me.'

'You are certainly descriptive. So alive in your writing... were you at the chapel for long?' I asked

'Long enough!' he said. Obviously, a sore point, and I presume Mrs Conley had something to do with his disdain.

'But you had such a passion to save people's souls?' I said.

He ordered tea.

The more questions I asked, the more he rebuffed me. He ended the discussion by talking about the appalling food at the care home. I have never eaten there so I couldn't comment but I knew he was distracting me from asking more questions.

Storytelling is a beautiful thing.

My mother was intent on us understanding our heritage of storytelling, known as the Dreamings. A timeless concept, one of many my British father found hard to embrace.

It is the very act of creation.

The Dreaming is always with you.

It is not set in time past or time present or time future... it is with us now in place and law. Knowledge, culture, and belief systems are passed on by way of song, dance, the arts, and stories of creation. In our home, our mother taught us intuitively, less bound by constraint or expectation. She enabled us to run freely to the shop, bathing our wounds if boys threw sticks at us. She stroked our hair with both hands and sang soothing lullabies. When people called us names, she prayed over our hearts and spoke the name of Jesus upon our foreheads. My mother calmed my father and held him back from his internal fire of revenge. She was a peacemaker and everyone in our small hub of houses on a piece of bush was a little frightened of her. I don't think it was because of the colour of her skin, I think it was because of the way in which she surpassed time. She held no grudges and she met everyone as if meeting them for the first time, even if they had been spiteful on previous occasions. When they were rude, she forgave them almost instantly. It was a strength that I have rarely met in anyone else, and I can only imagine that she learnt it from her parents who had no material wealth and who instructed her in the ways of the land and the Dreamings.

When she was presented with Jesus, an abused man, a victim of prejudice, not as white as she had first thought, who taught seventy times seventy forgiveness, she made the connection in her heart. She devoured the Bible from Genesis to Revelation and quoted the opening lines – repeating them like a mantra – *And the earth was without form, and void; and darkness was upon the face of the deep. And the Spirit of God moved upon the face of the waters.*

My mother married my father in a small welcoming church in Adelaide.

She was an activist, making strides in seeking justice for the oppressed First Peoples of this great land. She was a mediator and an influencer; her mission was to bring unity and peace beyond the glaring disparities of the First and Second Peoples.

The peace she managed in her marriage spilled out into her meetings and her dialogue was attractive. She was a genius in handling my father's traditionalism. To give him credit, he was a magnificent man because he saw her worth and he defied many obstacles in loving her. Their laughter was infectious, and it became the order of our household.

When my father was taken from us, the spiritual calling on my life flowed from my mother to me. As I walked towards my vocation as a nun, I felt the *Spirit of God soaring over me like a bird.*

I do hope Mr Walker finds the gift I placed in the Bible.

30. WREN

Tuesday 27 February 1990

In my twenties my mind was always a full larder packed with David, raising Patrick and Amy, and paying bills. It was so jammed tight with necessities that my father and Vivien were placed on the top shelf, in the dim light, out of reach.

I secured a job at a large comprehensive as a teacher's assistant and David was teaching full time, so we had to be rigid about getting the children into school. Patrick was an easy child as he enjoyed school and was happy to get up and get ready on his own. He was rarely sick and was an industrious student from a very young age and we had high hopes he would do well. But Amy was a sickly child. At four years old she had scarlet fever. At five and six, she had sore throat after sore throat. At seven, she had mumps. And when she was eight, she had six weeks of chickenpox. The doctor even had to pay a night time visit as she became delirious, seeing spiders climbing her bedroom wall. It was exhausting for David and I. Both trying to juggle work and Amy's time off.

My father, Henry, suggested she recoup with them in Spain. I wasn't sure about it but David thought the warm weather would do her good, so Amy and I flew out in the Whitsun break. Amy loved the villa, and she loved Vivien. They agreed to have her for the 6-week term and Amy was happy to stay. The hardest thing was to leave my daughter with my father. I wasn't convinced he could look after her. But Vivien reassured me that they would all have great fun. I was on the phone to Amy almost every day until my father put a stop to it. He told me that Amy found it unsettling and I should just let her be. I succumbed for a week and then called her for a chat. I didn't have a huge amount of faith that my father knew what he was doing. I could speak from experience. However, when I went to collect Amy, her health was totally restored.

31. HENRY

Tuesday 6 March 1990

My hands are a little puffy from typing each day and sometimes I wake in the night and continue by scribbling notes in pencil. Thinking back on my life, it doesn't always feel as if it happened to me; I feel disconnected, but as I write, I can remember those early years at the manse in Burrowbridge more clearly.

Memoirs 1935

Queenie wanted to restore many of the original features in the small house next to the Chapel. She painted the skirting boards in a sage green oil-based paint, flooding the house with a strong odour. Anticipating my annoyance, she placed small jugs of lavender in each room, and I was relieved when the scent finally won through. My task, meanwhile, included: filing all correspondence from the council and dealing with complaints from congregation members: setting up a committee for the forthcoming Spring Fair and taking minutes for said meeting; visiting the sick, taking funerals, weddings, baptisms, as well as writing a weekly sermon, as well as cleaning the cobwebs from the chapel ceiling. Deciding that Mrs Conley was an interfering busybody, I came up with a plan to keep her busy.

'Well Minister,' she said, 'if you think polishing the pews would give the place a lift, I shall organise a group of women straight away.' Six or seven women from the village, plied with dusters and thick brown polish, met outside the large front door and on entering proceeded to polish their way through the pews.

Life in the village of Burrowbridge was in many ways splendid and, except for a few pernicious individuals, one would be hard pushed to find a kinder bunch. The surrounding countryside was beautiful, and its abundant wildlife were frequent visitors at the manse. They included, foxes, hedgehogs and the occasional stray goat or lamb from the farm next door. The River Parrett flowed adjacent to the road directly opposite the chapel, while Burrow Mump, with its 15th century church ruin, loomed over St Michael's church and the village pub.

Organising the Centenary of the opening of the chapel, I established a special fund to raise money for the redecoration of the building. I was greatly cheered when I received close on £190 in subscriptions and collections. Unfortunately, the people's generosity meant they were reluctant to put money in the collection on Sunday which meant I didn't get paid. I was required to send a letter out to all the attendees asking them to bring a thank-offering.

Meanwhile, Queenie was busy with people in the village, often keeping it secret from me.

'What are you up to?' I asked on our first Easter Sunday.

'Just wait and see,' she replied, tapping the side of her nose.

At the end of my sermon, she stood and announced an Easter egg hunt for the children and their parents. During the week, she had gathered several mums in the baker's kitchen to make dozens of small chocolate eggs. During the cooking session, the baker's wife asked the group, 'What do you all prefer, Easter or Christmas?'

'Christmas,' the women replied, except for Queenie.

'Easter, every time,' she said. 'My father made it such an important occasion, with egg races and reenactments of the resurrection story. Don't you think it is remarkable that when Jesus rose from the dead, he appeared to two women and told them to take the news of his resurrection to the disciples? That may not seem so strange to us today, but two thousand years ago it was extraordinary that he gave such important news to women. The religious leaders at the time would not have been impressed, and the Gospel writers could have changed it to men, but they didn't.'

'I want to believe in the resurrection,' said one of the mums, 'but I'm just not sure if it is the truth.'

'Certain truths are so profound we find them impossible to accept,' said Queenie.

'Exactly,' said the baker's wife. 'How do I find the answers?'

'Seek and you will find,' said Queenie, dipping her forefinger into the pan and tapping the woman's nose with it, depositing a blob of chocolate.

'You are so naughty!' squealed the woman, as she chased Queenie around the table in the middle of the kitchen, scattering the other women in her path.

In the telling of the story Queenie concluded, 'Sometimes the answer is right in front of your nose.'

It was Queenie who had time for people. My 'calling' was in the academia of faith. I would have wanted to prove to the questioning woman that it was true by expounding on the historical evidence for the resurrection. Queenie gave people space. I was just too wrapped up in the preparation of the Sunday sermon, church politics, and the inexhaustible need to raise money for the chapel roof.

My brother Walter, and his wife, Florence, were due to arrive for lunch. Queenie popped out to get last minute provisions. On her return she realised the clock wasn't chiming the eleventh hour. 'Why can't you wind the clock, Henry? If I'm out, please be responsible. You can hear when it's winding down.'

'I have enough to do,' I said. 'Let it wind down so that neither of us have to do it! I find the chimes a little annoying in such a small house. They keep me awake through the night, and they disturb me when I am reading.'

'Don't be ridiculous, Henry. What's the point in having a clock if we don't wind it? Honestly, sometimes you are so apathetic.'

She was right, but I was stubborn and not prepared to stand down.

Queenie gave Florence such a hug that she nearly squashed the child hidden under her coat.

'How beautiful he is,' said Queenie, Florence unveiling George, her youngest, his auburn hair and pale complexion just like his mother. His cheeks, red and puffed out like a fist full of cherries. Fast asleep, he held onto a gold locket which hung from a long gold box chain around his mother's neck. He hardly stirred as Florence handed him to Queenie.

'He has his second birthday next week,' said Florence. 'Can't quite believe it.'

'Hello brother,' said Walter, interrupting his wife and handing me a bottle of Famous Grouse. 'I don't think I have ever been in a manse before.'

'It has its perks!' I replied, patting my brother on the back.

'Certainly! There is no travel to work,' he said.

Queenie peered into the car. 'Where are the boys?'

'We wanted a break from them for the day. We left them at the zoo,' said Walter, laughing at his own quip.

Florence playfully slapped Walter's arm. 'They would have behaved dreadfully in the car, and so we left them with a neighbour. We will only stay a few hours, so as not to be too late back.'

'It was worth every bump in the road,' said Walter. 'Maybe we can come back again soon?'

Queenie winked at me. 'Well, I'm not sure how long we will be here.'

'I saw that, Queenie. What's going on?' asked Walter.

'She's too modern for them. Isn't that right Queenie?' I said.

Queenie signaled for everyone to enter the manse, 'I'm trying to be patient, but some of the elders are so difficult. Whatever I suggest is ridiculed. We have a few more toddlers than when we started, but I want to reach the teenagers in the village. War is looking more and more likely. We need to be offering the young people some hope.'

Florence placed George, still full of sleep, on a leather chair in the front room, 'I agree with you, Queenie. Our boys refuse to go into Sunday school unless a particular helper is there. If she's away, they kick up a fuss and say it is too like being at school.'

'That's my point, Florence. Children are bright and discerning. We must show them the Gospel is relevant in their lives. I want to give them a sense of belonging – a place to have fun and do a little bit of Bible study, but my suggestions are always blocked.'

I was offended that anyone would criticise Queenie for bringing in changes. 'Do you want me to speak to Mrs Conley, I'm sure she is behind it? She is always complaining about everything we do.'

'No, my love, I need to win the elders round.'

'Win them round? We have been here two years. I think the time for *winning them round* has long gone.'

'Do they appreciate that you went to Cambridge?' said Walter.

'I hardly think that will gain me any favours,' said Queenie. 'Come on everybody we have so much to talk about, other than this.'

The next few hours were spent discussing the family, the political situation in Europe, and Edward VIII and Mrs Simpson. We shared a roast chicken, a spontaneous gift from James the farmer next door.

Florence and Queenie seemed to be talking for an age in the kitchen and that night I asked my wife what they had been discussing.

'It is private,' she told me.

'Really?' I said. 'What could be so private you can't tell me?'

'I'm not falling pregnant, and it is worrying me.'

'What did Florence say?'

'She asked me if we were trying at different times during the month?'

'I hope you assured her there was no lacking in that department... but maybe it is my fault.'

'It's not necessarily you.'

'It hardly matters. We may have to adopt.'

'Florence suggested adoption, but I want one of our own first. Am I being selfish?'

'No, Queenie. You are so hard on yourself. It's perfectly natural to want your own. It could happen yet. Just try and relax.'

'Henry?'

'Yes.'

'Mrs Conley apparently told the elders that I was barren.'

'What? Where did you hear that?'

'I have had several pity looks from people at the services and then Mrs Jefferson told me she knew a good home remedy for the barren condition!'

'Mrs Conley is becoming increasingly annoying. She is intent on gossiping about us. It was only last week that she was telling James that I wasn't sound in the scriptures, and that the last minister and his wife were far better. And yet James tells me that she moaned about them continually as well. She is exhausting and divisive. I will have to have a word with her.'

§

Sister Constance is hugely comforting. When she read this account, she sighed deeply and placing her head in her hands stayed there for a few minutes not talking. She then looked intensely at me and said, 'Poor Queenie, it's bad enough dealing with your own fertility issues without hearing other people's opinions on the matter.'

I went on to tell her about my stand-off with Mrs Conley... that wretched woman.

32. SISTER CONSTANCE

Tuesday 6 March 1990

I visited Mr Walker this morning.

I told him that I have very nearly finished the first section of his memoirs.

I thought it would be a task, but it has been a pleasure.

He let me read some recent reflections of how Queenie interacted with parishioners and how Mrs Conley was interfering and lowering for them both. He continued to tell me a tale of when Mrs Conley arrived at his house with a sheep's head.

'It was in a bucket,' he said.

'Was it a gift?'

'Well... that's what she said but considering Queenie had expressed a squeamishness for dealing with dead animals I believe it was a cruel act.'

'What did you do?' I asked.

'Well, I went to the butchers a few days later, on the Saturday morning, and presented Mrs Conley and her husband with a large casserole in front of six villagers who were cueing for meat.'

'Oh... that was kind, but I sense there is a twist?'

Mr Walker laughed. 'She lifted the lid and there was the head, cooked in a watery onion sauce. The surprise on her face was priceless. "This is for you and your family Mrs Conley," I said. It occurred to me that you and your husband rarely, if ever, get gifts and so Queenie and I wanted to bless you both.'

'Did Queenie cook it?' I asked.

'No! I gave it straight to the farmer's wife next door and she prepared it gladly! On my strict instructions. Queenie knew nothing about it.'

'I expect it went round the village how kind the minister and his wife were!' I chuckled.

'Absolutely! Precisely!' he said, 'she never messed with us again.'

§

Being in Christian ministry is often complicated. I witness it in the politics of running the convent. The nuns get offended, me included, by the smallest of things. I have counselled church leaders who have struggled with members of their congregation, coming across many Mrs Conleys in my time. They believe they are exposing truths about their ministers and their wives but most often they are stirring up trouble to get attention. Unfortunately, they have been the cause of many fractured parishes and even the catalyst for ministers having breakdowns. Of course, there are also situations where a minister is bullish and pompous and quite simply, lazy. They are not always blessed with great administrative skills or they have no heart for pastoral matters. Some can sit for hours with a weeping congregant only to be swamped with the logistics of running the building and organizing events and raising money. When the 'calling' comes upon your life it is hard to appreciate that much of your time will not be about spreading the love of Jesus. I've seen some good men and women pulled apart at the seams, both, clergy and parishioners. My advice is always the same BBBRR –

BOUNDARIES, BOUNDARIES, BOUNDARIES, REST AND REASSESS.

33. WREN

Tuesday 6 March 1990

Today, I met Amy for lunch. Afterwards she showed me around her work offices in Wardour Street and we walked through China Town. I enjoyed shopping in the supermarkets seeing the variety of noodles, woks, and cats with waving paws.

Visiting her tiny flat in Great Titchfield Street, we laughed and talked over a bottle of red wine and then I slept in one of her flatmate's beds because she had gone away for the weekend.

It is wonderful spending time with a grown-up daughter. She doesn't need me anymore, but we delight in each other's company. I do not take the relationship for granted as I know many of my friends struggle with their children. She rings me for a chat most nights, telling me that she is meeting lots of interesting people, and by that, she means, men. Although she has now been going out with her soldier, William, for four years, I don't expect it to last much longer. Apparently, having trained for the PT Corps, he took up a posting with The Royal Green Jackets and is now stationed in Gibraltar. I just don't understand their relationship, she only sees him occasionally. I'm not sure if I like him very much.

I am happy to hear that Amy is painting in her office after work, most evenings. I like to buy her work, as it gives her some extra money. David says we don't have any more wall space but I always find somewhere. I get enjoyment from the Mediterranean landscapes, in hues of primary colours, adorning our walls.

34. HENRY

Tuesday 13 March 1990

The weeks in this care home are flying by.

I can't say I am bored because I'm not.

Just getting out of bed, showering and getting dressed is like climbing Scafell Pike in the Lake District. Exhausting. When I was in my twenties and thirties my bones and muscles acted with great synchronicity. I felt invincible. Now I feel worn out and weighed down.

March is a hard month for me and I hope it flies by as quickly as February did.

After breakfast I sit back in the chair and have a snooze. Vivien has said she will be with me by 11am. My mind is filled with the Christmas of 1938 when Queenie's mother and father paid a visit. I start typing.

Memoirs 1938

The wicker basket was filled with homemade pies and treats and Betty's specialty, a pink and yellow checked Battenberg cake. 'This is the last one you will see for a while as I can't get the almonds for the marzipan anymore,' she said.

Honestly, you would think we were staying a week not just two nights,' added Bert as he unpacked the car.

'You are welcome to stay longer,' I said.

'We have to be back for the Sunday service as I must make a Victoria sponge and some fruit scones,' said Betty, 'If this country goes to war, it will prove difficult with rationing. I will be looking out some of my mother's recipes from the First World War. This place is adorable. You have made it so cosy.'

On Christmas day, after the morning service, we sat around the table in the kitchen enjoying roast beef and Yorkshire pudding. Betty left the table for a minute and returned with a gift wrapped in red paper. 'Open it,' she said to Queenie.

'Mum, we agreed, no presents.'

Betty grinned, 'It's only small.'

Queenie pulled off the paper revealing a slim blue box with a silver clasp. On opening it she was captivated by the delicate silver teaspoons resting in a bed of satin. 'These are beautiful,' she said.

'My mother gave them to me, but I could never bear to use them. I hope you will.'

'I'm sure I will,' Queenie said, knowing full well she probably wouldn't. 'I have something for you.'

Bert laughed, 'Honestly, you are both as bad as each other!'

'No point in making promises then?' I said, intrigued with what my wife would produce. We had all agreed not to buy presents for the very reason that money was tight. What had Queenie bought behind my back?

She appeared with a flat parcel about the same size as a book. On passing it to her mother she glanced at me. 'The frame was one of ours, so it didn't cost us a penny!'

Her mother handed it to Bert. 'You open it, darling.'

Sensing it was precious, Bert, unwrapped the gift carefully and read the penned words behind the thin pane of glass. 'How much more we might make of family life and of our friendships if every secret thought of love blossomed into a deed.'

'That's beautiful. Who is it by?' asked Betty.

'By Harriet Stowe, apparently,' said Bert, looking at the name beneath the quote.

'I found it in her book Little Foxes,' said Queenie, 'I wrote it with my own hand.'

'Where did you learn to write like that?' asked her father.

'At Homerton. Spent many dull evenings learning calligraphy! It is true though Henry, isn't it... *if every secret thought of love blossomed into a deed*, how much better the world would be?'

How could I answer my wife when every secret thought of love I had, was for her?

Queenie busied herself with her mother in the kitchen and Bert and I talked by the fire. He told me about Freddy's girlfriend, Martha, who had been at school with Queenie and Florence. 'Freddy is captivated with her blonde hair and green eyes. She has an exceptional capacity to recite all of Milton's Book 9 of Paradise Lost. She is short, like Queenie, and feisty too, challenging Freddy when he gets too silly. She keeps him grounded that's for sure,' said Bert.

'Freddy and I grew apart,' I said.

'You spent more time with his sister, and he was jealous.'

'We are all grown up now, and I should make more of an effort to see him.'

'He misses you and Queenie. I know because he told me.' Bert lowered his head for a moment and looked melancholic.

Two nights later the car was packed for their departure.

'Now, now, Mummy, please don't get upset. We shall meet again soon,' said Queenie.

'I know dear, but it is such a long time between visits. I know we have the telephone but it's not the same,' said Betty, through the tears.

For a few minutes they held each other fast as if their lives depended on it. Then Bert put his arms around them both. 'Come on girls, don't make too much of a fuss. Henry will wonder what the heck is going on.'

I waited awkwardly. Public displays of affection embarrassed me.

I became obsessed with cutting out news-worthy articles and making scrap books. In early January, 1939, America was looking at an increasingly fractured Europe. President Franklin D. Roosevelt gave the State of the Union Address to Congress. 'A war which threatened to envelop the world in flames has been averted but it has become increasingly clear that world peace is not a given.'

A family wedding took place in the spring. Queenie was delighted to be maid of honour while I was less excited. 'I just don't understand why Freddy didn't choose me to be his best man.'

'Oh, come on Henry, you know you haven't really been best friends since school. He has a new life now.'

Freddy had retained his boyish good looks and was also exceptionally fit, his chest and arms defined and muscular from running and doing numerous press-ups in the park each morning. Martha, his bride, came to me. 'Cheer up Henry!' she said. 'You know he loves you. You won't lose him.' Kissing me on the cheek she joined Freddy, throwing her posey into the crowd.

In July, Queenie spent the afternoon gathering Forget-me-nots, Cornflowers, long stemmed Day's Eye, Corncockle and Wild Carrot, Natural Thistles and Queen Anne's Lace, leaving them in the sink overnight. The next morning, she woke with the dawn, and I discovered her trimming the stems. 'It is so early, Queenie. What are you doing? Come back to bed for an hour.'

'I couldn't lie in bed on such a glorious morning.'

'You do remember that Florence has a garden full of flowers?'

'Every woman loves to receive flowers.'

'Unless they have hay fever!'

'Anyway, she doesn't grow these,' she replied, proudly holding up several wild bouquets.

'Why so many?'

'One is for Martha... one for my mother... Florence... and one for your mother?'

'We won't have time to see everyone, my darling. Let's concentrate on your family. Moving towards my wife, I put my arms around her waist as she wrapped the flowers in brown paper. Bending down, I rested my chin in the nape of her neck, a fusion of perfume filled my senses, while my lips caressed her warm skin. She giggled and turned around to face me, burying her head in my chest. 'Tell me we won't be going to war,' she said.

'Chamberlain will secure peace, my darling. You must not worry.'

'I do worry. I listen to the news every day, and it's not looking good.'

Letting go of my wife, I longed to reassure her. 'I'm sure Hitler will listen to Britain and France. He would be mad to invade Poland. I'd better go and get dressed.'

When we pulled up outside Freddy's house, he immediately opened his front door and ran towards the car. 'Hello you two lovebirds,' he shouted. 'Come and see Martha. We have some news for you.'

'She must be pregnant,' said Queenie, quietly.

Turning off the ignition I leant over and kissed my wife. 'Knowing your powers of deduction, I'll assume she is.'

Martha appeared with the biggest grin upon her small face and embraced my wife. 'Did you guess?' said Martha, tapping her tummy, her green eyes sparkling in the daylight.

'You beat us to it,' I said.

'I could beat you at most things,' laughed Freddy, punching me in the ribs.

'You never won a fight yet, you scoundrel,' I said, punching him back on his shoulder.

'Will they ever grow up?' said Martha. 'Do come in Queenie.'

'Flowers for my dear sister-in-law,' Queenie passed Martha one of the bouquets.

Martha placed her whole face into the flowers, taking a deep breath in. 'Oooh. Aren't they magnificent?'

After an hour and a half, we said our goodbyes and drove to Queenie's parents and then on to Craigmore to see my brother, Walter, and his family.

§

I have been typing for several hours and am rooted to the chair like a huge oak tree in a forest. I enjoy being immersed in my memories, even if some of my behaviour is hard to accept.

35. SISTER CONSTANCE

Tuesday 13 March 1990

It seems to me that Mr Walker may never have forgiven his parents for judging Queenie. He recounted a story from Christmas 1938. The Christmas before the outbreak of war on 1 September 1939.

Wounds from youth cut deep.

He obviously chose to avoid his parents on his visits to Southend.

Our parents do not always behave the way we would want.

But my parents were perfect enough for me.

Raised by a woman whose skin was as black as dark chocolate and by a father who was the colour of goat's milk, I became a drink of two tribes. I was neither black enough or white enough to please either culture, trapped in the middle like a moth between a window and a curtain.

I knew the Christian God as father and yet I was drawn to the mysteries my mother held, a Bush Queen with a palette of beliefs. Inherently, she believed in a God of love who sees into our hearts not into our faces or our colour. She told me that diversity is displayed in the flora and fauna – in the oceans – the deserts. It exists in the moon and the stars and in the broken body of Christ on the cross. It is held in the hands of a loving father and in the words of a kind mother and it survives in the breath of the Koala and in the cry of a newborn child.

My mother described me as the *Capparis spinosa*, the wild passionfruit, or caperbush. When it ripens, the skin turns orange and splits open and the little black seeds, when crushed, are hot and spicy. I have always been slightly alternative – a mix of parents – part desert and part city. I wrestle with injustice and yet I rest in the arms of Jesus. What can I say? I am a conundrum... I know.

What I do see is people's love for each other. The way Mr Walker talks about Queenie, I am anticipating the future for them was hard.

They struggled to have children, but I know they had a daughter.

I will read more tonight.

I am often asked if I miss not having children. Occasionally, my mind wonders to those places. But I am quick to pull it back. Refocus. It is not good to become too maudlin about things you cannot change. I was told I couldn't have children in my early twenties and so there was great power in resignation. And I have mothered so many more than I could have had myself in one lifetime. I have held the lonely and the lost. I have comforted the sick and the dying. I have mourned with the bereaved and laughed with the joyful. My life has been a quilt of colour – fabric cut from the shirts of the living and the dead – with no regrets. My heart is full for others to be in a place of peace. There is little conflict in my life because I have been able to cast my burdens upon Jesus knowing he cares for me.

36. WREN

Tuesday 13 March 1990

Five years ago, David and I moved to the Witterings near Chichester. We had both secured teaching jobs, and were drawn to the village of Itchenor right on the water's edge. Gradually I gained my sea legs. Taking a few sailing lessons in a Mirror, I soon realised that boats are very like birds in the way they use air to generate lift on the sail. From Itchenor Harbour I can now navigate a small boat along the Birdham Channel meandering past dry mud banks towards West Wittering beach to face the open mouth of the English Channel.

We often eat out. David, dipping into the Michelin food guide, surprises me with interesting culinary experiences at local restaurants and ones further afield. Three inches taller than me, at five foot ten, it doesn't matter what he eats, he never puts on any weight.

I wake most mornings with David's toes touching mine. His offer to make tea and read the poems of Seamus Heaney in whispers is always accepted.

I think when people see me, they think I am a privileged middle-class woman with very little experience. I am some of that. But I am also a myriad of thoughts and emotions which have been born out of trauma. No one truly knows someone else's life.

My therapist says I have an 'abandonment' issue.

It started many moons ago and rests on me like a stale perfume I cannot shake off.

I believe I will make my peace with it one day.

I hope to... at least.

David brings peace to my life. He is steady and reliable. A little crazy at times which is also refreshing.

37. HENRY

Tuesday 20 March 1990

Today, I realised I had forgotten Wren's birthday which had been on Sunday.

It was a big one. Her fiftieth.

I managed to send a telegram this morning, but she will know I have only just remembered. Not sure how I forgot.

After lunch I went to the chapel to light a candle. Not sure why, I just felt compelled to. It was a mistake. I knelt on the floor in front of the alter. I felt a bit foolish when I couldn't get back up and had to shout for help. It took two orderlies to lift me back into my wheelchair. I was like a beached whale. Growing old is so highly overrated.

When Sister Constance arrived, she handed me my memoirs. 'Let's talk about this,' she said, 'and can I have the next part?'

Memoirs 1939

When we arrived at Craigmore, Florence greeted Queenie who gave her a bouquet immediately. Queenie was alarmed because Florence had had her hair cut very short. 'Oh, Florence. What have you done?'

'I gave it to the war effort,' said Florence dryly, admiring the flowers.

'Really?' said Queenie. 'What do they need hair for?'

'She's only joking. We are not at war yet!' I interrupted.

'Well, I love it,' said Queenie. 'It suits you.'

'Thank you,' replied Florence. 'They are absolutely beautiful... from your garden?'

Queenie turned to me and nodded as if to say I told you so. 'Yes, and the surrounding area.'

'We have missed you both,' said Walter.

'I know. I'm sorry it has taken us so long to visit. The job is all consuming. Something has to change,' I replied.

George, six-years old, was sitting in the garden teasing worms out of the soil with a stick. Daniel, the eldest, at twelve, with his long legs and exceptional bowling technique was captain of the 2-man cricket team. His brother, ten-year-old Timothy, was missing the ball which meant it smashed into the heads of the peonies. Florence shouted at them to stop.

Later that afternoon we all sat, cross-legged on a rug, playing a game of Snap with Daniel and Timothy, while George spent the afternoon on Queenie's lap, playing with her hair, besotted.

Walter served tea and scones, fed the chickens in their pen, and didn't sit still until the children and the chickens were all in bed.

Walter, resting on the arm of a green velvet chair stroked the back of Florence's neck. Queenie and I sat on the sofa, our limbs entwined. I told stories about the intricate dynamics of various members of the chapel, and Walter joked about Hitler. Walter and Florence then quizzed us on the success of the fourth Spring Fair at Burrowbridge, and how on earth we had managed to collect the healthy sum of one thousand and thirty-five pounds.

'It has taken me four years to raise the money and of course I always tell a joke at the beginning of my speech, works every time,' I said.

'Don't listen to him,' said Queenie. 'He is a genius. The roof will get fixed very soon.'

Eventually, we retired to the guest room at the back of the house. Queenie, in her nightdress, knelt and opened her slim leather Bible, reading Psalm 130 under her breath. 'I wait for the Lord, my soul doth wait, and in his word, do I hope.' Placing her head on my chest she nestled her body under my arm. 'I know envy is a sin, but I do envy Florence and Walter for having three delightful, healthy children.'

'I agree. They seem to have it all. But what's wrong with our lives?'

'Nothing. Except I want us to have a baby, like Freddy and Martha. I don't understand why I haven't fallen pregnant. I am thirty-three, we need to get on with it.'

'I thought we had been getting on with it. Maybe we should go and see a doctor?'

Queenie added. 'I will pray for it to happen.'

'Well, let's help the good Lord with his role in creation. Anything Freddy can do I can do better.' I kissed her forehead. It was moist and warm to touch, and she smelt of Nivea Creme. Caressing the hollow created by her clavicle bone, I turned my body into hers. Longing to please her, I shifted position. Caressing the soft pale skin between her legs, I heard her delight. Unfortunately, the bed was noisy, 'Stop now, Henry, the bed is annoying me, it's so squeaky', she said. Placing a blanket on the floor, I beckoned my wife to join me.

It was past ten o'clock in the morning when we finally appeared in the breakfast room. Walter was sitting in his brown leather chair, by the fire, doing a crossword surrounded by plates, cups, and bowls from a breakfast feast. 'They have arisen,' he said.

'We needed a lie in,' I said.

Walter stood. 'Do come and join me. I've just made a fresh pot of coffee.'

'Where are the children?' asked Queenie.

'Florence has taken them to the park and onto the grocers. They make wonderful helpers and are very useful when it comes to carrying the shopping. You should have a few,' said Walter.

'We are trying to,' I said.

Walter smiled, 'We heard.'

Queenie blushed Geranium red.

§

On a hot summer's day, in late August, Queenie carried a tray to the chapel office. She was a little flushed. 'I thought we should celebrate!' Placing the tray of sandwiches on the table, she turned the radio off.

'There isn't much to celebrate, my darling.' I folded the newspaper and placed it down. 'We are on the brink of war with Germany. President Roosevelt has just sent a personal appeal to Adolf Hitler asking him to address the issue of Poland through diplomatic channels.'

'I don't believe Hitler wants peace. But there is still reason to celebrate.'

'Like what?'

'Can't you guess?'

I stared at her. She looked different. I couldn't put my finger on it. Then my heart raced tentatively towards excitement. 'No... you're not?'

'Yes, yes, I am. I'm pregnant. We're going to have a baby.'

'How wonderful. Aren't you clever? Aren't I clever!' Winding the gramophone up to play, The Blue Danube, our favourite Waltz, I took my wife in my arms and we danced down the aisle of the chapel, her frock moving in time with her body, showing no hint of pregnancy. We were full of faith and hope in the future despite the atrocious news reports.

In the manse, however, the minute hand continued to move around the face of the granddaughter clock, showing how time very quickly presents reason for doubt.

Queenie's parents, married for forty years, were planning on a happy retirement. Bert at the age of sixty-nine had been working part time for a small firm of local builders. Leaving work at lunchtime, he suddenly experienced a sharp pain in his chest alarming him enough to stop a passing lorry and ask the driver for a lift home. When Betty opened the door, he collapsed and died in her arms.

I received the phone call from Freddy, and it was I who broke the news to Queenie. She very nearly passed out. Fortunately, I steadied her, making her sit for a while, heaping sugar into a recently made cup of tea.

Queenie packed a small leather holdall and travelled by train to the family home on the Essex coast. She was to be gone for five days, assisting her mother with the funeral arrangements, helping her mother adjust to the unimaginable.

Dressed in my black suit and dog collar, I arrived early for the funeral and went immediately to talk to Reverend Tinsley, whose distress was apparent. 'What a terrible, terrible shock, so sudden! Bert was such a gentle man... such a humble man, I shall miss him dreadfully.'

The Avenue Baptist Church was full of friends and congregation members.

Bert was one of those discreet men whom you only really appreciate when they have gone. His concern for others, his love of his fellow man in the community, especially in the two chapels he had served at for nearly forty years.

During the hour-long service, five hymns were sung, including, *It Is Well with My Soul,* written by Horatio Spafford. It was a familiar hymn. In fact, I was fascinated by its origins. A wealthy businessman, who lost most of his investments in the Great Fire of Chicago, 1871, sent his wife, Anna, and four daughters, ahead of him on an ocean liner S.S. Ville de Havre, to have a holiday in England. On 21 November 1873, the liner was rammed by a

British vessel and sank immediately. Anna was picked out of the water, unconscious, but all four daughters drowned. One week later, Horatio received a telegram from Anna, who had arrived in Cardiff, simply stating. 'Saved. Alone. What shall I do?' As Horatio travelled, by boat, to meet his wife, the ship's captain pointed to the place where the tragedy occurred, and rather than looking into the icy water below, he looked to the heavens and composed the hymn.

I had referred to Horatio Spafford in several sermons as an example of resolute faith against unfathomable tragedy. Queenie and I talked about it many times, both of us unable to imagine losing four children. I admired Horatio for being able to produce something enduring: a hymn, which has been a great comfort to thousands, possibly millions, of people for decades.

Standing next to Queenie, I sang the opening stanza loudly. 'When peace like a river, attendeth my way, when sorrows like sea billows roll; whatever my lot, thou hast taught me to know, it is well, it is well, with my soul.'

At the end of the service the doors were opened, and a warm breeze rolled in. Queenie held her mother's arm, as we left the chapel, whispering. 'Mum, I have waited until Henry was with us to tell you, and forgive me if it is not the best time, but... I'm pregnant... and I'm due in mid-April.'

Betty clasped Queenie's hand tightly. 'Oh, my love, what wonderful news! I am so happy for you both. Freddy and Martha's baby is due in March. I will have two grandchildren to spoil. They will be friends, I'm sure of it.'

Queenie wept. 'I'm just so sad Daddy won't see the baby.'

'Maybe he is looking down on us all. You believe it, don't you?'

'Yes, with all my heart.'

'I miss him terribly, but it won't be too long before I join him. We mustn't be too sad, must we Henry? Death is inevitable, and so is new life. We should have hope for a better future. Be confident in the resurrection of the body.'

Taking Betty's arm, I passed it through my own, accompanying her to the graveside. 'I believe you have many more years left in you, but you are right, death comes to us all.' I thought of Doris, in heaven, dressed as an angel with her wings – Bert dressed in the same attire seemed a little ridiculous.

On the journey back, the pungent smell of smoke made Queenie sick several times. 'My darling, do you think you might give up smoking until the baby is born?' she said.

Immediately I flicked the cigarette out of the window, 'Anything for you. You can't afford to keep being sick, there is nothing of you.'

When we arrived back at the manse in the early hours of the morning, Queenie remained asleep, her head cushioned by her favourite blood orange scarf up against the window. Cradling my wife in my arms, I proceeded to the front door. When I carried her up the stairs, she stirred, but realising she was in my arms fell back into a deep sleep. Placing her down on the bed, I watched her for a while, her face lit by moonlight. Unclipping a small diamante grip, I marveled at how her soft wavy hair framed her face perfectly. I lifted her ankles up with one hand and gently prized off her shoes with the other. The button on her skirt unclasped effortlessly and I noticed how her belly was slightly rounder than usual. I unfastened her suspenders and removed her stockings, one at a time. I then lifted both legs with one arm, and raising the bedding with the other, slipped her in between the chilled sheets. Climbing into bed, I watched her for a while, thinking how exquisitely beautiful she was.

I wrestled with the thought of Bert dying. It seemed so unfair that he should die just as he was about to retire. Through all the years I had courted his daughter, he never once objected to my presence in the house, having in truth, welcomed me like a son. I considered it a great misfortune that Bert wouldn't get to see his grandchildren.

Queenie slept until eleven the next morning and was shocked when I woke her. Sobbing in my arms, she was deeply affected by her father's death, telephoning her mother every day from then on. 'I think it helps Mum that she will soon be a grandmother. It's something to look forward to.'

'I'm sure it is... but is it really necessary to ring her every day? You don't want her to become reliant on you?'

'Are you suggesting I shouldn't call my own mother daily when my father has just died? Henry, shame on you.'

Although fond of Betty, I was annoyed that Queenie was so attached to her, possibly not really appreciating that the very same qualities of attachment and affection I so loved in my wife were qualities that had been cultivated by her mother.

38. SISTER CONSTANCE

Tuesday 20 March 1990

M r Walker was in a strange mood today.

He mentioned to me that he had been to the chapel on Sunday to light a candle, but wouldn't say why. Subsequently, I met one of the orderlies on Monday who told me they had had to rescue him from the floor. He was sobbing when they arrived. He couldn't get up and was very agitated. Obviously, something had deeply unsettled him.

As soon as we said hello, he pushed his memoirs into my hands.

I found reading about Queenie's father dying very difficult. I know that pain. Loss of a loved one, however long ago, remains in the breeze. Despite someone's age, death is always difficult. If their love has been given, then you miss it. If it has been absent, you miss the potential there could have been. Fragments of their life float upon the air or clog the soil. That is why we commemorate events and have anniversaries; a form of gardening, digging up and turning over the earth, adding oxygen. When we are impacted by a person's contribution to the world, their parting is a deep wound, often to more people than they could ever have imagined.

When a plane crashes in a distant land you may find yourself aching for the dead, wondering, even just momentarily, what they must have suffered and what their last thoughts were. Their last actions? Did they speak to the stranger next to them? Did they hold hands? Did they say a prayer? Did the agnostic suddenly believe? Did the believer have doubts? Those tragedies always move me to tears.

Placing down the memoirs, I decided to be more open with Mr Walker. There was a deep sense in me that I was running out of time.

'When my father died, he was in the prime of his life,' I said. 'A Yorkshireman, a plain speaker which always got him into trouble. My mother loved him for it. But the gubba, the white men from the outback who raced their trucks in front of the house, full up on alcohol and baccy, resented his choice of wife. "Blasted Pommy!" they called out, "You come out here and take our abos! You try to civilise them!" They were always bullying him.'

Mr Walker was animated, 'I'm sorry he suffered.'

'It happened many times growing up. Against my mother's advice, in retaliation, he took hold of a spade and raising it above his head like a mighty sword of truth threatened the men– *Teach us to number our days*–swinging above his head as he called down the mighty wrath of God.'

'I learnt that scaring people into the kingdom very rarely works!'

'I agree.'

Mr Walker softened. 'Please go on. Tell me what happened.'

He placed his hand upon my hand and I continued. 'Four men came at him and taking his sword of truth beat him to death with it. My mother was away at the time, and the twins were on a sleep over. I was nineteen years old and like St. Margaret Mary Alacoque, I had been out dancing. Yes, dancing! In the early hours of the morning, with a large moon lighting the sky, my friend and I arrived back home in her car. Approaching the house, I could see my father face down, wrapped in what looked like a fine linen cloth. Running to him, I quickly realised he had been stripped naked and his shroud was sand from a light desert storm: his face and body bloodied, a shovel laying at his feet.'

'Oh, how shocking! That's dreadful.' Mr Walker gasped, 'What did you do?'

'I fell on the floor next to his body and I screamed a scream that went to the very moon and back. My friend, a willowy girl of my age, sped to the police station and raised the alarm. "What is wrong with these men, intent on causing trouble?" My father had asked my mother that morning. She replied, "They have small brains and are not open to the essential fact that love has no colour." My father had replied, "I won't let them hurt you," only to be murdered eight hours later.'

'People are so cruel. How did you cope? You were so young!'

'For months and months, I tried to comfort my mother and then one day, I left her with the twins and went on walk-about. I needed to find myself. It was several years later, that I went to a convent, fleeing into the arms of Jesus, who, like my father, had been blooded and wrapped in a shroud. I needed a sanctuary from hate and loathing. It was here that I took my vows and trained in counselling. Delving into the human psyche, I studied bereavement and found my purpose. I gradually blossomed like a field of pink everlastings after a downpour in the outback. At last, I was able to give something to those struggling with grief. I had found my direction, a clear path on which I could guide others.'

'I am pleased that you found solace here and also that you found a calling to help others. You have a talent. I am even happy to say you have a God-given gift.'

'That's a huge compliment coming from you! I am grateful.' Casting her eyes to the floor, she continued, 'Do tell me what happened after Bert died.'

'I remember it was 11:15 a.m. on 3 September. Neville Chamberlain gave his long-awaited speech to the nation. "You can imagine what a bitter blow it is to me that all my long struggle to win peace has failed." Britain was at war with Germany. Queenie dropped the milk jug. I swore out loud.'

'Such a blow for so many.'

'Queenie wrote a list of all the young men in the village who might be called to fight. There were fifteen names. I reminded her that the Royal Ordnance Factory, between the villages of Puriton and Woolavington, would soon be open, supplying a radical new form of high explosive. I told her not to worry as some of the lads would get work at the factory. She was heartbroken. She was concerned we were bringing a child into this world.'

'There is never a perfect time to have a baby,' said the nun.

'That's what I told her. During the pregnancy, we grew even closer, and Queenie, with characteristic fervor embraced up-to-date ideas on how to keep fit, eat well and plan for the baby's birth. Following all the advice to the letter. The following month, I was furious to hear that a German submarine had penetrated Scapa Flow and HMS Royal Oak had been sunk in Scapa Bay. They were the first major losses in Scotland. Eight hundred and thirty-three men dead.'

I had to stop Mr Walker there. I could tell he was annoyed that I had to leave. But I have so many people to visit, boundaries need to be observed. I do confess, I am enjoying our time together so much. He is really opening up to me and for this, I feel truly privileged.

39. WREN

Tuesday 20 March 1990

Two days ago, I celebrated my fiftieth birthday.

David booked a restaurant and suggested a walk on the beach with Patchou. We are expecting a visit from Amy. My son Patrick sent me a wonderful bouquet.

I thought on my mother and on my name.

The Royal Society for the Protection of Birds describes the wren as, 'A tiny brown bird; although it is heavier, less slim, than the even smaller goldcrest. It is dumpy, almost rounded, with a fine bill, quite long legs and toes, very short round wings and a short, narrow tail which is sometimes cocked up vertically.'

I certainly inherited Henry's long legs and Queenie's cupid lips. Unfortunately, I lack wings and a tail, which would have been useful when faced with my finely-honed flight response. If I were a bird, I would have chosen to be a dove, "*Oh, for the wings of a dove.*" Fortunately, Wren is a better name; given to me by my mother, whose fluttering heart comforted me before she flew away to a place unknown.

Oh, and by the way, the day after my birthday I received a telegram from my father wishing me a happy one.

I have decided to write down what I know of what happened to my mother. My therapist suggested I do this years ago and yet I am only deciding to do it now. Maybe it has something to do with the telegram and the echoes of time!

40. HENRY

Wednesday 27 March 1990

It seems to be a pattern now that I tell a lot of my story to Sister Constance. It is becoming quite cathartic.

When she arrived yesterday afternoon, she was in a happy mood. I asked her what had tickled her.

'Do I look tickled?' she laughed.

'Well, yes you do. Come on tell me.'

'It's silly really, but I won the egg and spoon race at the Saturday fete which meant I won a bottle of malt whisky.'

'I hope you brought it with you.'

'As a matter of fact, I did.'

From her cassock she took out a small silver hipflask. I could have fallen off my chair with sheer amazement and delight at her kindness. I begged her for a sip. Not even my wife will sneak me in a tipple.

Unscrewing the flask, she handed it to me with the biggest grin on her face. 'Here,' she said, 'enjoy.'

The liquid ran down my throat, bypassing my tongue. It was heavenly— a taste of youth and happier times—the smell alone conjured up decades. My mind ran through the years in a montage. It was strangely alarming but also pleasurable. I hadn't had any alcohol since Boxing Day, twelve weeks previously.

'Isn't it wonderful!' said the nun.

I was so grateful.

'Now, do tell me what happened after Bert died.'

I had missed Bert terribly. 'It was January 1940, four months after his death, when Queenie organised a table in the Chapel so that people could leave food for those who were struggling. James, the elderly farmer next door, left gifts of eggs and potatoes.'

'People were so kind during the war years, sharing what they had,' said my nun.

'People are still kind,' I said. 'Especially when sharing their whisky!'

I resumed my tale, reminding her that it was the news from Freddy that Queenie was longing to hear. It was early March when he telephoned the manse. I answered the phone and he roared with laughter as usual. 'Martha gave birth to a girl last night. We named her Eve. Thought you might approve.'

'You just need an Adam, and you will have the set,' I said.

'What a wit,' said Sister Constance.

'Freddy had not wanted to tell Queenie the difficulties he had witnessed during his daughter's birth.' He had told me how he had a newfound respect for women since being present at the birth. Queenie had asked him the details but he had replied he thought it best to talk about it once she had been through it. 'Nothing to fret about,' he said.

Queenie secretly yearned for a daughter, calling 'the bump' numerous names, and describing the movements in her tummy like a bird fluttering in her womb. She was fond of the birds which had visited the garden, especially the tiny secretive wren, singing from the top of the pear tree with its powerful voice, in the early hours of the morning. I drove Queenie to her antenatal appointments at the Mary Stanley Nursing Home on Castle Street in Bridgwater; a beautiful set of houses, red and yellow Flemish-bond brick, similar in scale and ambition to houses in London's West End. I waited in the local library until it was time to meet her. Afterwards we strolled, arm in arm, to the Blake Museum with its exhibition on, The General at Sea: Robert Blake, and on to Blake Gardens for a pot of tea at the refectory.

'I noticed you have removed the seascape painting from the wall? What was the reason for that? asked Sister Constance.

'Let's not talk about that now. I need to get through this.'

'Did the birth make you fret?' She said, and asked me to continue.

My thoughts went back to when it all happened. The doctor at the nursing home had considered that Queenie's height and frame necessitated a caesarean, and she was therefore booked for one in the first week of April. 'Three weeks before the operation date, Queenie persuaded me to visit my dear friend, Ralph, in Dartmouth. "Better to go now before the baby comes," she told me. Preparing to leave the manse straight after lunch, I noticed how round she was looking. The pregnancy had the effect of filling out her delicate features, and because she was so small, her bump looked huge. When I left the manse, I told her she looked rather like a duck as she had a distinct waddle when she walked. "I don't appreciate that comment. I feel so un-appealing and gargantuan!" she protested. I told her she was the most gorgeous woman in Burrowbridge! "Don't you mean England?" she said. But I truly believed she was the most gorgeous woman in the whole world!

'After leaving Ralph, I arrived home late that evening in a relaxed mood but was alarmed to find a note, written in an unfamiliar hand, on the kitchen table. I noticed a puddle of water on the floor by the granddaughter clock as it chimed the hour. Dashing to the car, I sped along the narrow twisting lanes towards the Nursing Home in Bridgwater seven miles from our home. Earlier that day, Queenie had pushed me out of the front door and as I drove away, I watched her at the window. I was intensely proud as she waved goodbye, all smiles and as pretty as a picture, framed by the criss-cross of small windows. But within a few hours, and unbeknownst to me, she was taking her coat from the hat stand

and was knocking on the door of the neighbour's front door. James, the farmer, answered. Queenie had pleaded with him to take her to the nursing home. He later told me that he had wished his Mrs had been there but that she had gone to stay with her brother for a few days. Apparently, he ran to the manse, grabbed the case from the bedroom and went immediately to the kitchen where he scribbled the note. Within minutes he was helping my wife climb into his old truck. He then drove, as fast as he dared, to Bridgwater. He could see Queenie was in pain, and although he had been present at the birth of numerous calves and lambs, he did not feel equipped to deal with his Minister's wife giving birth in his truck.'

'So, your wife had gone into labour prematurely? How concerning for you,' said Sister Constance.

At that moment, we were rudely interrupted by an orderly knocking loudly and bursting in. He asked Sister Constance to come quickly. Sister Jennifer had collapsed and they needed my nun back at the convent. She got up, took hold of my hand, and said she would come back to see me the next day.

I felt cut off at such a crucial moment.

I felt sick to the core as if I had been stopped exiting a house on fire and the only option was to jump from a top floor window.

I had supper delivered to my room as I didn't want to eat with the other residents. I devoured a plate of red snapper, brown bread and two ripe figs. The food was improving.

The night duty receptionist knocked on the door and told me that Vivien had a migraine and wouldn't be visiting. From experience I knew that I might not see her for a few days. 'I feel so useless,' I told the receptionist. 'I should be looking after my wife.'

Taking a tablet for indigestion I was concerned enough to pull the emergency cord. On arrival, the orderly poured me a glass of water but when I didn't improve, he went for the nurse on duty.

A young Chinese woman with a short bob arrived and was quick to ascertain that I wasn't having a heart attack. 'You seem very anxious. Your blood pressure is rather high, and it might be good if you take it easy. Your heart sounds fine, and everything else is good. So why not do some deep breathing?'

'Don't you think I should see a doctor? You look as if you have just left school.'

'Mr Walker. I'm a qualified nurse. You must relax. I'm sure you have a few years in you yet!'

None of us can possibly know that! I was annoyed with her but she sat with me for the next ten minutes.

One hour later, I rang my buzzer, and because my legs were swollen more than usual, I asked the orderly if he would help me get undressed. Although a short man, he was exceptionally strong and was able to set me down on the seat inside the shower.

On his return he helped me with my pyjamas and settled me into bed. 'Can you place my typewriter on the table for me?' I asked him, 'and pass me the Bible.'

'Yes of course. I didn't know you were a religious man, Mr Walker,' he said, picking up the Bible from the Formica table.

I told him I wasn't but that I had been once.

Memories and reflections poured out of me at a fast rate. To what purpose? I am not sure. Who will read my ramblings? Hopefully Vivien will give them to Wren. I must mention it to her.

On opening the Bible, a postcard of *The Light of the World* fell onto my lap. It made me grin, recognising the nun's desire to wake me up spiritually by giving me irresistible reminders of Jesus.

After reading for ten minutes, I placed the thin chord marker at Psalm 23, and on closing my eyes scripture circled my mind like a Ferris wheel—*Yea, though I walk through the valley of the shadow of death, I will fear no evil.*

Closing the book, I drifted off to sleep with shards of evening light across the bedroom wall.

In the early hours of this morning, I woke with a start, perspiration dripping from my forehead, my pyjamas drenched in sweat. A care worker, a plump woman with a penchant for macadamia nuts, heard my cry, and asked me what was the matter.

'I saw her!'

'Who did you see?'

'My wife... she was drowning.'

'Your wife is fine... it's just a headache.'

'No... not Vivien. My first wife.'

'How many wives are there?'

'Three.'

'Oh my,' she said, and offered to change the sheets as they were soaked through. I told her I needed Sister Constance urgently.

'It's two 'o' clock in the morning. I won't ring the convent at this time. I will call her first thing. Now stay there while I get some help and some fresh bed linen.'

Exhausted, I slumped back on the pillow.

As I typed more of my memoirs, I found the tapping soothing, the rhythm reminding me of the tick tock of the granddaughter clock before the chimes had a chance to disturb my peace.

41. SISTER CONSTANCE

Wednesday 28 March 1990

Yesterday was a highly charged day that's for sure. Mr Walker's story was interrupted by an orderly informing me that Sister Jennifer had collapsed. When I arrived at her room, the paramedics were doing CPR. There was an awful moment when we thought she was gone but then after the second blast with the heart defibrillator she came round. Sister Jennifer is only fifty-five, she is too young to go to heaven. She has such a gifting with the old folk in the home. I wonder what brought on a heart attack? I am quite shocked.

I had planned to go and see Mr Walker in the afternoon but when I received an urgent call at 8.30 a.m. from the receptionist I went immediately.

His confession was to arise out of the dust like a rare Hopping mouse in the bush.

On entering his room, he was sitting up in bed with his hands busy at his old typewriter, tap... tap... tapping.

'I hear from the nurse that you had a very disturbed night. Are you alright?' I said.

'No, I'm not. I had such an awful nightmare about Queenie, I couldn't get to her.'

Taking a chair to the bed, I sat down next to him, 'I'm sorry I had to leave you yesterday.'

'How was Sister Jennifer?' said Henry.

'She is doing okay, thank you for asking. Now why don't you tell me about your nightmare.'

'I don't know what's wrong with me. I have had a good life. I was very high up in the United Nations you know. By the time I retired I was managing one hundred people. I was important.'

'I'm sure you were but that's not what's concerning you. Why did you want to see me in the middle of the night?' He was silent, stuck like a needle in the groove of a spinning record. Playing with the cross around my neck, I said, 'Do you know what your Christian name means?'

'Queenie told me once, but I don't remember.'

'One of its meanings is hero.'

'Oh yes. I must confess I don't feel like a hero. What is your name? I presume Constance is your saint's name?'

'Yes, it is.' I paused for a moment, letting go of the cross. Giving him my name felt intimate, but I needed to let him know something of myself if I was to get him to open up. 'My name is Amandyo Smith.'

'Can you elaborate?'

'Smith was my father's family name from Yorkshire.'

'Yorkshire? Oh yes, you said he was from Yorkshire. Whereabouts?'

'From Haworth. I went there once... a place of great beauty.'

'And your Christian name?'

'Given by my mother. It's from the Amangu people, the indigenous Yamatji people of the mid-western region of Australia. My mother was a woman of greatness. Rather like the Yorkshire moors, although she never saw them, she was rugged and imposing.'

'You loved your parents, I can tell.'

'Yes... yes I did.'

Tentatively, I took hold of his right hand. 'Tell me about your nightmare.'

And at last, the record was jolted out of its groove.

'I saw Queenie. She was drowning in the sea, but I couldn't get to her.'

'I know the farmer took her to the nursing home, but what happened to her?' I said.

'I thought no one on the planet loved Jesus as much as I did, that is, until I met Queenie.' Taking a laboured breath in, his body shook.

I passed him a cup of water, which he sipped dutifully.

'I was trying to find her in the Atlantic Ocean, but the boat was going too fast, and I left her to drown.' He started to cry and couldn't stop.

'It's alright Mr Walker, you are in a safe place.'

'You don't understand,' he replied forcefully. 'I should never have left her.'

'You mean when you went to see Ralph?'

He nodded and was eager to confess everything, 'Queenie was the love of my life.' He said as he handed me the recently typed sheets of paper. 'I wrote this in the night. Please forgive the mistakes. I had to get it down.'

Familiar with Mr Walker's desire to let me read his memoirs, I took the three sheets of typed A4 and sat at the window while he lay in his bed.

His breathing was shallow.

42. WREN

Wednesday 28 March 1990

I am not so sure where to begin. Do I start on the day I was born? Or do I start a bit later?

It may seem obvious to someone looking on, but to me, I am hesitant. I don't want to tell what I imagine happened rather than what actually happened, and so as I was a baby, it is best to go with Florence's account. Walter was also a reliable source of information. He was very honest and straight with me and gave me wonderful snippets of insight into who my mother was. My Uncle Freddy gave me insights into my father's behaviour and grief during the 1940s. He was sad to tell me that they had lost touch, "drifted apart" were his words.

There is a certain amount of confusion for me as I think about writing it all down. My loyalty is to my aunt and uncle, to keep them at the centre of the narrative.

I will begin with Florence in her favourite place.

In the garden.

43. HENRY

Wednesday 28 March 1990

Memoirs 1940

Castle Street was empty of cars. Parking directly outside the nursing home I banged on the front door. 'I'm Reverend Walker,' I said to a young woman, 'can you please take me to my wife?'

I was shown to the birthing room and as I entered, I heard Queenie cry out. Rushing to her side, I said, 'Darling, why didn't you telephone Ralph... to let me know... I could have left earlier?'

Sweating profusely, she mustered a smile, 'I couldn't find Ralph's number. I searched through the drawer. Don't worry. You are here now.'

'But this wasn't meant to happen for at least a month,' I said feeling panicked.

'You must telephone my mother tomorrow. I spoke to her tonight, and she wants to come down and help but she has no idea I am in labour. I was about to make up the bed when my waters broke. You will ring her, Henry, won't you?'

'Yes, yes, of course, I will.'

A young doctor wearing a standard white medical jacket addressed Queenie, 'Mrs Walker, you are going to have to push this baby out naturally. I know you were booked for a caesarean, but unfortunately our surgeon is away on holiday, and we have been unsuccessful in locating another. You don't need to worry, the midwife has informed me that the baby is small, we will both help you.' Turning to me, he said, 'Reverend Walker would you like to go to the waiting room? It is customary for the father not to be present at the birth.'

'Absolutely not. Queenie needs me by her side. Isn't that right, Queenie?'

'I would like my husband to stay with me. I'm in a lot of pain.'

The doctor nodded, 'Then I am fine with it. I will need to examine you now.'

He proceeded to lift the sheets, covering my wife's lower half. 'Bend your knees, Mrs Walker.'

'Is everything all right doctor?' I asked.

'Yes of course... Mrs Walker, it is time... you have dilated very quickly. The midwife will tell you when to push.'

The midwife, a tall thin woman with a kind face, placed her hand onto Queenie's tummy, near the top, in the dip. 'Right, there we are, Mrs Walker, push now,' she said.

Queenie gritted her teeth, squeezing my hand with surprising strength. She was silent, but the perspiration soaked her forehead, neck, and chest as she pushed deep into her pelvis.

'You can do it my darling. It will be over soon, and you will be a mummy.'

Within thirty minutes, at a quarter past midnight, a baby with a head of black hair and a faint cry arrived prematurely into the world. 'It's a girl,' said the doctor.

'A girl?' said Queenie.

'A girl?' I repeated.

Wrapped in a standard white cotton blanket, she was placed into Queenie's arms. 'Wren... let's call her Wren... you know like the bird, my little bird.'

I was so relieved. 'My brave darling. You did so well. Just rest now.'

Queenie was exhausted. A young nurse took the baby from the room.

With my forefinger and thumb, I peeled some strands of hair from the sweat that acted like glue on the side of my wife's face. The doctor then signalled for me to follow him out of the room. 'What is your blood group, Reverend Walker?'

'Rhesus negative, group A, the same as Queenie... what's the matter?'

'Your wife is losing blood and she needs a transfusion straight away.'

'But she will be alright?' I said, seeing how unnerved he looked.

'Yes, I'm sure she will be fine. Wait there. We will sort this out.'

An orderly wheeled in a bed and placed it next to my wife. He then attached me to a rubber tube up to a glass bottle suspended on a metal frame. For thirty minutes, I was motionless, staring at the ice blue walls, I grew cold and nauseous. I began to watch Queenie closely and noticed how pale she was and how her eyes flickered under transparent eyelids. A drop of saliva travelled in a thin line from her mouth to the pillow and so with my little finger I wiped it away. Her vulnerability made me gasp. 'It's all right my darling, I will save you,' I whispered, while stretching out my hand to touch her cheek.

The nurse, taking a full bag of blood, hooked it up to Queenie – casualties on a battlefield. Ten minutes later I sat up, suddenly aware of the tangible panic in the room.

'Mrs Walker, can you hear me?' The young doctor began to shake her. She is un-conscious! 'Get Dr Moore, nurse,' he shouted.

The midwife took me firmly by the arm. 'You need to leave the room, Reverend. Please.'

'What's going on? What's the matter with her?'

'She is unconscious. Please leave so that we can concentrate on helping her.'

'I need to be with her. Let me stay here, I won't be any trouble.' Turning away from the nurse I moved to the corner of the room. Clasping my hands together, I prayed fervently. *Though I walk through the valley of the shadow of death... Lord please help my wife... Lord don't abandon her... I need her Lord.'*

Dr Moore entered. He was a fatherly man with thinning white hair and silver rimmed glasses. Instantly, he scanned the room, and on registering the pool of blood on the floor, he shouted, 'What is going on here? Get this cleaned up immediately.'

The madness, the chaos began.

I was in a foreign country, among people who spoke a different language, I couldn't understand what was happening. What I did know was... it wasn't good. What I could fathom was... Dr Moore, who had appeared from nowhere, had a mastery of this language and so my hope rested in him. On his instructions, nurses ran back and forth, with medical instruments and towels.

Dr Moore leant over Queenie's face, his head moving swiftly from her mouth to her chest, checking signs of life with his fingers, his eyes, his ears, barking orders to the young doctor who left the room. But soon there were no more words. Just the sound of Dr Moore's hands flattened over Queenie's bare chest, pushing down, forcing the strange noise of breath out. Over and over, his voice counting one, two, three.

I was locked in disbelief—as if in a straight-jacket—*Lord don't let Queenie die. I beg you, Lord, don't let Queenie die. I can't bear it. Have pity on me wretched soul that I am. Please, Lord, save my wife, take pity on us both. I will do anything for you, Lord, if you save her, anything.'*

Finally, there was silence.

No one spoke.

Queenie's arms were outstretched over the narrow bed as if she was floating in an ocean after a storm, her face pale and her blue lips parted.

Dr Moore turned to me and taking hold of my arms said firmly. 'I am so dreadfully sorry.'

'No,' I screamed. 'You can't let her die.'

Pushing the doctor aside, I rushed to my wife and taking her in my arms rocked her back and forth like a father comforting a sick child, muttering. 'Don't leave me Queenie. Don't leave me.'

A young nurse let out a cry and the senior midwife escorted her quickly from the room.

No words of apology, explanation, or condolence brought any relief.

I could hardly breathe.

Eventually, Dr Moore took hold of my arm and escorted me to a waiting room where I sat for a time with my head in my hands, every thought blurred as if I was submerged in the cold Atlantic with no way up. My body jolted—my arms fell from my knees—I sat upright, then stood, my body a dead weight. *What the hell just happened?* Thumping the wall over and over, my hand throbbing with pain.

After what seemed an age, Dr Moore appeared, 'Reverend Walker, may I suggest you stay here tonight as you are in no condition to drive home.'

'What about Queenie?'

Shaking his head from side to side he said, 'There is nothing we can do for her now. I'm so sorry. I truly am. It is a tragedy.'

I was speechless, caught between two worlds, the world of the living and the world of the dead. I wanted to be with Queenie. The thought of remaining alive was unbearable. 'I will go home. I can't stay here.'

'If, you are sure. You will need to return within a day or two to collect the death certificate.'

'I will ring you. I can't think about it now.'

'Of course. We will take care of the baby until you decide what to do.'

'Thank you,' I said, unable to register the presence of my daughter who was swaddled in the arms of a shadow behind the doctor.

44. SISTER CONSTANCE

Wednesday 28 March 1990

Pulling several tissues out of the box, I wiped my face as if I had just finished a long race. Turning to Mr Walker, I blubbed, 'I am so dreadfully sorry. You, poor dear man.'

'I was a mess for a long time,' he said.

'You must have been grieving for years.'

'I have never stopped.'

An hour had passed and Mr Walker was still in bed.

The orderly knocked on the door. 'Would you like some coffee?'

'Yes please,' I said, 'I will go and have a word with the nurse. Could you help Mr Walker get dressed, and maybe we can sit by the patio doors and get some fresh air?'

'You don't have to come back, Sister, you must need to see other residents.'

'I will be back,' I reassured him.

At that point in the day, I was feeling a little under the weather and although I had planned to do a 10k walk in preparation for a charity event, I decided I would rather be with Mr Walker. After having a chat with the nurse, I returned to the room, 'Goodness me, you look smart. You are wearing a tie?'

'Have to keep up appearances,' he smiled.

'It must have been your daughter's birthday last week. Just turned fifty?'

'Yes, it was.'

'Did you send her a card?'

'No... I sent a telegram. But it was a day late,' he said, and I could see he was sad about it.

A cafetière was placed on the table with two shortbread biscuits. Handing him a napkin, I simply said, 'Aren't they kind to do this for us?'

'I pay them enough,' he replied.

PART TWO

When yet I had not walked above
A mile or two from my first love,
And looking back, at that short space,
Could see a glimpse of His bright face;

The Retreat by Henry Vaughan 1621–1695

45. HENRY

Tuesday 3 April 1990

Since Sister Constance left me last Wednesday, I have been prolific. My mind is swiftly recounting the time immediately after Queenie's death. I had blocked it out for decades but now the memories are pouring out of me and every day since our last meeting, I have been documenting the events so she can read it. Vivien asked me what I was working on but I have no desire to share it with her.

Sister Constance arrived a little flustered. 'I cannot fathom some people,' she said.

'By some people I wonder who you mean?'

'I won't moan to you Mr Walker, it wouldn't be professional or fair,' she said plonking herself down next to me in her usual chair.

Respecting her privacy, I said, 'Shall I make you some Earl Grey tea and you can read my ramblings. The ink is only just dry.'

I proceeded to make her some tea and she began to read.

Memoirs, 19 March, 1940

It was three o'clock in the morning when I stumbled down the stone steps of the nursing home onto the pavement. I began to shiver and couldn't stop. Like an actor who had forgotten his next line I kept repeating the same one over and over, 'Queenie, I can't live without you'. But there was no prompt, human or divine. As

I leant against the car I vomited, collapsing to the ground, drunk with grief.

Somehow, I managed to drive home, the darkness of the night veiling my thoughts. Back in the manse I sat at the bureau, writing a brief letter, addressing it to Walter and Florence. I then rummaged through the same drawer Queenie had looked through a few hours earlier. Pulling out bits of string and notes and a screwdriver, I found an old stamp and some glue and my small address book. Ralph's number was written in large black numbers on the front page. Throwing it across the room, I continued to search. I came across a flattened 'Passing Clouds' packet left over from Christmas. I knew there was one left, in case of an emergency, and concluded it was as bad as it could get.

On opening the front door, I took the letter, and lighting the cigarette walked as fast as I could to the village post box. My mouth tasted of ash as my lungs filled with smoke and I immediately felt nauseous. All was quiet except for the clicking of my shoes on the pavement. On my return, the clock chimed four times. Opening the small door at the back, I stopped the pendulum from swinging. I went to the larder and poured myself a large whisky, downing it in one. Climbing the stairs to the bedroom, I stripped off down to my underpants and climbed into bed. Pulling the eiderdown over my head, I clutched Queenie's nightdress, and cried myself to sleep.

Hours passed, sleeping, and waking, I relived my wife's death. Furious at the surgeon for being on holiday, I shouted, *how incompetent! How dare you go on holiday when you were to do an imminent caesarean. How could you let her die? A fit and healthy woman of thirty-three!* Tossing and turning, my sheets became wet with perspiration.

The dawn arrived, followed by the blaze of the midday sun but I remained frozen in bed, in a living hell, with no relief, no answers. I screamed at God, *you abandoned her, and you failed me! You are not a loving father! You are cruel and heartless!*

When I finally got up, I looked at my wristwatch and realised it was five o'clock in the afternoon. Pulling on some trousers and a shirt I went quickly to the telephone and dialled Ralph's number.

'What's the matter, Henry, I can't understand you?'

'She's dead, Ralph. Queenie died giving birth.'

'I don't understand. When?'

'In the early hours of this morning.'

'But I only saw you yesterday. Oh God, Henry... I should never have asked you to come over.'

'It's not your fault, Ralph.'

'Where are you now?'

'At home.'

'I shall drive to you immediately. Don't go anywhere. I can be with you within two hours.'

Slumping down in front of the ash filled fireplace, I waited for my friend.

When Ralph pulled up outside the manse it was nearing eight o'clock at night. I opened the front door. Ralph strode forcefully through the darkness to the dim light of the porch and as I collapsed into him, he managed to embrace my full weight.

'It's all right my dear man. I'm here now,' he said. 'Let's go inside and you can tell me what happened.'

I took the bottle of Johnnie Walker from the mantelpiece, wiped two unclean glasses with my shirt sleeve and poured out the amber liquid.

Ralph listened attentively, anticipating a squall of grief. He then realised something. 'Am I the only person you have spoken to, Henry?'

'Yes, although I have written to Walter and Florence.'

'Have you told the elders or James?'

'No, not yet. What do I say?'

'Let me call on James for you. I won't be long,' he said, putting on his coat and going directly to the farm next door.

Within ten minutes he returned.

'I have not been a good man, Ralph! Maybe if I had been a better person, Queenie would have lived. I asked God to give her life, raise her from the dead.'

Ralph is taken aback. 'Now, now, you can't blame yourself. Queenie died as a tragic consequence of labour. It is nothing to do with you.'

'But if we pray, Ralph. Pray that she will come back. If we get down on our knees and cry out to God to raise Queenie.'

'I think you need to calm yourself, Henry. You are becoming a little hysterical.'

'I mean it, Ralph. Isn't that what faith is, believing in the miraculous? That's what Queenie would do.'

'I think you have to accept what has happened. It is dreadful for you, but you need to accept that she has gone... to a better place.'

'A better place? She should be here by my side! Don't you see Ralph, this was not meant to happen.'

'You are so right, my dear chap. It was not meant to happen, but it has happened, and you are going to have to accept it.' Getting up, Ralph walked to the kitchen. He turned, adding, 'I have to go back in the morning. I'm so sorry. What will you do?'

I paused, I was exhausted and Ralph wasn't helping me. My body started to shake. 'I'm sure Walter will telephone me in the morning when he gets my letter. I will go and register her death on Tuesday, and then go straight to Westcliff. Get some sleep, you must be exhausted. I shall see you at the funeral.' I left the room and went to bed without washing.

In the morning, Ralph made me a cup of tea and left it on the bedside cabinet.

Not stirring, I remained still, like a fractured shell on a beach.

46. SISTER CONSTANCE

Tuesday 3 April 1990

The fact that Mr Walker has written the account of his wife's death many years after it happened has enabled him to write a moving account which I believe he wouldn't have been able to muster at the time.

As part of my bereavement counselling, I studied the five stages of grief, a model of behaviour by Swiss American psychiatrist Elisabeth Kubler Ross in her 1969 book *On Death and Dying*. It presents the hypothesis that those experiencing grief go through a series of five emotions: denial, anger, bargaining, depression, and acceptance. There is much criticism of this theory, however, I believe there is still some merit in it. In my own experience the order may vary but the components are all usually present to varying degrees.

Certainly, for Mr Walker, his memoirs express the first four but as I see him now in his eighty third year, I think maybe he has never experienced the last one; acceptance. This often comes several years after the death for many people, but I have met others who never embrace it fully. Maybe that is the flaw of the '5 stages' model.

Some confuse acceptance with eradication. Acceptance takes imagination, courage, and risk. It devours the rational. It defies the mind and its need for justice and answers. I sense, however, that this is possibly Mr Walker's 'half of it' and that he is trapped in the trauma of Queenie's death.

On the surface, he has made a new life for himself, and everything appears normal. But he is like men who have been through war and lost their friends in conflict. It doesn't take much for them to tear up as they remember their comrades fifty years after their death. The mind has the staggering ability to retain tiny bits of information for decades which indent into the psyche – a laugh – an embrace – the nape of a neck – a scent – the unique tone of a loved one's cry.

Grief is not a simple thing to go through.

It rests upon the soul and won't be shaken off, and if you compartmentalize it, it will seep out like oil from an ill-fitting lid.

More and more, I believe, the weight of death must be given away to a higher power, because without that act, it remains a wound which festers.

And in Mr Walker's case he still bears the wounds of battle. His soul entombed in 1940.

47. WREN

Tuesday 3 April 1990

It was 1940 and Florence was in the garden, looking at the new vegetable beds which replaced the magnificent magenta peonies. Having experienced years of rationing during WW1, she knew what she had to do. She dug the earth over and with her three sons planted carrots, turnips, and radishes as well as seed potatoes in the greenhouse next to the rosemary, chives, and mint.

Making her way back to the hall, she shouted, 'Boys, are you ready?' They appeared suddenly, running down the stairs like charging bulls. 'Daniel, collect the sandwiches from the kitchen, and don't forget to tell George's teacher that I will pick him up earlier today. He has a dental appointment.'

'Yes, Mum,' Daniel said, picking up three brown paper bags from the kitchen table. Followed by his two young charges, he slammed the door behind him.

Florence then went to the front room and taking a cloth from the pocket of her apron began dusting the three large pottery gurgle jugs on the mantelpiece. In the mirror she saw the postman open the gate and walk to the front door. Pinning up her unruly hair on one side, she listened to Walter's steel caps clip clopping on the resin-speckled floor, 'Goodbye Florence,' he shouted, 'I'm off to work.'

Walter, dressed in his usual attire, a smart grey suit, gabardine coat and black felt trilby, met the postman at the door. Exchanging pleasantries, the postman handed Walter a small white envelope.

Recognizing my father's handwriting, Walter shut the door and went to the sideboard to get the letter knife. On scanning the words, he collapsed in the hall chair, shouting, 'Florence! Come quickly!'

Florence rushed to his side. On handing her the letter, she read:

> *Dear Walter and Florence, Queenie died today after I gave a blood transfusion. The baby is fine. I can't write more now. Henry*

Walter clung shipwrecked to his wife's waist. Florence began to weep. 'This letter is dated the eighteenth. She died yesterday, and we didn't know. Why didn't he use the telephone? Poor Henry, poor Queenie, poor baby.' Stroking her husband's hair, she added, 'Walter, you must call him and find out what has happened.'

'He has told us what happened, Queenie died giving birth, that is all he can say.' He pushed past his wife and took off his hat and coat and went straight out to the garden. He hit the trellis with such fury that it snapped in several places. Florence was shocked as he was not a man prone to outbursts. She went upstairs to the lavatory, locking the door behind her.

Walter wept non-stop for thirty minutes, pacing up and down the garden, searching for the right words. He then went with a sense of purpose to the telephone.

'Henry... Henry I am in shock. I don't understand what happened.'

'You received my letter then?'

'Yes. You must be devastated.'

Henry groaned.

'I will drive down?' said Walter, 'You mustn't be on your own.'

'No, stay there. Ralph has been here. I will come to you in a couple of days.'

'Of course. Where will you hold the funeral?'

'I'm not sure.'

'What a mess,' Walter paused. 'The Avenue Baptist Chapel will be nearest for Betty. Poor Betty. How did she take it? Have you told her, Henry?'

'Not yet. I don't think I can bear to.'

'I will go and see her this morning. It's the least I can do for you.'

'Can I stay with you, Walter?'

'Yes, of course you can. Florence and I will help you all we can. How's the baby? Is it girl or a boy?'

'A girl... Queenie named her Wren.'

'Henry, come as soon as you can.'

Walter placed the receiver down just in time to catch Florence as she passed out.

48. HENRY

Tuesday 10 April 1990

Memoirs 1940

I sank back into the chair by the fire, I noticed the basket was empty of wood. I opened the back door and went to the small outhouse with its old porcelain lavatory and picked up some of the logs that James replenished on a regular basis. When I entered the manse I shivered, and after lighting the fire filled my glass with a double whisky. There was something I felt compelled to do before I could sit and rest. I reached for the telephone and dialled the nursing home. Someone eventually picked up. 'Hello,' I said.

'Good morning, who do you wish to speak to?'

'Who is speaking?'

'It's Jenny, one of the trainee midwives, sir... how can I help you?'

'I remember you, Jenny. It's Reverend Walker. How is my daughter faring?'

'Hello Reverend, Wren is thriving. She loves the formula.'

'That's good.'

'Will you be coming to visit her, sir?'

'At some point... I intend on making enquiries for her to go to a Baptist orphanage.'

'Oh... I see... But you have family she could go to?'

'I think that is a matter for me to decide, don't you nurse?'

'Yes, Reverend. I didn't mean to interfere. Would you like to speak to the doctor?'

'No, not now... later,' I said, putting the receiver down abruptly.

After adding a log to the fire, I took a framed photograph from the mantelpiece and slumped down into the leather armchair set at right angles to the hearth. Staring at a photograph of my wife, wearing her favourite blue dress and a matching small felt hat, I thought back to the day it was taken. It was a glorious day in Cuckfield—in the graveyard, at the back of the church—the day I proposed.

The fire in the manse was faltering. Placing the photograph down, I prodded the ashes, and added another log and a few bits of kindling. I noticed my green jumper was splattered with dried egg. What did it matter? No one would see it. My thoughts turned to the granddaughter clock and an argument I had had with Queenie, when she reproached me for not winding it. I knew I was apathetic about many things. The clock faced me with silence. I needed it to be mute. The Westminster chimes, marking the hours of the day, reminded me too much of my wife and our life together. In the evening, ten chimes meant time for bed. Seven chimes in the morning signalled time to get up. One chime called me to lunch. Now the clock had no purpose in telling me what I could not share with my wife.

I imagined her busying herself with letters at the bureau. I stretched out a hand as if to touch her. But like a mirage, she disappeared, and my arm fell with the weight of disbelief.

I arrived at the nursing home and the receptionist showed me into the waiting room. The condensation dripped down the old windowpanes, and I saw Queenie wiping them and tutting, 'Come on, Henry, give me a hand. They will rot if we leave them.' Shaking my head, I assumed I was going mad.

Dr Moore appeared looking pallid and tired. The strain of losing a patient had taken its toll. I was not in the place to reassure him that he had done everything possible to save her as I was not convinced that he had.

'Dear Reverend Walker,' he said, clutching a file close to his chest, 'please come this way.'

Following him up the large stone staircase, my thighs burned with fatigue. The office door was ajar, and as we entered, I spied Mrs Elsie Walker written on the front of the cardboard file placed on the desk. The doctor signalled for me to sit down. 'How have you been keeping?'

'I just don't understand how she could have died. She was perfectly well in the morning.' My eyes rested on the file, the name Elsie, so foreign to me.

'I'm afraid it had nothing to do with her not being well. It was purely a result of a very quick labour.'

I protested. 'But if a surgeon had been here, she would have lived?'

'Possibly... but as you know, we did all we could to save her. She lost so much blood.'

'But I gave her my blood.'

'It was too late... I'm so sorry... there was nothing we could do.' His voice trailed off into his chest. On opening the file, he handed me an envelope. 'Her death certificate... you will need this for the burial.'

I read the medical reason for my wife's death, but it made no sense. I folded it over, along the crease and placed it back in the envelope.

Returning to the manse, I lit the fire and sat in the chair for the next six hours, my head filling with a myriad of thoughts. *Had Queenie not always loved the Lord? Was she not a good person? All her care for others? All her discipline and restraint during the long engagement, for what purpose? Hadn't we deserved a long life together? What was the point in following Christ if He let us down so badly?*

The only time I rose was to use the lavatory or collect more wood or get a slice of bread and a whisky. When the sky turned black and the owl hooted in the night, it was as if a wilderness had entered the manse and my survival depended on the fire staying lit. Eventually, I turned on the radio; listening to the Home Service helped fill the overwhelming silence.

Early the next morning, there was an unexpected knock at the door. Peering through my bedroom window, I saw Mrs Conley. Reluctantly, I opened the door and she held her gift up high for my approval. 'Another sheep's head?' I said.

'No Minister,' she flushed red, 'I brought you one of my husband's pies.'

'Thank you, so kind of you.' Turning, I walked to the larder knowing she would follow.

Her short legs took twice as many steps as mine, her heels clip-clopping across the flagstones. 'Now, Minister, you must reheat this thoroughly for at least half an hour.'

Directing her back to the front door, I thanked her for her trouble.

'Your friend, Ralph, told James, and James told us. My husband and I are so sorry for your loss. When is the funeral?'

'This Saturday in Westcliff-on-Sea. The elders have the details.'

'Easter Saturday? I don't think we can make it. Mr Conley will be working, I'm afraid. It's the busiest day of the week.'

'I understand.'

Reaching out, she held onto my shirtsleeve. 'We loved her, you know, Minister.'

Her cologne was pungent, musty, and instinctively I pulled away. 'Really? I don't think she felt loved by you Mrs Conley. I think she felt constantly judged.'

Mrs Conley gasped. 'Queenie was loved Minister, but we had to put a stop to some of her ideas. You can't just waltz into a village and tell us how to worship or how to run Sunday school. You have to do things slowly.'

'We've been here five years,' I scoffed, 'she was trying to bring some life to this place, God knows it needs it!'

Mrs Conley's face drained of all colour as she tightened her features. 'The elders believed that your love for one another was your strength. They considered a couple would bring a family dynamic to the chapel.'

'Well, I shall be of no use to you now, not without the family dynamic!'

Leaning forward she touched my arm. 'Minister, I am so sorry. Forgive me? I spoke out of turn.' Capitulating I nodded and ushered her to the front door. 'Some of the elders will visit you tomorrow,' she said.

'I am driving to my brother's house tomorrow. Goodbye Mrs Conley.' Closing the door, I brought the meeting to an end.

Standing on the step she said out loud. 'Strange man, never did like him.'

On hearing her spite, I collapsed onto the wooden chair in the hall. My mind, spinning. *Why on earth would I stay here? How can I face the congregation? All the years of serving God, to what purpose?*

It wasn't that I no longer believed in God or in the divinity of Jesus, but the cruelty of watching Queenie die had hurled my faith into an abyss. Queenie was, after all, the centre of my world and I considered Martin Luther was right in his Catechism of 1529 that *Whatever your heart clings to and confides in, that is really your God.*

It was at that moment that I made the decision – I will no longer serve a God who makes no sense to me – if I can't have Queenie then God isn't going to have me. The fine thread of faith which runs through the suffering inside one's very being had snapped.

What will become of me?

Sinking to my knees I let out a primal cry for my dead wife, before spread-eagling myself out on the flagstones.

'Henry?'

'Queenie is that you?' I said, lifting my head and looking around the room. Did I imagine it? There was silence. 'Queenie, come back to me,' silence... 'Queenie, I wish you hadn't got pregnant. It was a mistake.'

Silence. Then a familiar voice. 'Henry. Wren is not a mistake.'

Whether she spoke the words, or whether I made her voice up in my head, I do not know for sure.

Either way, her words eased me from the floor and onto my knees. I went to the oven and opened the door wide.

Overwhelmed by hunger, I took Mrs Conley's pie from the shelf in the larder and walked back to the Rayburn.

§

The dawn light shimmered across the bonnet of my Austin as it sped along the main road towards the east coast. Easter fell early that year. It was colder than usual and there were only a few buds on the trees. Fortunately, I discovered a pair of brown leather gloves in the glove compartment. Unfortunately, due to the heating in the Austin having packed up, my legs were in a draft as the wind whistled through the vents. Twice I had to stop at petrol stations and stamp up and down on the forecourt just to get my circulation moving.

Driving in the early hours of Maundy Thursday meant I would miss the holiday traffic. It also meant that I would have two days with my brother before the funeral. I was concerned about my state of mind, insomnia having crept into my bed, pawing at me like a hungry dog. I was hoping Walter might be able to calm my nerves enough for me to be able to sleep.

Pulling up outside Craigmore, I sat for a few minutes, the engine ticking over. I was nervous at the prospect of seeing family members who loved Queenie. After living in my own world for the past few days, I was unsure how to deal with another person's grief. The front door opened, and Walter walked at a fast pace towards me, tapping on the window to get my attention. 'Henry, are you all right in there?'

Walter's presence moved me to tears.

49. SISTER CONSTANCE

Tuesday 10 April 1990

Mr Walker was melancholic when we met today. I think looking into the past can be lowering. But I know, in Mr Walker's case, this event has not been visited in many years and so he needs closure to be able to live in the present.

He mentioned Vivien is visiting him less frequently and he believes she is making excuses to not visit him. I try and reassure him but as I have never met her it's difficult for me to comment. I see it often at the care home. Some spouses come every day, for several years, until their loved one dies, while others start visiting regularly but after a month or two pass the visits diminish. It can be exhausting for them and I totally understand. But it is hard on our guests when visits tail off. So, Mr Walker, bereft from his past, is now sensing his wife is reluctant to see him, resulting in another bereavement.

With regards to Mr Walker hearing Queenie speak to him, it is not uncommon during a trauma. There are many accounts of people hearing the voice of God or a departed loved one. I appreciate the brain is a powerful weapon and can be for us or against us and often voices can be accusatory, while the voice of the Holy Spirit (God) is more instructive, uplifting and comforting. 'Wren is not a mistake,' are the words of a mother. I reassured Mr Walker. He smiled at me and nodded.

It seems obvious to me that Wren should go to Florence and Walter. How did he not see it at the time?

50. WREN

Tuesday 10 April 1990

My father turned up outside Craigmore two days before my mother's funeral.

Apparently, Walter opened his car door and had to prize my father's hands from the steering wheel.

Florence appeared and embraced him, saying, 'I'm so terribly sorry. I am lost for words.'

'So am I, Florence. Thank you.'

Once inside the house, his three nephews appeared. Daniel, the oldest boy, spoke first. 'I'm so sorry for your loss, Uncle Henry.'

'Thank you, Daniel.' Reaching out he shook the boy's hand.

Timothy, the middle one, also stretched out his hand, but said nothing.

Then George, the youngest, threw himself into Henry's arms, taking him off guard.

'Come now, George. Try not to burden Uncle Henry,' said Florence.

My father stroked the boy's mop of sandy coloured hair. 'You're just sad like me, aren't you George?'

George's tears flushed his cheeks. 'Yes,' he said, moving back to his mother.

After a brief conversation, Walter ushered Henry into the breakfast room and poured him some tea. Florence spooned in three sugars thinking he must need them.

'I hate to talk about it now, Henry, but I need to get the service sheet printed off soon. We will need to make some decisions on the order of service and the hymns,' said Walter.

'I trust you, Walter. Just sort it out for me... with Reverend Tinsley,' said my father.

'Yes, of course, you must be tired after your long drive. Let me show you to your room,' said Florence.

'I know where it is. You must have to deal with the boys.' Picking up his leather suitcase he went upstairs to the guest room he had shared with Queenie just eight months earlier.

Florence knew he was in deep shock, but she had no idea how to reach him.

51. HENRY

Tuesday 17 April 1990

Memoirs 1940

On Good Friday morning Walter invited me to chapel. 'No thank you,' I said, 'I was just thinking about the sermon I had prepared for today.'

'Tell me', said Walter, sitting on the bed next to me.

'I was to speak on Peter, the disciple who denied the Lord in the courtyard of the High Priest's house before the cock crowed three times.'

'Oh, yes.'

'I expect you imagine cockerels in the courtyard crowing?'

'Well, yes,' said Walter, 'of course.'

'But you see, having read numerous commentaries, one of them suggested the possibility that 'cockcrow' was actually a trumpet sounding for the changing of the Roman guards at 3 a.m. And that it was unlikely that cockerels were even allowed in the holy city. Interestingly, the trumpet call in Latin *gallicinium* and in Greek *alektorophonia*, both mean cockcrow. It is therefore possible that what Jesus said to Peter was, *before the trumpet sounds the cockcrow, you will deny me three times.*'

Walter was intrigued. 'I've never heard it put like that before.'

'Nor had I. I was so excited to tell my congregation. Stupid really because in the next part of my sermon I berate Peter for his cowardice in abandoning Jesus, stating that it is a matter of discipline to face the trials of this world and not to deny Christ when things get tough. Now I realise I am no better than Peter... I would deny Christ if I could have Queenie back.'

Walter placed his arm on my chest and began to weep, we then shared the same embrace we had shared when our sister Doris died all those years before.

I went to the bathroom and splashed my face with cold water. I heard Florence, Walter, and the three boys leave the house. Back in the bedroom, daylight peeped through the faded rose print curtains onto the rug, buckled from having been kicked earlier. After straightening the rug, I tried making the bed, but instead took off my slippers and collapsed back down, the wooden frame creaking under my weight. The sound reminded me of when Queenie and I made love on our last visit and how embarrassed Queenie was when Walter said he heard us.

Deep in thought, I cried out, 'Help me! My soul is overwhelmed with sorrow to the point of death.'

I began to shiver and perspire like a man with flu.

Sitting up suddenly, I put my shoes and jacket on and went downstairs and out of the house. My legs carried me down to the seafront at Chalkwell. My pace grew faster, and I found myself close to my parent's house on Ambleside Drive. What on earth would I say to them? They must have heard the news from somebody, but not having spoken to either of them for a good six months or seen them for at least four years I was not sure how they would respond to my visit.

Father opened the door. I was surprised to see his hair had turned white and that he was a little stooped. 'Hello, Henry its rather early. Your mother was very disappointed that you didn't ring us and tell us the news yourself.'

'I'm sorry to disappoint you, Father. Who told you?'

'Walter, of course.'

'Yes, of course.'

'What's happening with the baby?'

'I'm not sure. But I can't raise her.'

'I'm not expecting you to. I'm just asking a civil question.'

'I'm sorry. Maybe a Baptist orphanage would be good?'

'Yes, maybe."

At that moment Mother appeared in the hallway. 'Aren't you going to ask Henry to come in?' Embracing me, she exclaimed, 'Oh, my goodness, Henry you are a rake. You can't be eating enough. Let me get you some food.'

'No, Mother, Florence and Walter gave me strict instructions to return for lunch.'

'Right then,' said Father.

The rest of the meeting was as tense as its onset. I let them know the time of the funeral but apart from that I had very little information. I made my excuses and left.

52. SISTER CONSTANCE

Tuesday 17 April 1990

Goodness me, I have never heard an explanation before about the cockcrow in the courtyard and that it may have been a trumpet sounding. I'm not sure how true that is but it does make a lot of sense. I will have to do some further research on that matter and must inform Sister Agnes as she loves all thing related to hermeneutics.

There is so much about Mr Walker's story that I identify with. Although we are from such different backgrounds and life experiences, I do recognize the overpowering and inexhaustible weight of grief.

When my father died, I remember doing what Mr Walker describes, sitting on the bed, reflecting on Maundy Thursday, the day Jesus wrestled with God on the Mount of Olives, crying out, *"Father, if you are willing, take this cup from me: yet not my will but yours be done"*. I too, was unable to relinquish my will.

The intimacy Mr Walker had shared with his wife does not escape me either, and the fact they made love on the floor because of a squeaky bed must be such a wonderful memory to have. At Craigmore he slept for hours; the change of room and bedding anesthetising him. It's extraordinary that he has such a memory for detail. He wrote, 'At two o'clock the following morning I got up to go to the lavatory, tripping on the rug by the bed. My grey wool suit, creased like a dry leaf, as was my face'.

Walter then knocked on the bedroom door and invited his brother to the Easter morning service at the Baptist chapel. 'I thought you two were Church of England,' said Mr Walker.

'We are, but we need to discuss the funeral with Reverend Tinsley,' said Walter.

Good Friday, a solemn day in the church calendar, was the day Christ was crucified on the cross in between two criminals. The day Jesus invited one of them to be with him in paradise. A sinful man, who had never been confirmed or taken communion, or followed the catechism. He had accomplished little and his only achievement was to be placed on a cross next to our Saviour and he was instantly invited into heaven by Jesus because he was repentant and asked to be remembered. None of us want to be forgotten. How gloriously simple.

Mr Walker declined his brother's invitation to chapel. He was very much incapacitated.

I find it strange that he was bothered by denominational differences. It is an age-old issue for some Christians. Catholics, Protestants, Baptists Methodists, Pentecostals... the list is endless. So much infighting puts people right off. We have more that unites us than separates us but a stranger to the Christian faith must look on with amusement. Although I am a nun, to be quite honest, I could have fallen into the arms of any kind-hearted denomination. It just so happens I met the nuns who led me home. It is Jesus at the heart of these ministries. The Spirit. The air I breathe.

Religion is, unfortunately, thwart with politics, wars, and divisions.

Jesus is the sanctuary.

The pearl.

53. WREN

Tuesday 17 April 1990

Although my father paid a visit to his parents, Florence never knew the details. It remained a mystery.

When he returned, he appeared vacant. Lunch was a little strained, as no one knew what to say.

Florence broke the silence, 'Henry. You are doing remarkably well, considering.'

'I'm not sure what that means' he said... 'but thank you'. This is good food, Florence. I must give you my ration book. It will help you get more provisions.'

'No, certainly not,' replied Florence who had prepared a sausage hot pot with vegetables and seasoning from her herb garden. Rationing, only having recently been introduced, meant everybody, especially three growing boys, were feeling the pinch.

§

It was many decades later that I pieced together what had happened in Burrowbridge on that Easter Friday. Visiting the area, David and I discovered that the chapel had been turned into a delightful bed and breakfast and the manse was occupied by a lovely family who showed us around. The farm next door was being run by James's grandson, James having long since passed away.

Later that day we took a trip to Bridgwater library and searching through the microfiche archives I discovered a report of my mother's memorial service.

I was amazed to read that over one hundred people attended, representing all the churches and organisations of the district including most of the village, all of whom were packed into the chapel like 'Pippins in a box'. The previous minister, Reverend Wilson, a tall well-built man who had an air of authority took the service. 'I commend our dear bereaved pastor Reverend Henry Walker to the comfort and love of God. He is not present because he is with his family in Westcliff-on-Sea as Mrs Walker's funeral is tomorrow.'

There followed the first hymn, The King of Love My Shepherd Is, *whose goodness faileth never.*

In his tribute, the Reverend reflected on how Mrs Walker captured the hearts of the elders when she came with her fiancé to the interview almost six years previously.

> *From first to last, she had been found faithful, faithful to the purest ideals of Christian character, faithful in all kinds of womanly service, faithful in that which was least and in that which was much. She was, indeed, a capable, charming, and winning personality. She had a heart that was full of tender sympathy and her relationship with her husband in their service of the Church and community was ideal. The life of a minister's wife is never easy, and not to be envied. Few people know what a lonely and hard life it is, and Mrs Walker's life was not the exception. Yet she took a vital interest in the work of the district and won the admiration and affection of all. The young people in the district would say of her, as Jesus did of Mary, she hath done what she could. She lived a happy, a hard,*

a holy, and a hopeful life... I must remind you of the truth of Eastertide, so that in our sorrow we can rejoice and proclaim the note of victory. "For Jesus Christ hath abolished death and brought life and immortality to light through the Gospel."

§

The Reverend's words brought my mother to life. I cried reading the impact she had made on others.

54. HENRY

Tuesday 24 April 1990

The community in Westcliff, like me, was stunned by Queenie's death into an eerie silence but I was grateful for it. However, when the coffin was set at the front, suspended on wooden trestles as if floating on air, the congregation began to speak in whispers.

I sat in the front row next to Ralph, while Walter and Florence sat in the row behind with Mother and Father and my two other brothers, no longer referred to as the rascals. Across the aisle on the left sat Betty with Freddy and Martha by her side, and behind them sat scores of people.

The service began and Reverend Tinsley, a consummate professional, led the event with a sensitivity remarked upon for years.

Betty was barely able to look at her daughter's coffin. It was only six months earlier that she had attended her husband's funeral. She, like me, was surely bereft of all happiness.

During the second hymn, my mother, recognising Betty's grief at the loss of a daughter, broke convention, and crossing the aisle, slid into the pew next to her. Placing her spare hanky upon Betty's black gloved hand, they wept quietly in unison and forged a firm friendship from that day on—for death can either ignite a flame of resentment or indeed extinguish it as a blanket puts out a fire.

Freddy walked to the pulpit and climbing the stairs placed his sheet of paper on the lectern. Pausing, he looked out at the mourners. 'There are no words to sum up my sister's life, and I would not be so presumptuous as to imagine how you all feel about her, especially Henry, so I shall keep this short... I want to read a letter she wrote to me just six months ago, when she was staying with my mother, after my father had died.' Freddy looked at his mother. 'I hope, Mother, you will be comforted by it and all of you will witness Queenie's strong faith.'

Clearing his throat, he began.

> *Dearest Freddy,*
>
> *You cannot imagine the anguish mother is going through. Father was precious to us all but the love she has for him is humbling. It is as if they are connected in their souls and now father has gone, her soul is wilting.*
>
> *Flicking through the Bible, I am desperately seeking comfort and truth, and there I find it, in a way I cannot find it from within my own being.*
>
> *It states very clearly in Romans 8: 'The Spirit itself beareth witness with our spirit, that we are the children of God: And if children, then heirs; heirs of God, and joint heirs with Christ; if so be that we suffer with him, that we may be also glorified together. For I reckon that the sufferings of this present time are not worthy to be compared with the glory, which shall be revealed in us.'*
>
> *I will trust in God, Freddy, as Jesus' mother, Mary, did. Trusting, whatever the outcome, even when it is not good.*

Freddy's voice cracked. 'Queenie was my big sister, and she was a mighty woman of faith.' Leaving the pulpit, he walked over to the coffin and kissed it... 'I will miss you, my darling. Rest in peace.'

I cannot remember much of what happened after that. Tinsley said a few kind words, and then the final hymn was announced.

I was mortified.

At Bert's funeral, having sung loudly, It is Well with my Soul, I could now barely hold my head up. After the first stanza, I sat down, deaf to the words, gazing at the coffin, which held my wife, cold and still, when only a matter of days before she had taken my hand in hers and pressed it to her full belly.

Sitting down, I put my elbows on my knees and covered my head with my arms. The woman who had been my companion, my flesh, was being buried on Holy Saturday, the day Christ was placed in a tomb. In blackness, Jesus lay on a slab with a stone rolled across the entrance, separated from God. I was cut off from my wife, retreating into bitterness. On opening my eyes, in that fleeting moment when vision is unclear, I saw Queenie's smiling face. She was waving goodbye at the window of the manse.

I wept.

At the end of the service, I stood, and along with my three brothers, Freddy, and a man from the funeral parlour, I walked towards the front of the coffin. Lifting Queenie high, we placed her upon our shoulders. I shivered; my wife's face separated by less than an inch of oak. Slowly, we walked out to the waiting hearse.

55. SISTER CONSTANCE

Tuesday 24 April 1990

On the morning of Queenie's funeral, Holy Saturday, Mr Walker, for a moment, upon waking, forgot he was at Craigmore. Ralph, his dear friend, arrived from Devon in the early hours of the morning. It's a rather sad fact that Mr Walker decided against wearing his dog collar for the service, but I do understand.

I was relieved to read that when he arrived at the Avenue Baptist Church, he took Betty's arm, and they followed the coffin into the chapel together. And no real surprise that the building was full to overflowing, people having travelled from across the borough and up from Somerset. I asked Mr Walker if he remembered what the congregants whispered at the funeral. He replied, 'Things like, why is it always the good ones who go first? And the doctors should have saved her, and, that poor man, how will he ever cope?' All very familiar.

My meeting with Mr Walker was shorter than usual. I had a Chiropodist appointment for an ingrowing toenail which was causing me untold pain and I had to get it seen to. Mr Walker was miserable. I suggested I could return this evening and he was delighted. *Be still, my soul; the Lord is on thy side; bear patiently the cross of grief or pain.*

56. WREN

Tuesday 24 April 1990

The funeral party followed in six black cars to the cemetery three miles away. Florence told me of the rain that poured down in late March, black umbrellas opening in a synchronised flurry as the coffin was lowered into the hollowed-out earth. One of the women from the choir sang, 'Amazing grace how sweet the sound that saved a wretch like me.'

The minister threw a handful of earth onto the coffin saying, 'In sure and certain hope of the resurrection to eternal life through our Lord Jesus Christ, we commit our dear Queenie to the ground. Ashes to ashes, dust to dust...'

Turning away, my father refused to throw earth onto her coffin. Walter took his arm, later informing me that he had at that moment whispered, 'I have never told you this, Henry, but do you remember when Doris died?'

'Of course.'

'That night, as I lay in bed, she came to me and stroked my head... have faith. Florence and I can take care of Wren. We can raise her for you.'

'I have decided she will go to a Baptist orphanage.'

Walter was so shocked by this announcement that he said nothing. Instead, he tugged at his brother's arm. 'Come now, come with me.' Back at Craigmore, standing in the hall, my father made himself available to the hordes of mourners who greeted him. Old school friends of Queenie's, each taking his hand in theirs. Some cried and said too little while others said too much.

The elders from the Burrowbridge chapel lined up to speak to him, but it was my father's response of turning his back on an odd-looking couple, that concerned Florence the most. Mrs Conley, the butcher's wife from my father's village, looked embarrassed and tugged at her husband's arm, having decorum enough to know it was not the time, nor place, to make a scene.

My father said to Walter, 'I thought they weren't coming! I have to go now. I can hardly bear it. Would you mind awfully if I went home?'

'No, of course not, but are you in a fit state to drive?'

'I will be all right. I'm not in a fit state to stay here any longer. I have to do something.'

'When will you come back?'

'Very soon. Very soon.'

He took his hat and coat from the stand in the hall, picked up his leather bag and left the house via the side door in the front room.

When all the guests had left Craigmore, Florence sat alone by the fire. Walter appeared. 'I know they are taking care of Wren in the nursing home, but I wonder if she is being loved as much as we could love her.'

'I don't see how they would have time for her. They must be busy. Henry will have to make a decision about Wren soon,' said Florence.

'Henry wants her placed in a Baptist orphanage.'

'He what? No! I won't let that happen.'

Walter walked to the hall and picked up the telephone. 'I must speak to them.'

'But you only rang them yesterday, and it's late now,' said Florence, following behind him.

Walter picked up the receiver. 'Hello, is Jenny there please?'

'Hello, Jenny speaking.'

'Hello, Jenny, it's Walter Walker here. I wanted to enquire about Wren.'

'The same as yesterday, Mr Walker. She is so lovely. Bright as a button.' Pausing, she added, 'You asked me for the official reason for Mrs Walker's death, and because you are not immediate family, I was told I couldn't tell you.'

'Have you changed your mind, Jenny?' Walter signalled for Florence to listen in.

'Well, yes sir, I have. Considering you have called every day since Wren was born, I think it is important for you and your wife to know what happened. I managed to look through the file.'

'And?'

'The coroner put the cause of death as a pulmonary embolus, a precipitate birth and an adherent placenta.'

'What does that mean in layman's terms?'

'It means that the baby came extremely fast, resulting in severe loss of blood, and heart failure. I'm so sorry Mr Walker.'

'But my brother gave her blood.'

'One of the midwives told me that the only way her death could have been prevented was if someone had performed an immediate hysterectomy after the birth but unfortunately it all happened so quickly.'

'Thank you, Jenny, for being so candid and of course for helping with Wren.'

'I did speak with Mr Walker in the week, and he mentioned that he was enquiring about placing Wren in a Baptist orphanage.'

'I'm sorry, Jenny, but I have to go. I'll speak with you again tomorrow.' Walter replaced the receiver and turned to face Florence. 'I just don't understand how he can leave her at the nursing home and keep suggesting that she should go to an orphanage. Surely, the fact that we have offered to have her should be enough for him. I am his brother, and he is very fond of you, Florence.'

'Let's pray he comes to his senses,' said Florence.

57. HENRY

Tuesday 1 May 1990

Sister Constance had to leave me rather early last week but she promised to return that evening, which she did. We had a productive meeting. By that I mean, she asked me more about the events of the funeral and I was happy to hand over my memoirs. I made her a hot chocolate and she read for a little then we talked well into the evening. I am growing very fond of her. She has such insight. I am looking forward to seeing her later today so I can show her the next part of my memoirs.

Memoirs 1940
The long drive home enabled me to smoke, and the monotony of the journey brought some solace. Arriving back at the manse, I saw a wicker basket on the doorstep, filled with fresh bread, a pint of milk, some homemade biscuits, and eggs. Although there was no note, I presumed correctly that James had left it.

Inside the manse nothing much had changed. The clock was silent, and the condensation on the criss-cross windows had worsened. I took a handkerchief out of my pocket and began to wipe away the drizzle. After two windows I stopped, my handkerchief dripping wet. Inspecting the room, I observed the house was looking dusty and shabby. However, I was relieved to be at home, away from the crowds at Craigmore. In the bathroom I splashed my face with water so cold it took my breath away. I then went to the bedroom and sat on the unmade bed, falling back exhausted. On hearing a lone bird tweet, a monotonous, irritating tone, I covered my head with a pillow and fell asleep.

On Easter Sunday I was awakened by the Church of England bells sounding in the village. Although my chapel didn't have bells, I knew parishioners would be turning up for the morning service and assumed one of the elders would be standing in for me. The sermon wouldn't be as interesting as mine, but it was of little importance. I remembered back to last year's Easter morning when Queenie jumped out of bed, excited for the day ahead. 'He is risen!' she said, enthusiastically, not content until I had replied with, 'He is risen, indeed!'

I refused to answer the door when several elders knocked. Over the next few days, I became a recluse, venturing out in the early hours of the morning or after dark for a quick dash around the village, like a ghost, or something hollowed out. During the day, I drove for miles, as far as my petrol coupons would allow. Visiting places where I was unknown and where I didn't have to answer questions. I sat in teashops, read the newspaper, and discussed the War with strangers, enjoying some anonymity. Too much Red Label always preceded bed and sleep was always broken and fractious.

After a vivid and unsettling dream, I woke with a sense of purpose, and went to the telephone. 'Walter, I have to talk to you.'

'Yes, Henry, I'm listening.'

'I dreamt I was Horatio Spafford. I saw myself at the helm...'

Walter interrupted me. 'Hold on, who is Horatio Spafford?'

'He wrote that song It Is Well with My Soul. We sang it at Queenie's funeral. His four daughters drowned at sea, and last night I dreamt I was looking for them in the Atlantic. I saw the faces of four young girls struggling to breathe in the icy waters, and I sat bolt upright in a panic.'

'That's understandable.'

'I need to discuss how you and Florence might take care of Wren.'

'Of course, Henry, we would be delighted to have her.'

'I haven't time to talk now, but I will ring the nursing home and advise them of my decision.'

'What will you do with yourself?'

'I am not exactly sure what I will do, but I am clear about what I need to do now. I have to leave the Church, Walter, have time away somewhere.'

'You mean leave Burrowbridge?'

'No, I mean leave the ministry. Give up being a Baptist minister.'

'Are you sure, Henry?'

'Yes, I'm sure. We will speak again tomorrow.' Replacing the receiver down, I picked it back up and dialled the nursing home.

58. SISTER CONSTANCE

Tuesday 1 May 1990

After spending a couple of hours with Henry this afternoon, I decided to do a little research.

In the early hours of the morning, I am often restless, and more recently I have been singing It Is Well with My Soul, to get myself back to sleep.

It is such a resounding hymn.

It makes me cry.

I cannot stop thinking of Horatio and his wife Anna and what pain they must have gone through to have four precious daughters, Annie, Maggie, Bessie, and Tanetta, drown at sea.

My time with Mr Walker is, I believe, coming to an end. I can't tell you exactly why but I just sense it. I spend more time with him than any other resident because he knows he doesn't have long and he is almost desperate to have a conclusion to his dilemma of faith. He needs to tell his story to someone and that happens to be me.

Through many dangers' toils and snares, we have already come. 'Twas grace hath brought us safe thus far and grace will lead us home.

Funerals are so familiar to me that if I haven't been to one in a month, I wonder what is wrong. How strange that is. I suppose it comes with my vocation. The living. The dying. The dead.

The first funeral I attended was my father's. I was nineteen years old. The second was that of a close friend. Then my mother died and then one of the twins.

Bethany was short and feisty.

When she was a child, she loved taking the Lilly Pilly from the trees, gorging on the small pink berries, the front of her tunic often stained red, betraying her feast to our mother. She had the prettiest smile, and she never went unnoticed. She braided my hair and looked up to me with a reverence I didn't deserve.

My mother tried to hide it, but we all knew that Bethany was her favourite. They had a closeness I envied. Beth had an intensity about everything, and after my father's death my mother often indulged her. But it was okay. It meant when I left my mother, I could let her go to Beth.

But Beth hated exercise and loved food. In her thirties she was twice the size of her twin. On one visit to the house, I found her cutting up her clothes in a rage. She proceeded to cut her hair and her arms and legs. It was Me that called for the doctor... Me that had her sectioned... and when she died it was Me that held her sobbing twin – my remaining sister from a family of five.

Now I attend the funerals of the residents in the chapel within a few years, sometimes within a few months of their arrival. Many of them have lived unremarkable lives and yet exude grace and wisdom. I have learnt so much from them and been loved by them too. It has been hard to see them go.

I wonder about the order of death. How some people leave early, and some people outstay their welcome, and which is worse. *When we've been there ten thousand years bright shining as the sun, we'll have no less days to sing God's praise, than when we first begun.*

I understand Mr Walker's desire to run from pain – but pain catches up with you, and if you are not careful, even overtakes you. It is like the proverbial tortoise and hare story – we all know the tortoise beats the hare to the finish line. It is inevitable. None of us escape pain. The answer is not to see pain as the enemy but rather as something you must ride, like a wave. You may fall off your surfboard numerous times, but if you keep getting back on you will gradually master the fear and have glimpses of joy.

59. WREN

Tuesday 1 May 1990

Walter went immediately to the front room where Florence was sitting by the fire prodding the coals with a long-burnished bronze poker, trying to get the most heat out of each piece. 'I've got some news,' he said. Florence looked at Walter quizzically but said nothing. 'Henry has asked if we can have Wren.'

'Oh, my goodness. What did you say?' Florence rose from her chair and walked towards her husband.

'I said, of course, we would have her. He was distressed about a man who had lost four daughters at sea, something to do with one of the hymns we sang at Queenie's funeral.'

'It Is Well with My Soul,' Florence replied, taking her husband's hands in hers. 'Don't you remember? He sat down and placed his head in his hands. Poor man.'

Walter thought for a moment. 'Yes, I remember now. It seems our prayers have been answered. We can go and collect her whenever we are ready.'

'No, Walter. I think I should go by train. It is a far quicker journey. Maybe Henry can drive me back with the baby.' Florence kissed Walter and left the room; she didn't have a moment to spare.

Later that evening, Walter telephoned Henry to let him know that Florence would be arriving on the twelve o'clock train the day after next.

When Florence left the house, it was pouring with rain but it stopped just as the train pulled into the station, the steam from the smokestack mingling with the low-lying fog. Florence leant out of the window, her mop of auburn hair blowing back in her face. My father ran to open the door, and removing his trilby, embraced her. She handed him a small tin. 'I baked you some potato scones, but with no sugar they are rather plain.'

'Thank you, Florence, you must be thirsty. We can stop for a drink.'

'Walter made me a flask for the train, and we will have a long drive back to Westcliff. We had better get going.'

Florence mentioned my father was unkempt.

Before heading off on the ten-minute drive to the nursing home, Florence's eyes rested upon the full ashtray. 'How have you been?' she asked.

'I don't know the answer to that question.'

'Have you managed to get any sleep?'

'On and off,' he muttered. 'I have a lot of nightmares.'

'Walter mentioned the one about that poor man who lost his four daughters at sea. I had no idea of the hymn's origins. It must have upset you dreadfully at the funeral.'

'Horatio Spafford? Yes, but I don't suppose it would have mattered what hymns were sung.'

'No,' she said, quietly.

They continued the journey in silence. When they arrived at the nursing home, Dr Moore appeared greeting them with an outstretched hand. After a few pleasantries, a young trainee midwife appeared with me in her arms, wrapped in a yellow wool blanket. Florence's face flushed red as she moved towards the young nurse holding the tiny parcel. 'Jenny?' she said.

Jenny was not yet twenty years old. Her skin, unblemished except for the dark circles under her eyes. 'Yes, Mrs Walker, I am so pleased to finally meet you.'

'And I'm so pleased to meet you. What a darling she is!' Jenny placed me into my aunt's arms. Florence was transfixed by my dark blue eyes and mass of raven hair.

'I have grown very fond of her,' said Jenny.

'Yes, I'm sure you have. Are there many babies to take care of?' asked Florence.

Jenny shook her head. 'They usually go home with their mothers.' Tenderly she added. 'My mother died in childbirth, Mrs Walker.'

Florence told me that seeing this young midwife moved her deeply. 'Oh dear, dear! I am so sorry!'

'I think that is why I am training to be a midwife.' She paused... 'I wept for hours the day Mrs Walker died... it was so dreadful. The Reverend was beside himself.'

'Oh, Jenny, what a terrible thing for you to have to witness,' said Florence placing her hand on the young woman's arm. 'You must have grown attached to Wren.'

'Probably too attached for my own good.'

'I will take good care of her.'

'Yes of course you will, Mrs Walker.'

'And thank you, Jenny, for speaking to my husband every day. You have been a great comfort during this testing time.'

'I am so sorry for your family.'

'Thank you, Jenny. Queenie is sorely missed.'

When the time came to leave, my father asked Florence to carry me down the stone steps of the nursing home. Florence told me how nervous she had been, taking great care not to drop her precious bundle. Placing me in a straw bassinette on the back seat of the car she then covered me with a knitted blanket.

Florence asked my father if some of the congregation would like to see me.

'No,' he said, abruptly. 'Only James and Edith can see her.'

'Who are they?' asked Florence.

'The farmers next door. James took Queenie to the nursing home on the night of her labour.'

'Were they at the funeral?'

'No... I don't think they were.' He thought for a moment, 'I haven't seen James since before Queenie died.'

Carrying the bassinette to the front door of the farmhouse he signalled for Florence to knock. On opening the door, James, without looking at either of them, peered inside the crib. Stepping back, his eyes filled with tears. 'Isn't she bonny,' he said. Reaching out he touched my cheek but retracted his hand quickly. 'I have something for the baby. Please come in.'

'We won't. Thank you, James. I just wanted you to see her. We have a long drive back to Westcliff,' said my father.

'Wait there, Minister, please.' James disappeared into the back room and returned promptly with a small, wooden bread crate. 'I picked these from the riverbank, this morning. I know how much Queenie loved wildflowers.'

On the drive back to Craigmore, there were two bundles on the back seat, a sleeping baby, and a crate of cowslips with tall stems and tiny yellow flower heads. In the boot of the car was the small suitcase Queenie had taken to the hospital, full of towelling nappies, booties, leggings and two knitted matinee sets.

It was early in the evening when they pulled up outside Craigmore. Walter appeared. 'Hello both of you,' he said eagerly. 'Where is she?' Opening the passenger door, he lifted the bassinette from the back seat. 'Let me carry her into the house and get her by the fire... I always forget how tiny newborn babies are.'

'She needs feeding straightaway,' said Florence.

The three boys appeared from the front room and gathered around Walter, who bent down to show them their cousin.

'She is so small,' said Daniel.

'Her hands are so sweet,' said Timothy.

'Can I hold her?' said George.

The house became a hive of activity, but my father was nowhere to be seen. Walter discovered him an hour later splayed out on the bed in the spare room, fast sleep.

60. HENRY

Tuesday 8 May 1990

Sister Constance was 5 minutes late and I was a bit annoyed with her. I apologized for being grumpy and she politely nodded. She continued to tell me of some internal politics at the convent but I wasn't really interested. I needed to carry on with my tale. I have been having some palpitations in the night and hot sweats. I do not feel well. Each day I think maybe it will be my last.

'Do go on Mr Walker. Where were we up to? What did you do after the funeral?'

'A few days later I telephoned Ralph and asked him if he could help me pack up the manse? "Where are you going?" said Ralph. I told him I had secured a position in Bermondsey. To help the homeless find accommodation. He said it was a bit soon and so I shouted at him that there was great need in London.'

Memoirs 1940
Ralph may have been used to my curt manner, but he was becoming concerned about my state of mind. He arrived at the manse within a few hours. Placing his holdall in the hall he took off his coat. 'I have been thinking that a new job will help you heal. I worry that if you stay here your melancholy will turn into deep depression.'

'I know, Ralph, that is what I was trying to tell you, but it is also hard for me to leave this place so soon. It's as if I am wiping Queenie's life out,' I said, removing the books from the shelves one by one.

'Can I put the kettle on? I am so thirsty,' said Ralph.

'How about whisky?'

Ralph reached into his bag. 'I have a bottle of your namesake and a tin of smokes.'

Taking the bottle of Johnnie Walker from him, I placed the cigarettes on the table, 'You always know what I need.'

Later that evening, books strewn across the floor, Ralph held up a theology book. 'Where shall I put this one?'

'I shall leave it for the minister who takes my place. In fact, let's put them all back, I don't want any of them.'

I packed some kitchen items and then disappeared upstairs. Ralph found me sitting on the bed clutching the orange scarf to my face. 'My dear man, let me take that from you,' he said.

'When I was five years old, a few days after Doris died, my mother filled a large steel saucepan with oranges and sugar. The fragrance of oranges saturated the house till the next day.'

Passing the scarf to Ralph I picked up my wife's nightdress and holding it to my face, I tried to breathe Queenie back in, 'I'm losing her scent, Ralph. I can't smell her anymore.'

Everything shouted Queenie's absence. Her dresses hanging in the wardrobe, her combs and hair slides on the bedside table. Three pairs of shoes, half the size of mine, sat in a row under the bed. If I stay in Burrowbridge, I might go mad with the loss of her. If I leave and start a new life, I might have a chance to swim to safety... hold on to a rock with my fragile sanity. 'When will the pain stop?' I said in desperation.

'Not for a long time,' said Ralph, sitting down next to me on the bed. 'You will have to take one day at a time.'

'It's exhausting, I'm so tired.' I said, placing my head on Ralph's shoulder.

Ralph raised his hand and gently patted my face. 'Once you have settled in to your new flat, I will come and visit you.' He then stood. 'Now let us finish off up here, and I will cook us some food.' He picked up a slim blue box with a silver clasp. 'Which bag do you want this in?'

'In my suitcase. I shall take it with me.'

The next morning, I packed my clothes and a few more personal items and went to the office in the chapel. It didn't take long for us to clear out my desk and pack the Remington and the gramophone in the boot of the car. Ralph cooked up a couple of rashers of bacon and two eggs. It was a feast. We drank a large pot of tea between us and devoured several pieces of toast. 'You will miss living next to a farm, Henry, that's for sure. London won't be so generous to you on the food front. You must take your ration book with you.'

Once Ralph had left the manse, I sat for several hours by the fire. Plumes of smoke from a cigarette enveloped me. I stood, and taking the dog collar from the mantelpiece dropped it in the fire watching it as it curled up within seconds. 'I don't know you,' I said under my breath.

Later in the afternoon there was a knock on the door. James stood awkwardly with his cap in hand, his mass of grey hair sticking out in all directions.

'Hello James, do come in.'

He stood opposite me. 'I don't know what to say to you, Minister. That's why I didn't call round before now.'

'Call me Henry, please. And you don't have to say anything. Thank you for the baskets of food. They have been greatly appreciated.'

'That's all right. Me misses insisted,' he said, scratching his head. 'Queenie was such a sweetheart. I just keep saying to the misses, I don't understand it.'

'I know James. Nobody does. I wanted to thank you for driving Queenie to the nursing home.'

'I just wish she had called on me earlier. It might have made a difference. I feel so guilty. Me misses feels bad because she was away that evening and thinks she could have helped her give birth at home.'

'You mustn't blame yourself, James, and neither must your wife. Not even the doctors were able to save her.'

James scratched his head again. 'I heard you are leaving us?'

'Yes, I have secured a job in Bermondsey, as part of the war effort. I need to leave here. I'm sorry James. You have been the best neighbour we could have asked for and Queenie adored you both.'

'I shan't forget you and Queenie. You made such a difference to this place despite what Mrs Conley said. You will be missed.'

'What did she say?'

'Oh, it's nothing.'

'No, James, please tell me.'

'Well, you know what she can be like. She used to ring me misses to spread gossip, but Edith never did listen... well she listened... but never agreed with her. Some people are never satisfied with who is running the chapel, there is always someone better... usually the person who went before them... and yet... they weren't satisfied with them either.'

'Queenie found Mrs Conley's criticism of me so tedious. She was always trying to protect me from her negativity... but I knew what she was like. You are kind, James, thank you, although I don't think we made much difference to Burrowbridge.'

James was shocked. 'No, you are wrong there, Minister, you made the world of difference to a lot of people. You and Queenie brought life to the village. You made going to chapel a real joy, and everybody loved Queenie. Me missis says she was uncanny. She always knew what was wrong. "I'll pray for you," she would say at any opportunity. When Edith lost her sister, your Queenie was round our 'ouse every morning, for a month, putting the kettle on and giving her a well needed hug. This place won't be the same without you both.' Dropping his head to his chin, he wiped his nose on his sleeve.

'That's kind of you to say... but...'

'And the way you took the funeral for me sister-in-law was... exceptional. I know you didn't know her well, but you was so caring to our family. I shan't forget what you said.'

'James... I...'

'And thank you, Minister, for helping me find God again. I had lost me faith you see, that is, until you and Queenie arrived. Funny really, spent decades denying God's existence, but I still couldn't stop meself from praying to Him every day. It's either all meaningless or there is some meaning somewhere. I don't understand why she had to die, and if I did, I don't think it would hurt any less... but I am hopeful that I will see her again, and I am forever grateful to you, Minister.'

'I am glad we helped you and Edith, James, that was always the intention.' I changed the subject. 'Will you help me pack the rest of my things into the car? I am leaving tomorrow morning, and I want to get the granddaughter clock and a couple of boxes in tonight.'

'What time will you be leaving?' he said, following me over to the clock.

'About nine. I'll just creep away. Don't want any fuss.'

I took the head of the clock while James took the bottom end and we maneuvered the clock out of the manse into the garden. I was struck by the display of Forget-me-nots. James paused with me.

I carefully placed the clock on the back seat of the car and covered it with my black preaching suit and Queenie's winter coat. Only the face of the clock was left uncovered, staring upwards in silence. James took a box full of novels and personal belongings, while I took a holdall and a leather suitcase out to the car. On returning to the manse, James bent down at the hearth, and started to clean the grate, tipping the debris into newspaper. I was thankful not to be dealing with ash.

A restless night followed, I gathered up my wash bag and comb and threw the empty tin of Brylcreem in the bin. I stripped the bed and put the linen in a large paper bag ready to put in the car. Opening the wardrobe, I took a clean shirt off its hanger but left behind my two clerical shirts. I dressed in the same clothes I had worn for the past month and went downstairs. After a cup of coffee and a crust of toast, I looked around the manse for the last time. I had arranged to leave the furniture, and the elders kindly agreed that I didn't have to serve my notice. Realising I hadn't packed the radio, and with no intention of leaving it behind, I put it under my arm, along with the bag of linen. I shut the front door firmly behind me posting the key through the letterbox. It wasn't until I got to the gate that I saw people lining the streets on both sides.

James stepped forward. 'I only told me misses you was leaving at nine. You know what a village is like.'

'I wanted to leave without a fuss.'

'I know, Minister, but what could I do?' Edith, stood next to James, blowing her nose and wiping the tears away with her handkerchief.

A young girl with red hair, from Sunday school, was pushed gently forward by her mother, 'Minister?' she said.

'Yes dear.'

'Please don't go.'

Stroking the girl's cheek with my thumb I said, 'I'm sorry, but I can't stay.'

Her mother, a woman in her mid-thirties, dressed smartly in a three-quarter length black coat and small black hat, stepped forward. 'We will miss you, Minister. My daughter cried for days when I told her that Mrs Walker had passed away.'

I turned to the crowd, 'Thank you. Thank you for coming. It means a great deal to me.' I placed the radio on the passenger seat, along with the bag of linen and as I drove slowly past the gathering more and more people came out of their houses, waving as I passed them.

The villagers were as bewildered as I was. Queenie may not have been a member of their family, but she was many things to many people, and her absence was felt deeply. Her death, like a storm, had forced the banks of the River Parrett to break.

The car sped through the English countryside on A-roads, the rain beating a percussive rhythm on the windscreen, hypnotising me. After nodding off for a brief second, I hardly cared if I made it to Betty's house. The clock protested with clanking sounds every time I braked, the pendulum loose in the box, muffled slightly by the coats, but still an irritation.

61. SISTER CONSTANCE

Tuesday 8 May 1990

Mr Walker visited Betty, his mother-in-law, only briefly. When Freddy arrived, it gave Mr Walker permission to leave the house. How sad that would have been for her. It appears that he was unable to engage in someone else's grief because he hadn't acknowledged his own. Can you imagine what overwhelming pain Betty must have experienced not only to lose her husband but within six months to lose her only daughter? It must have been a Tsunami of grief.

Mr Walker appears grateful to Walter and Florence for having Wren, but from the way he describes those meetings he wants little to do with her.

Standing in the hall of Craigmore with the granddaughter clock dripping wet, Walter patted his brother on the back. 'These are hard times, Henry, and we will help you and Wren in any way we can.'

Florence, asked him if he had seen Betty. 'Not for long. I shall visit her again when I am more composed,' he said.

Florence took his hand and led him into the front room. Peering into the crib, Mr Walker did not recognise his daughter. Like a sleeping cherub, her cheeks had filled out and her hair was thick and wavy. Hardly daring to touch her, he placed his forefinger under her right hand, and she sprang awake. He was surprised by the strength of her grip. Suddenly, a flashback of Queenie giving birth hit him like a vehicle out of control, he swerved, darting away, seeking refuge in the bathroom.

It wasn't long before Walter knocked on the door and pushing it open said, 'Are you all right, Henry? You went so pale.'

Seated on the floor, with his head in his hands he answered the best he could, 'I can't seem to look at Wren without seeing Queenie in pain.'

Walter asked him to come and have a cup of tea. 'I have had so much bloody tea, Walter, and it doesn't seem to make any difference.'

Walter's answer is the best I have heard, 'I don't think tea will make a difference. It's just something for us to do.'

Taking his brother's hand, Mr Walker let himself be pulled up from the floor, reflecting on the fact that drinking copious amounts of tea with numerous different people was possibly the only way he could deal with his grief.

Mr Walker was awoken by his daughter's cries in the early hours and decided to dress and drive back to the manse. Florence appeared with Wren in her arms. 'Come and sit with me for a moment Henry. I have just given her a bottle.'

Following them into the front room Henry said he had to get home. Florence was agitated, because it was 3 a.m.

'I was awake and assumed it must be about seven,' he replied.

Florence explained that newborns need feeding in the night. 'Come back soon. She needs to know her father...' she said. She repeated the request. 'She needs her father, Henry.'

Mr Walker heard her the first time but was unable to commit to much.

§

I have found the offer of tea is an ideal vehicle for healing. It is certainly part of ritual and ritual is hugely important in our everyday living. Think of your own rituals, repeated daily, maybe with slight variations but still all very similar. An alarm wakes you. You raise your head, maybe reluctantly, from the pillow. You open the curtains. You go the bathroom and wash your face and clean your teeth. You put the kettle on. You cut the toast or fruit or pour out the cereal. You turn a radio on or the television and catch up with the morning news. You think of the day ahead and the meetings or the gatherings or the tasks: washing, food shopping etc. And then in the evening you take a walk, draw the curtains, and light a fire, cook a meal, ring a friend, read a book, and step into a bath or shower, and finally rest your head back on the pillow after setting the morning alarm.

DEATH interrupts this ritual.

Like a plague, it stultifies life, jarring the mind out of its pattern. In fact, it denies ritual. It threatens everything normal. The heart bleeds because it has been squeezed of the regular, the mundane and what is left? Chaos.

Even if it is just a cup of tea... from a host who has nothing much else to offer, it is at least the reinstatement of ritual.

Of course, I have a hope to offer more than just tea. But it is a good place to start.

I had to stop reading Mr Walker's memoirs as I had a few people to meet but I find it all so frustrating. On an emotional level Mr Walker was so abandoned, so disconnected from everyone. He needed professional help. I feel as if I failed him, and I didn't even know him back then. Where were those able to minister to him? Florence and Walter were obviously an extraordinary couple to embrace his daughter. But Mr Walker was traumatised and needed help.

62. WREN

Tuesday 8 May 1990

I used to visit my grandmother, Betty, as a teenager, because she was living with my Uncle Freddy and I spent a lot of time with Eve. One Sunday afternoon she whispered in my ear. 'Your father came to see me just the once after your mother died. When I lived in Kenilworth Gardens. It was pouring with rain... He handed me your mother's coat and I couldn't let go of it even when I went to put the kettle on.'

'What was he like?' I said.

'He offered to make me tea... and then I told him that I had been to see you and couldn't believe how you were so like Queenie as a baby. Florence was wonderful with you... I asked your father just one question.'

'What was that?'

'Did my girl suffer?'

'What did he say?'

'He said that she hadn't and that she had fallen into a deep sleep. At that moment, I just wept... your father moved towards me, but I stepped back holding the coat up to my face. I didn't want him to comfort me.'

'Why not?'

'I think I was angry with him. He should have called me and let me stay with my daughter... to help her. It was her first baby.'

'I'm so sorry, Granny.' I said, sensing the weight of sorrow on my grandmother's lips.

'My only consolation is that my husband never knew of it. It would have broken his heart.'

'Did my father make you tea?' I asked.

'Your Uncle Freddy arrived but the interruption meant your father had an excuse to leave. He never did make me that tea.'

Walter told me the story of when Henry bought the clock to Craigmore. My father, having left the manse in Somerset, had delivered the clock on an exceptionally wet day. Once he had left after breakfast, Florence sat with Walter in the front room. 'I just hope he hasn't acted too quickly in giving up his home and his community,' she said.

'It seems to me he has made the decision rather impulsively, but I can't imagine what he must feel,' said Walter. 'The thought of losing you terrifies me.' The clock remained in the hall. 'Let's put it in the front room, by the fireplace. It will have pride of place!' said Walter, bending at the knees and lifting the clock. 'It's not heavy at all.'

'Not too near the fire, Walter. It will dry it out,' said Florence.

Moving it a foot to the right, away from the heat, Walter took a brass key from his trouser pocket. 'I don't know how to wind the clock. Do you know, Florence?'

'We had a mantle clock with Westminster chimes, and my mother always wound it from left to right.'

Walter proceeded to wind while Florence opened the small door at the back and lightly flicked the pendulum with her forefinger. The clock beat out a familiar rhythm and they were both relieved as if successfully bringing it to life. Florence then moved the large hand through quarter past, and suddenly the chimes geared up and rang out, reminding her of her parent's home.

'I think it needs a polish,' she said, leaving the room to get a duster. On her return she knelt and began dusting the clock, examining it all over and caressing the small flower heads on the beading. She was still for a moment. 'I remember Queenie telling me she had been given a clock by the elders. I dismissed her for some reason, and she said I was jealous. I said I wouldn't want your clock for all the tea in China... it's just another thing to polish...'

Florence started to weep.

63. HENRY

Tuesday 15 May 1990

The London Embankment was overcast. Dark grey clouds fused together with the muddy brown waters of the River Thames. Only a thin line of pale pink paint was visible on the body of the Albert Bridge—its suspension cables fanning out from four posts—a half spider's web.

It was a Sunday morning in April, and I was in my new but sparsely furnished flat on the third floor of Cheyne Place, SW3. Having secured a six-month let, in a large modern Art Deco block with rounded casement windows, I looked out over the Physic Gardens towards the Chelsea Embankment. It was a stone's throw from the Albert Bridge and Chelsea Bridge and a thirty-minute walk to the Houses of Parliament and Big Ben. The new job at the rest centre in Bermondsey took up most of my time, and as the journey back to Chelsea took an age, I occasionally slept on a camp bed at the Centre during the week.

For the month of August, London was peaceful until 7 September when the appearance of German bombers in the sky heralded Hitler's attempt to subdue Britain by destroying London. All hell was released, and I spent the next few months dodging death as incendiary bombs rained down over the East End and central London. Having lived in a serene part of England for many years, I questioned why I had chosen to be in utter bedlam. But it suited me, suited my mood. I was able to focus on other people's troubles instead of my own. A neighbour advised me to take cover in the underground at Westminster, and even though the government attempted to stop the public from using the tube stations as shelters, they were forced to back down as people continued to purchase platform tickets and defy the ruling. Staying at work until seven, I returned home on the tube for around eight. On leaving the flat an hour later, I walked for thirty-minutes to Westminster, becoming one of the hundred and seventy-seven thousand who lined the platforms of the London Underground, nightly, during the next five months. Women served up cocoa and men played accordions and violins to keep the children entertained. Surprisingly, I slept quite well on the hard platform. The proximity of people lying nearby a comfort and the banter and camaraderie distracted me from thinking of Queenie.

One time, arriving late, I purchased a platform ticket for a halfpenny, but since the platform was full, I slept on the escalator. My long limbs twisted on the wooden slats – people all around groaning – body parts numb, burning and tingling. Shifting and changing positions enabled me to sleep for half an hour at a time before the pain set back in. I vowed never to be late again, my body, aching and bruised for several days. Back on the platform at night, I enjoyed stretching out on a flat surface and once the thundering of the trains stopped at around 10 p.m. everyone settled down to sleep.

I decided I would get a better sleep at Craigmore and so drove there one evening. Walter embraced me and gave me some toast and a whisky by the fire. The next morning, the boys appeared at the door of the breakfast room. George, dressed in a pair of red knee length shorts and a blue knitted jumper, stood in front of me. 'You must be turning seven soon George. Are you having a party, or is the war putting your mother off?'

'Yes, I am... next Saturday. Mother says that every seven-year-old should have a party.'

Reaching into my pocket, I took out a florin. 'Do you think you can buy yourself something with this?'

'Oh yes! Thank you! Will you come to my party?'

'I'm afraid not. I am working in London.'

'What are you doing exactly?' said Walter.

'Helping people get accommodation when their houses are blasted to pieces.'

'Please come to my party,' said George.

Daniel took hold of his younger brother's shirtsleeve and pulled him away. 'Enough now. Leave Uncle Henry alone.'

'That's all right, Daniel. Remind me how old you are?'

'I'm fourteen in September.'

'And how old are you, Timothy?'

'I'll be twelve soon.'

'What's it like having a baby in the house?' I said.

Timothy smiled. 'She is very sweet, and it makes a change from having brothers.' He playfully smacked George on his arm.

Florence interrupted, 'That's enough horse play. Now go and get ready for church.'

'I must be going,' I said, determined to leave the house.

'So soon?' said Walter.

'I think it's for the best.'

'You need to stay for Sunday lunch, Henry, there is nothing of you,' said Florence.

She was right, I had lost a lot of weight within a short period of time. I was happy to sit in the front room and wait for them to come back from the service.

In September, word soon spread of various tragedies in the underground. Twenty people sheltering in Marble Arch station were killed when a bomb blast ripped the white tiles from the walls turning them into deadly projectiles. In October, an explosion at Balham station burst the water pipes and sixty-eight people drowned. Everybody knew the facts, but what could we do? We had little choice. It was either go underground or make use of small private shelters.

Much of London was devastated. Taking a train to Westminster I viewed the shattered walls of Whitehall and Buckingham Palace. Walking down Oxford Street, I came across parts of John Lewis and Selfridges lying in rubble: water jets blasting into the sky, putting out smoldering bricks and furniture.

On returning to my sparse and uninviting flat each morning, I experienced an overwhelming weight in my chest. The cigarette I smoked on the walk produced a little pleasure, but when it was finished, I was left with the familiar taste of ash and a need to clean my teeth. During those bleak months, I only used a teapot, one cup, one plate for toast, a razor and flannel in the bathroom, and the obligatory lavatory paper. After shaving I looked in the mirror, smoothing my hair back with water as my staple supply of Brylcreem had run out and could not be replaced. I was receding a little faster than I would have liked and lines that once inferred their residence were now firmly squatting on my face.

I noticed an imbedded frown between my eyebrows and tried to smooth it out with my forefinger, but it fell back into a deep ridge. I smiled falsely seeing the face of a young man who was happy. At only thirty-four years old, I looked nearer forty. However, I considered that looking miserable suited the time I was living in, and no one would question why I was morose.

London suffered terribly during the Blitz with nearly thirty thousand deaths and fifty thousand seriously injured. At the Bermondsey Rest Centre, I came across families who had lost their homes and only had each other. Sometimes they were even stripped of each other. Watching women arrive at the Centre in deep shock at having lost their husband or a child during the raids I soon realised that the best way to help them was by using my skills in administration by swamping the Metropolitan Borough of Bermondsey with paperwork, letters, and phone calls; demanding families had their plights acknowledged. Local housing organisations dreaded my impromptu visits as my internal anger expressed itself on the stage of a destroyed London. Gradually I got a name for myself and respect from the local community and the authorities.

Henry Walker is not to be messed with.

Henry Walker demands to be listened to.

Henry Walker fights for justice.

An elderly couple arrived at the Centre one morning after their house had been blasted to Timbuktu, but a few hours later they went missing. On their return they explained to me that they had gone back to their house to look at the damage. Although the roof was blown off and the windows were shattered, several walls collapsed, and furniture stolen, by some miracle the gas oven still functioned and so they cooked a meal. 'Had to do something for ourselves, Hitler or no Hitler.'

I was never a prayerful person, having relied on Queenie to pray for family and congregants. I had (like most people) prayed emergency prayers and (un-like most people) liturgical prayers, but soon after Queenie died, I stopped praying altogether. Every incident I read about in the paper or heard on the news, which pertained to an answered prayer, I balked at, believing that mankind had been abandoned.

64. SISTER CONSTANCE

Tuesday 15 May 1990

I'm sitting up in bed and have just read a section of Mr Walker's memoirs and I sense his pain grew daily.

He mentions the bombing of St Paul's Cathedral in the autumn of 1940 and how firefighters worked through the night, as more than 10,000 incendiary bombs fell from the sky like a meteor shower. Notwithstanding all the devastation in London, St Paul's remained intact, despite a direct hit which destroyed the high altar. Many Londoners considered it a miracle and St Paul's became a symbol of strength and goodness but Mr Walker thought this was ridiculous. 'Surely it was the twenty thousand firefighters helped by numerous soldiers using 2,300 pumps who had put out the raging fires. God was nowhere to be seen.'

He decided to take a look for himself. Taking a tube to Mansion House, the smell of fire and wreckage hit him as soon as he started up the escalators. Looking skyward, he watched as smoke fused with monochrome clouds blanketing the cathedral in fine dust. The Home Guard directed him away with a 'God bless.' But he persevered, pushing his way towards the dome. Chairs were scattered, and debris littered the polished floor. Fortunately, most of the valuable paintings were packed and stored in the crypt, and he was strangely relieved to know that The Light of the World had not been hit.

What surprised me when I read his account was his indifference towards God. After years of preaching and caring for people going through personal suffering, it seems he could no longer believe. His faith had shrivelled up and he passed off any divine involvement amid appalling calamity as nothing other than co-incidence.

Extending the lease on his flat, he was unaware that he was about to meet Cécile Croze, the woman who was to become his second wife!

65. WREN

Tuesday 15 May 1990

Florence prepared a table fit for a king. George invited eight friends for his birthday party, five of them girls. Unfortunately for George, as soon as the girls saw me in the crib, they cooed over my podgy hands and pretty clothes. George could have been put out, but he was proud to show off his cousin.

Florence placed the cake in the middle of the oak table. It was a triumph, the neighbours having contributed towards the fat and sugar, with a few chocolate drops placed on top of paper-thin icing.

It wasn't long before coaches arrived outside Southend High School collecting the Walker boys and three hundred other children from the surrounding area. Over eight thousand children were taken from the south of England to Mansfield and the countryside in the North of England. Florence's heart was broken, but the War Office said children should be away from Southend as its geographical position made it one of the most vulnerable towns in England, for either bomb attacks or invasion. Florence, however, decided to stay with Walter after she heard that a neighbour, having gone to the Midlands with her four children had, within three months, been informed that her husband was having an affair.

'I have no intention of losing you, not over this silly war!' said Florence.

'I know, my dear, but you should trust me.'

'You will be vulnerable, Walter. The war will end some day and it is not good for us to be apart when we don't have to be.'

Florence believed that I was better off staying with them. After all, I had been born into crisis and what I needed now was stable parenting, something, which she knew she and Walter could provide. If bombs were to fall, I would have to take my chances with my aunt and uncle.

I wasn't aware of one such incident because I was too young to remember, but Florence told me how one night when they were sleeping under a green floral eiderdown and my cot was on the landing, they heard the rich droning sound of a German bomber. It was rumbling above the house as it headed for the channel. Suddenly, a noise like a fire-cracker blasted through the roof and debris fell to the floor. On hearing me scream, Walter jumped out of bed and Florence followed quickly after. 'There, there, Wren... Uncle Pop is here... don't cry.'

'Look Walter, look!' said Florence, pointing at the floor. 'It missed Wren by inches. It would have killed her. It's lodged itself into the floorboards.'

'The plane must have been discarding its shell casings.'

Walter checked me over for any wounds. 'Thank God, she is not harmed,' he said, 'I'll have to get a builder into fix the roof tomorrow.'

'It's as if someone is watching out for her,' said Florence.

'Yes, yes I think you're right, darling.'

Walter carried me back to their bed and placing me between them for the night, stroked my hair and soothed me with sweet words as I was calmed and drifted off to sleep.

66. HENRY

Tuesday 22 May 1990

I woke up this morning having had a good night's sleep and I certainly feel refreshed. The sun is blazing through the patio doors and I am happy that Vivien is paying a visit. She is bringing some homemade flapjacks which I am partial to. *Not too much of that Mr Walker* I hear my nun telling me. I had an hour without any interruption so I sat at the table and started to type. I was reminded that even though I would rather wipe out the memory of my second wife she is relevant to the story and so I must push on and tell it.

Memoirs 1941
I met Cécile Croze on the stairs at Cheyne Place. She had locked herself out of her flat and I had invited her in to have a cup of tea (there you go again, tea on the menu!).

She began, 'I fled my home in the Luberon when Hitler's forces were advancing. I arrived by ferry from France with my life's savings of fifty-four pounds, wearing my one suit and my foxy, given to me by my mother,' she said, 'I wanted a better life for myself. I left my parents and six siblings behind. I thought London would be a safe refuge.'

'Ah, like me,' I said, 'we were both wrong.'

Cécile reminded me of Queenie, but on reflection the former lacked the elegance of Queenie's bone structure and her joie de vivre.

Thirty-seven years old, with slim legs and a small waist, Cécile wore the same sage green wool suit every day accompanied by a fox stole; her constant companion. She was taller than Queenie by four inches; pale skin, white as bone, with large brown button eyes sunk deep into a rectangular face. Her shoulder length chestnut hair, her most striking feature, was set each evening in curlers and headscarf. Her lips, although full, missed being attractive due to the slight grimace they held. However, when she opened her mouth and spoke, her sing-song voice redeemed her.

I was certainly seduced by it, or rather beguiled by it, but as we all know someone must have more about them than just a sensual voice. Cécile managed to secure a position as a translator at the French Embassy in South Kensington but was less delighted when Charles de Gaulle announced the surrender of France to the Germans and the Embassy was shut down.

I can acknowledge that she was a little unstable, but for some reason I still pushed on with the relationship. Each night we agreed to meet at my flat at around eight, and after a light supper, with bedding, walked for thirty minutes to the underground. We soon realised we had been sleeping a matter of feet away from each other for a couple of months. Gradually, we established a routine, and a particular spot to bed down, making polite conversation with others. I placed two blankets on the station platform to soften the ground for our hips, followed by more blankets and two pillows. People assumed we were married and neither of us contradicted the presumption. Lying together, fully dressed, under the blanket was comforting for us both.

When I mentioned the possibility of marriage, Cécile jumped at it. I quickly realised two things about my fiancée. Firstly, she was not overly tactile, a quality in Queenie I had taken for granted.

And secondly, she had an abrupt manner. Some would say rude. Marriage may have been premature, but once the question has been put it is hard to retract.

Of course, I talked of Queenie and Wren to Cécile and her response was fitting. 'You, poor, poor man.' And although Cécile was not to replace Queenie, she at least gave me a morsel of kindness.

But no one knew about Cécile at my place of work, and I had no intention of mentioning her to Walter or Florence. I assumed they would be horrified, and therefore wanted to delay judgment. It was my secret, and I would tell people in my own time.

Not wishing to draw attention to my relationship status, I managed to find subjects on which my brother and Florence could be distracted, however, I never anticipated that they would have an agenda for my daughter. On a visit to Craigmore, we discussed Pearl Harbour.

Florence was playing Patience.

'It was the best thing that could have happened,' I said.

Walter looked up from his newspaper, 'Henry! What do you mean? The bombing of Pearl Harbour is a travesty. Over two thousand naval men and women wiped out.'

'It will bring the Americans into the war,' I insisted.

'President Roosevelt called it a day of infamy,' said Florence.

'You don't understand,' I said, 'it was an unprovoked attack, and the result is that Roosevelt has declared that a state of war now exists between the United Sates and the Japanese Empire. Don't you see? It means the war has gone from being a European war to a World War.'

'Well, I hope some good will come out of it. We could do with some help,' said Walter, and then he changed the subject. 'Henry, there is something Florence and I wish to talk to you about.'

'Oh yes, fire away.'

'How would you feel about us getting Wren christened?'

'No... definitely not!' I said.

'Surely every child should be christened,' said Florence.

'Absolutely NO to a christening,' I bellowed.

Walter stared at me in disbelief. 'All right, but please explain.'

'Explain? Do I really need to? You two may well be Anglican, but as a Baptist... a lapsed Baptist... I still believe that a child should decide on baptism when they become an adult. I want Wren to be free to make up her own mind. She is only ten months old. She may decide it is all baloney.'

'What about Queenie? What would she have wanted for Wren?' said Florence.

'Queenie would never have agreed to infant baptism, and as she is not here, it falls to me to make the decision.' I paused and tried to soften my tone. 'Look, both of you, I appreciate everything you do for Wren. She is in the best place, but who knows when that may change. I must go now. I have to get to a petrol station before they close.' Walking to the hall I took my raincoat from the hat stand. 'I'll be in touch,' I said, slamming the front door behind me.

§

As I write these memoirs, I do question my attitude. I am trying to be as truthful to my memory as I can be and upon reflection, I think maybe my actions and words were often severe. When Sister Constance arrives, I will ask her opinion.

She is always clear with me.

67. SISTER CONSTANCE

Tuesday 22 May 1990

Mr Walker, was in a strange mood today. He made me sit down and immediately thrust some A4 into my hands. On reading the opening few sentences, I looked up and said, 'Tea would nice.'

He obliged.

I assumed he wanted my opinion on his attitude towards infant baptism; that I would disagree with him because I am a Catholic. But I am not one for insisting on religious superiority.

'Was I too harsh in opposing that Wren be christened?' he asked.

I thought for a moment. 'I have spent time researching this and I have found no scriptural insistence either way.'

'Go on.'

'As I understand it. Historically, New Testament baptism replaced the Jewish ritual of circumcision for infant boys on the eighth day. Baptism was a new ritual/practice that Jesus and the early apostles presented to include girls, women and gentiles and, yes, even babies.

'But...' said Henry.

'Baptism is symbolic of the water of life and the Holy Spirit and it was St Peter, the fisherman and close friend of Jesus who said, "Repent and be baptised, every one of you, in the name of Jesus Christ for the forgiveness of your sins".'

'Exactly, babies can't repent of anything.'

'But they don't have to. The Godparents do it on their behalf. I understand that some priests have lorded it over their congregation insisting that children may end up in purgatory if a child dies and is not baptised. Can you imagine a situation where an infant dies and has not been christened? Would Jesus, who stated, "let the children come to me; do not hinder them, for to such belongs the kingdom of God," let one perish? Look at the thief on the cross, he had not been christened and yet Jesus took him to heaven with him.'

'But as a Baptist, I believed that someone should be old enough to repent of their bad behaviour in order to be baptised.'

'Well, you are right. But historically, if whole families were being baptised including the babies, then the church practise has developed from a biblical practise. It is a free gift.'

Henry was pensive, 'A free gift? How did I miss that?'

'It's offered to everyone, irrelevant of one's age or status.'

'I get that... it was unfair of me to stop Walter and Florence baptising Wren. They were caring for her.'

'Maybe it gave you a bit of control?' I asked.

'Not really. I think I just truly believed it was wrong.'

'Each denomination thinks their way is the only way to God. It seems very narrow to me. It is such a shame because we have more that unites us than divides us.'

'Remember, I was also very angry with God at that time in my life.'

'Are you less angry now?'

He looked at me, his eyes filling with tears. 'I am beginning to see myself more clearly and I don't like what I see.'

'God sees you very clearly, Henry, and I believe he is loving you each and every day.'

He nodded slowly and changed the subject.

§

I am very aware that wartime heightens emotions, and back in 1941, Mr Walker's emotions were unhinged.

If he had told Walter about his relationship, I feel sure Walter would have given him some perspective, but unfortunately, he chose not to.

Leaving Mr Walker alone for a few minutes I went and used the staff toilet. His tale was exhausting me. It felt as if there was a black cloud hovering over the events of his daughter, Wren, and I am beginning to understand her story despite only hearing it from his perspective.

He is predictably going to marry someone highly unsuited to him and that marriage will cause untold misery. It doesn't take a genius to work that out.

On my return, he continued. 'It was in 1943 on a bright autumn morning when the large wooden doors of the Chelsea Registry Office opened, and Cécile and I appeared. I wore a pale grey wool suit, and she was dressed in a popular tartan skirt suit, a 'siren suit', made by Incorporated Society of Fashion Designers... With limited stocks of material, they created suits that were less boxy and more contoured to a woman's figure...'

'Can I stop you there a minute? You speak as if you are an advising agent for a fashion show. You married Cécile without informing your brother?'

Henry was in a trance, 'She wore a cream blouse and a small posy of yellow roses, she looked bonny enough and I was happy that she was more than willing to pay for both suits out of her savings.'

'Who were your witnesses?' I asked him.

'Ralph, of course, and the maid of honour was one of Cécile's work colleagues. It was a modest affair... she kept the bouquet for a month, until it began to rot, and she had to throw it away.'

'Did you inform your parents?' I asked him.

'I did not like keeping secrets from Florence and Walter, or from my mother, who by this time was a widow – my father's death having passed over me like a cloud driven by the wind – but I knew I would have to tell them of my marriage to Cécile very soon and decided to inform Walter by letter.

A few weeks later, I received a letter from Florence.

68. WREN

Tuesday 22 May 1990

Florence wasn't a very religious woman and certainly didn't understand denominational differences, but my father's harshness over the matter of me being christened, wounded her. Walter, however, was not surprised by his brother's outburst. 'He will soften with time, dear. Don't be so offended by him. Sometimes he reminds me of my father.'

'I'm not offended. But we have charge of her. He should allow us to make certain decisions. Hasn't he left the Baptist Church? Why can't he just let her be christened? It wouldn't do any harm.'

'We were raised as strict Baptists, Florence. I have become an Anglican partly because of you and partly because I don't mind either way what church I attend, but despite Henry's lack of faith he is still very much a Baptist.'

Florence went straight to the granddaughter clock and taking the key from a small porcelain bowl began to wind each of the three mechanisms until they resisted. 'Oh blast,' she said, 'it's stopped.'

'I think you are over winding it my darling,' said Walter, gently. 'It will right itself. Just give it time.'

Meanwhile, Walter, was concerned with what I should be calling Florence, 'Don't you think Wren should grow up calling you something better than Auntie Flo?'

'Like what? She can hardly call me, Mum. Anyway, Henry wouldn't agree.'

'What about Auntie Mum?' he said.

'That sounds good, but I insist you ask Henry's permission.'

Walter went immediately to the telephone. 'I need to catch him before he leaves for work. Hello Henry is that you?'

'Yes, Walter. What is it?'

'I wanted to ask you a favour.'

'Yes of course, what is it?'

'At two and a half, Wren is talking a lot more now, and I thought it might be nice if she grows up calling Florence, Auntie Mum, as it is a bit more endearing than Auntie Flo. I know she can never replace Queenie, but she is acting as her mother.'

'Yes... yes. Is that all? I need to get on. Would you excuse me, Walter, I must dash?' The receiver went dead.

'What did he say?' said Florence, appearing from the kitchen.

'He is fine with it. He is exceptionally busy, my dear. I think we can safely say that Wren can call you Auntie Mum.'

§

From photographs of my third birthday, I was slight in build with a round face and bright eyes. My hair, jet black at birth, was now a lighter shade, and my fingers were long like my father's: Florence calling them 'violin fingers'. As usual Florence made a fuss and because my birthday fell on a Thursday, Walter left work early to stop off at Harrods, purchasing a teddy and some yellow ribbon. A teddy I kept by my side for many years.

Before the war, Florence played the violin in the Southend Symphony Orchestra and was considered a good reliable player. She was delighted to have a little protégé, and it was therefore no surprise that she put me on a quarter size violin, teaching me the rudiments of the instrument at such a young age. 'You were as bright as a button', she told me 'a delight to teach.'

Standing between the slats of the five-bar gate at Craigmore, wearing a thick navy-blue coat, a woolly hat, and a bright red scarf I sang Florence's favourite song, 'Sunshine, my only sunshine, you make me happy when skies are blue.'

The postman handed me a letter. 'Now Sunshine do you think you could deliver this letter to your Auntie?'

Bolting to the open door, I yelled, 'Auntie Mum, you have a letter.' I then ran to the kitchen and handed her the small white envelope. Recognising the writing she said, 'It's from your Daddy. Walter! Walter come, quickly!' Walter arrived from the garden in his shirtsleeves, holding a rake. 'You open it, Walter. I'm never sure what your brother is going to say next.'

Leaving the rake against the back door, he walked to the cabinet in the hall and picked up the letter knife. Within a few seconds he exclaimed, 'Oh my goodness, what on earth has he done now!' His jaw dropping open. 'Married? He's got married!'

'What?' Florence said, rolling her eyes.

I appeared. 'Has my Daddy got married?'

'Yes dear, it would seem he has.' Apparently, I went and clung to Walter's trouser leg. Sitting down on the chair in the hall, I straddled his leg, and he held my hands, rocking me up and down. 'Horsey, horsey, don't you stop, just let your feet go clipity clop.' Screaming with joy, I flew high as if on a swing boat at a fun fair.

Climbing up his leg I took his face in my tiny hands, and gazing intently into his eyes, pleaded for him to do it again. Kissing me sweetly on the forehead, he set me down gently, and reached for the phone. 'I must ring your Daddy.'

'Not now,' I said.

'No, Wren, be a good girl. This is important.'

I understand from Walter that he was deeply shocked that my father had remarried. He asked his brother if they could meet his new wife. The call ended abruptly without Henry telling Walter any details of the wedding.

Florence understood he was lonely but that he certainly wasn't in the best frame of mind to pick a wife. Florence was concerned that he would now spend even less time visiting me, whereas Walter, had other concerns which were proven to be right.

Florence's attention soon turned to her oldest son Daniel.

At seventeen he was struck down with polio and rushed by ambulance from the farm in Mansfield to Southend General Hospital. Even though it was a six-hour journey, Florence insisted that her son be near her. Penicillin was couriered by a policeman on a motorbike all the way from The London Hospital in Whitechapel. Cycling to the hospital, twice daily, meant she had to leave me with a neighbour, but neighbours were scarce, as most people had left Southend due to the bombing.

One evening, after she had prepared a light meal for Walter, Florence sat down at the desk in the dining room and composed a letter to my father. It was a letter that she was always to regret sending.

69. HENRY

Tuesday 29 May 1990

Memoirs 1943

My dear Henry,
*   I was surprised to hear of your recent wedding but also delighted for you. I know the last few years can't have been easy, and I am acutely aware that we all need a companion in life, never so true as now, so I am sending belated congratulations to you both.*

*   I am sorry that you missed Wren's third birthday celebration but understand you have been very busy with the war effort. I am therefore not sure if my request will be at all possible, considering your newly married status.*

*   Daniel has been in Southend General suffering with polio for the last few weeks and the prognosis is not good. As it is proving exceptionally difficult for me to get Wren cared for during my twice-daily visits I am appealing to you to take charge of her for two weeks. We would tell her that she is to have a holiday with her Daddy and his new wife.*

*   Do please say if it is not convenient for you both. I will understand completely.*

*   Love from Florence.*

Telephoning Craigmore immediately, I spoke to Walter. 'I'm sorry to hear about Daniel. How is the poor chap?'

Walter's voice shook with distress, 'He is seriously ill. It's a rare form of polio; the doctors say he may not walk again.'

'That's dreadful! I'm so sorry. What are they doing for him?'

'They are trying a radical new treatment. But they have said it will be very punishing to his system.'

'I'm sorry. I understand Florence needs some help with Wren. Cécile and I are happy to have her.'

'Just for two weeks. Florence will manage after that,' insisted Walter.

'Of course,' I said, and I meant it.

§

Placing the memoirs down, the nun gazed at me for a moment. 'I'm so glad you were able to help Florence. She seems such a wonderful woman. I can quite imagine her.'

I blushed and bowed my head, 'You need to read on,' I said, 'You may not be that pleased with me after all.'

70. SISTER CONSTANCE

Tuesday 29 May 1990

Unable to stay with Mr Walker for as long as I would have liked, he let me take his memoirs away with him. They are *hot off the press*, so to speak.

Memoirs 1943
Within a matter of twenty-four hours after receiving the letter from Florence, Cécile and I arrived at Craigmore. Walter and Florence made pleasantries about the weather and the war while Wren wrapped her arms around Florence's legs. Cécile leant forward to greet Wren and the dead glass eyes of the fox stole loomed into her face. Screaming, she ran into the kitchen, and Walter had to coax her out of the pantry.

Florence broke the ice. 'Wren, why don't you go and get a book from the cupboard, and let Cécile read you a story?'

'No,' she said, stomping off.

'I'm sorry,' said Florence.

'Oh, don't worry. We will become good friends. She is adorable,' replied Cécile.

I don't think Wren reciprocated the admiration and when it was time to leave could not be found anywhere. It was Walter who discovered her, hiding in the hall box-seat. 'Come out now. It is time for you to go on your holiday,' he said.

Burying her head in Walter's chest, she sobbed, 'I want to stay with you.'

'You will be back very soon. Your Daddy wants to spoil you. Don't you, Daddy?' Walter nodded at me to join in.

'Yes. We will take you to the park, and you can see the swans,' I said.

'I hate swans.'

'Wren!' said Florence. 'Don't be rude to your Daddy. He has come to take you on holiday. We shall all meet in Harrods, and you will be home before you know it.'

§

Gradually, Wren was cajoled into Mr Walker's arms. Why do I sense this is not going to end well?

71. WREN

Tuesday 29 May 1990

Walter told me that he had watched me clamber up on to the back seat and wave at him and Florence through the oval window of my father's Austin. Apparently, I had the look of a lost child. Florence, meanwhile, watched the car disappear, and she too had that same lost look. Walter, recognising the expression, put both arms around his wife and led her back to the house.

That evening, Florence sat brushing her hair at the dressing table, wondering how I was faring in a different home and a different bed. Opening the window for some fresh air, she breathed in the cool dry night of early winter and recognised *You Are My Sunshine*, playing on a neighbour's radio. Straining to hear, she listened to the words, as if for the first time. *You are my sunshine, my only sunshine you make me happy, when skies are grey. You'll never know dear how much I love you. Please don't take my sunshine away.* Florence wept in Walter's arms, and Walter felt a deep unease.

72. HENRY

Tuesday 5 June 1990

Memoirs 1943

As soon as we arrived back at the London flat, Cécile went straight to the kitchen and put a small pan of water on the stove to cook my daughter an egg for supper.

Wren shrugged her shoulders. 'Auntie Mum gives me an egg every day.'

'That's because she has room to keep chickens, unfortunately, we do not,' said Cécile.

Later that evening, I went to Wren's bedroom. Peering in, I saw her tossing and turning, obviously unsettled by the day's events. Closing the door, I sat down next to Cécile. 'I'm not sure I can do this my dear.'

'Don't you worry,' she said, patting my leg. 'We will do it together.'

I admit that Cécile was overbearing; the way she washed Wren's face with a flannel as if she was trying to rub her out, smothering her with kisses and affection one minute, then quickly changing her tone to a harsh one the next. After seeing Wren flinch once too often I had to speak up. 'Cécile my dear, maybe you need to relax with her a little. Give her time to adapt.'

'I am doing my best.'

'I know, my love, but Wren hasn't known you long. She will need time to adjust to our environment and our ways.'

'Yes, yes, of course, you are right. I will try better tomorrow.'

Tomorrow, however, was not much different, or the next day.

Cécile poured herself over Wren who was swamped like a small bird in a deluge.

Two weeks later I was due to take Wren to Harrods, a large red brick department store on the Brompton Road in Knightsbridge.

Florence greeted me in the tearoom. 'What, no Wren, Henry? Where is she?'

'That's what I have come to talk about. Is Walter not coming?'

Florence stumbled over her words. 'I'm not sure why he's late.'

'Let's sit and have some coffee'

'I'd rather have tea,' she replied, looking pale.

After ten minutes of discussing the weather, as only the English can, I realised Walter may not be coming and so decided to impart my news. 'You and Walter have been wonderful looking after Wren, but I think it's time for me to take over the role of being her father... and Cécile is eager to be her mother.'

'But wait a minute, Henry,' said Florence, 'I only needed a break for two weeks. Surely you can't just take her from us. That would be unkind to her. After all, she has been with us since she was a month old.'

Placing my hand tenderly on Florence's arm I said as clearly as I could, 'I know and I am grateful, but I need to do this. I want her to be with me now... it has taken me too long already to make this decision.' Unable to meet her gaze I added, 'And as far as helping Wren to adjust, I believe it is necessary for her not to see you for six months.'

At this news something in Florence's strong English resolve never to cry in public was shattered; the tears came fast. 'Florence?' I shouted as she fell to the floor taking the pot of Darjeeling with her.

The waitress ran to her, waving a napkin in her face. 'Is she all right, sir? Shall I call an ambulance?'

'No... no, she will be fine. She just had a shock, nothing to worry about. Maybe a glass of water, please.'

Picking up several pieces of broken teapot, the waitress ran off to the kitchen. The couples seated a few feet away dithered about whether to get involved or not. There was a war on, and people were used to seeing strangers receive bad news. Not wanting the whole thing to escalate, I said firmly, 'Don't worry everybody she will be fine, just a small shock. It's all under control.'

Florence began to come round. The waitress knelt. 'Here you are Madam. Take a sip.'

'Thank you... I'm not sure what happened,' said Florence, clutching the glass of water.

Reaching down I tried to pull her up. 'Let's get you to your feet.' But she was having none of it.

'I can manage!' she said with a scowl, slapping my hand away.

Walking towards the escalators in silence we were like warring factions with no negotiator.

At the back of the building, I hailed a taxi, giving the driver enough money to get Florence back to Westcliff.

I then went immediately to a red telephone box at the back of the store and rang Walter. 'Walter, why are you still at work?'

'Henry is that you?'

'Yes, of course, it's me. Why didn't you come to Harrods?'

'We had a problem with a member of staff. A clerk stole some petty cash, and I had to deal with it.'

'You need to get back to Florence. I have sent her home in a taxi.'

'Why, what's wrong with her?'

'I told her that Cécile and I are going to keep Wren. She passed out.'

'She passed out. Where?' said Walter.

'In Harrods. She's fine now. I made sure she was all right before I put her in a taxi. But she needs you Walter, you must get home to her immediately.'

Walter was flabbergasted. 'I will leave straight away.'

I was unnerved by Florence's apparent vulnerability, but there was nothing to be done. Hailing a taxi, I headed back to Chelsea.

73. SISTER CONSTANCE

Tuesday 12 June 1990

Oh, for goodness' sake! What a thing to do to a child! Poor Wren! Poor Florence! Poor Walter! And to take her to someone who is obviously not going to manage her well. I can tell already this is not going to be a happy ending. What was Mr Walker thinking?

I discovered from Mr Walker that on his return to the flat he took Cécile to one side. 'I had expected Florence to be a little relieved to give up her charge. I hadn't appreciated the bond she had made with my daughter.'

Cécile was firm. 'It is better to do it now than to leave her to get more attached in a few years' time. You are her father, Henry.'

Mr Walker learned more about his wife that evening. She told him how she was one of seven children from a strict Catholic family and her parents had failed to supply her with any love or affection. 'I was lonely all my life until I found you,' she told him. 'I was much younger than my siblings, raised as an only child. That is why we should have children together. Wren will need some siblings. It is imperative.'

Mr Walker was reluctant to agree with this suggestion, 'I want some time with you before we have children. After all, Wren will need our attention.'

She replied impatiently. 'But we must not wait too long.'

The following evening, he plucked up the courage to talk to Wren. 'How would you like to stay with Daddy and have Cécile as your new Mummy?'

Hurling herself to the floor, she banged and kicked, screaming out, 'No! I want to go home to Auntie Mum and Uncle Pop.'

Picking her up, her arms flailing, Mr Walker took her to the bedroom and placed her on the bed. Not knowing what to do next he shut the door and left the room. An hour later he returned and picked her up from the floor where she had fallen asleep. Her face was stained with tears. 'What am I doing with this child?' he thought. 'How fragile she is.' Placing his daughter under the sheets, he gazed at her for a while, her bobbed hair framing her face, and for the first time he did not want to move away from the memory of Queenie.

74. WREN

Tuesday 12 June 1990

The Georgian Restaurant, first opened in 1911 and situated on the third floor of Harrods, is the largest in London. It can seat almost a thousand people, but on the day Florence was due to collect me, there must have been no more than six couples.

Scanning the menu, Florence raised her head upwards admiring the Art Deco skylight with its ornamental wrought ironwork, supporting a magnificent chandelier.

The waitress approached Florence for her order.

'I'd like to wait for my husband and relatives to arrive. Thank you,' she said.

The waitress turned away, and my father appeared... alone.

He was curt. Florence describing him as unflinching.

My father had had no intention of returning me to my aunt and uncle.

I am still angry about it all these years later.

In the taxi home Florence stared out of the window, her face fixed in disbelief, tears streaming down. Approaching Westcliff, she watched the sailing boats bobbing up and down, the metal lines beating against the masts making the familiar clicking and clacking. She wanted to halt time and reverse it, but knew it was futile as it had already expired.

At Craigmore, she opened her front door and walked into the front room. As if on cue, the clock chimed six. The doorbell then rang, breaking her stillness.

'I saw you get out of the taxi, Florence,' said her friendly neighbour, who was too busy with her elderly mother to take care of me. 'You don't look yourself. Are you all right? I thought you were going to collect Wren.'

'He's decided to keep her,' said Florence.

'But he can't just take her from you. You raised that little poppet since she was four weeks old!'

'Well, it seems he can, and he has. I must go now. I will speak to you tomorrow.'

Not waiting for a reply, she closed the door and went with purpose to her bed.

Walter arrived within the hour to find her curled up under the covers, drained with red swollen eyes. He held her tight as an internal sorrow reverberated, a tremor that wouldn't subside. He had never seen her in such a state. 'It's my fault,' she repeated over and over.

'No, my love, it's not your fault.'

'I should never have written the letter,' she said.

'He would have taken her anyway.'

'You must ring him, Walter. You must tell him he was only meant to have her for two weeks.'

'What can I say? He will tell me she is his child, not ours. We have three children. Wren is all he has. I am not able to ask him for his daughter back.'

Walter would never know if his brother might have given me back because he remained wordless–like a blank crossword.

Florence retreated. The opposition too strong. She decided she must recover for her own sake and for the sake of her boys. The very next day she folded the rest of my clothes into a brown leather case, careful to include Queenie's vanity set, and Walter delivered them to his brother within the week.

Back in the front room, Florence was on her knees polishing the clock. 'If he wants the clock he will have to come and get it. We will not be inconvenienced... it is all I have of Queenie. All I have of Wren.'

The clock chimed ten times and Florence found it strangely comforting.

Florence became consumed with visits to the hospital, Polio debilitating poor Daniel, who was delirious through the night, telling his mother that he had heard the nurses discussing who should lay him out. Each night, back at Craigmore, Florence climbed the ladder up to the attic, and peering through a tiny window watched to see if any bombs were dropping on the hospital. Daniel was making slow progress, and they wouldn't know if the penicillin had worked for many more months, or whether he would ever walk again.

75. HENRY

Tuesday 19 June 1990

Vivien arrived at her usual time and we played *Patience*, something she told me I have very little of. This made her laugh and laugh and I found it slightly annoying. I was quite glad when she left the room to get her hair done.

When Sister Constance arrived, I told her of how my wife had annoyed me and the reference to Patience and she laughed too.

'Mr Walker,' she said as she gasped for air, 'We have to be able to laugh at ourselves sometimes, otherwise life is just too serious.'

'I know,' I replied. 'I don't know why it gets me down. I feel foolish.'

'Maybe you could let go a little and join in with the humour. It might make you happier.' She then leant over and stroked my hand.

I smiled.

'Smiling is so good for you.'

She was right.

She is often right.

'Tell me about Wren living with you in London.'

'On Wren's first morning with us the bed sheets were sodden, and it continued every morning for one month, until Cécile decided enough was enough and marched Wren off to the local doctor. The doctor assured her that it was bound to be related to the *poor child's state of mind*, but Cécile insisted Wren should be observed in hospital. After two nights of no bedwetting, they handed her back, but after one night in her own bed the sheets were soaked again. It became a routine every morning for Cécile to strip the bed and wipe Dettol over the plastic sheet before re-making it.

After six months, I could see Wren was still unhappy, but I had no idea of how to change things for her. I decided we should take a trip to see Florence and believed it was enough time for Wren to have forgotten her a little. I arranged with Walter that I would bring Wren to them every month, choosing to meet, not at Craigmore, but rather, on Southend Pier.'

'I'm not so sure she would forget them,' said the nun.

'We arrived to see Walter standing gormlessly holding a bucket of pebbles. Wren, struggling to be released from Cécile's grip was dressed from head to toe in brown wool clothing. The bonnet was rather silly, but I suppose it was practical as the wind was bitter. Florence cleverly engaged Cécile in conversation and Wren trotted off with Walter. I watched them sitting together on the boardwalk, snuggling up, while she threw pebbles from the bucket into the ocean below. He had a way with her that I couldn't manifest. I knew she loved him more than me.'

'Were you jealous of your brother?' said Sister Constance.

'Yes, I was. When it was time to leave, she clung to his legs, screaming out, "Let me stay! Please, please, let me stay with you." Cécile prized her strong grip from Walter's coat. Florence was calm, but firm, "No, Wren, you live with your Daddy and Mummy now. You must go home with them, but don't worry we will see you soon."'

'I can appreciate that would have been hard for you.'

'Then in January 44', the 'Little Blitz' or 'Baby Blitz' began. Four hundred German aircraft flew in two waves, dropping tons of high explosive bombs and thousands of incendiaries on South East England and London, hitting the Houses of Parliament, the

Embankment, New Scotland Yard, and parts of Pimlico. Along the brick wall of the Embankment shrapnel ricocheted off the granite façade, chasing Wren and very nearly catching up with her, Cécile screaming her loudest. 'Get down, Wren! Get down! For Wren's fourth birthday, I gave her a watch. It was Cécile's idea as she wanted to teach Wren to tell the time. It felt inappropriate for such a small child. I should have bought her a dolly or something.'

'Yes, maybe more appropriate,' said the nun.

'When Wren was four and a half years old, I enrolled her into the City of London School for Girls. Cécile had the task of getting my daughter ready for school, Wren dressed in a grey pinafore, a wool coat and a snug fitting felt hat. Each morning the two of them caught the red Route Master, which stopped opposite the flat on the Embankment.'

I told Sister Constance how Wren became obsessed with Battersea Power Station with its three cream towers jutting into the sky, the frame of the building, looking like a giant painted cardboard box.

'There are four towers... no?' she said.

'Battersea Power Station was in fact two power stations, side by side. The first one was completed in 1935, while the second one, with the fourth tower, wasn't completed until 1955.'

'Oh, I see,' she said.

'In September 44', British troops suffered a major blow when Operation Market Garden failed, and troops had to pull out of Arnhem resulting in 6,000 paratroopers being captured. My hope of the war ending was abandoned. Civilians were also paying a high price as local men were not returning home. For Cécile's sake, I took the decision to only listen to the radio broadcasts once a day as she found the news alarming.'

'Goodness me, your memory of war events is astounding!'

'I lived it, Sister, I can't forget it!'

76. SISTER CONSTANCE

Tuesday 19 June 1990

I did so laugh with Mr Walker today. Or rather I laughed at his po face to do with his wife inferring he wasn't at all patient. Maybe I shouldn't have, but sometimes I can't be that serious. Eventually, he softened and smiled with me. I asked him about his daughter, Wren.

He went on to tell me about what they did when the War ended in August 1945. 'I took Cécile and Wren to Trafalgar Square. Loud and overwhelming, the car horns blasting out. I lifted my daughter up onto one of the bronze lions and clinging to the hard-black mane, adult bodies squashed her in. Everyone was laughing and crying and hugging one another.'

When Mr Walker told me his account of Victory in Europe Day, I thought back to where I was at that time. With the family crowded around the radio listening to the news, my father and mother danced their version of a swing in jubilation. I was eleven years old and excited to be going to a thanksgiving service at church. It was packed full to the rafters with people singing and clapping. However, with Australian soldiers still incarcerated in camps in Japan, there was a restraint on big celebrations taking place. Liberation didn't happen until Japan had accepted the Allied demand for unconditional surrender. The very next day, 15 August, Victory in the Pacific Day (VP Day), took place.

Tensions were growing between Mr Walker and Cécile. She was irritated by little things, such as Wren drawing the same picture repeatedly: the front of Craigmore with its black gate and geranium pots in every window. 'Can't you draw something else? You live in a flat now!' shouted Cécile. 'We have to leave this city. We must go to America. It will be better for Wren. Better for all of us!'

And when Mr Walker punched the keys on his Remington, with his forefingers, Cécile screamed at him, 'You've got to stop the noise. That awful typing! It must stop! I cannot live in this country anymore!'

Mr Walker decided to apply to the United Nations for work.

I went to the care home library to see if I could find any information on the UN and discovered it was officially opened in New York on 24 October 1945, when the UN Charter had been ratified by a majority of the original fifty-one Member States. At this point in the conversation, I noticed how animated Mr Walker became when he described the UN. 'Its aim was to bring the nations of the world together, to work for peace and development,' he said. 'I was delighted when I received a reply to my letter and was able to say to Cécile, they have accepted me, I was to start within two months. Cécile danced around the room and jumped into my arms. I was so relieved that something had at last made her joyful.'

Mr Walker flew to New York to find a house not too far from the UN headquarters at the Sperry Corporation's offices in Lake Success, Long Island. He presumed he had secured the job by impressing the board with his management role at the Bermondsey Rest Centre, however, it turned out it was his degree in theology and the five years of being a Baptist minister that had really impressed them.

As part of his employment package, Cécile and Wren travelled first class across the ocean on the Gripsholm. During the war, the ship had been chartered to the US State Department, under the protection of the Red Cross, and having only just returned to its luxury status, his wife and daughter were two of the first civilian passengers.

So now they are heading for New York.

My mind is focussed on Wren and all the disruption she would face.

77. WREN

Tuesday 19 June 1990

I piped up, 'Is New York near to my Auntie Florence and Uncle Walter?'

'No! No! You silly girl! It is on the other side of the ocean!' said Cécile, who by now, insisted I call her, Mum! I burst into tears.

'I will buy you a bunny rabbit once we get to our new home in America, and I promise we shall visit your aunt and uncle tomorrow,' said my father, trying to repair the damage.

Walter and Florence were not impressed with Henry's decision to leave the country, but they said very little.

In Portsmouth Harbour, the Gripsholm creaked and groaned against the dock as hundreds of passengers began to board. Cécile asked one of the professional photographers to take a photograph of us both in front of two lifeboats suspended one on top of the other, on the wooden upper deck. I am six years old and smiling, wearing a dress with delicate smocking and puff sleeves. My right-hand hangs by my waist, my thumb tucked in closed fingers, and my left hand holds onto a metal cable which visually splits Cécile in two. Cécile's recently cut fringe acts like a basin on her head and there is a perceptible smile on her angular face. She is wearing a plain blouse cut off at the elbows and tied with a bow at the neck, a mid-length wool skirt and a pair of low-heeled black shoes. Over her right shoulder is a thin strap holding a camera box with a round metal clasp.

During the first few days of the journey, the morning mist rose like a curtain from the sea as Cécile helped me into a life jacket for the lifeboat drill. In the first-class dining room, with its polished floorboards and chandeliers, breakfast was in abundance, but I was 'monitored' on my food intake in case it damaged my 'constitution'. We then spent at least two hours on the loungers, blankets across our legs, Cécile reading aloud from a French novel, her words fusing with the Prussian blue waves of the ocean while I daydreamed about Alice and rabbits and tea parties. Sleeping on the top bunk in our small but beautiful cabin, I enjoyed switching the overhead lights on and off until Cécile smacked my hand. Eventually, I was rocked to sleep by the deep hum of the ship's engines and the swell of the Atlantic.

We arrived in New York on 27 May 1946. I remember seeing the Statue of Liberty. My mouth hung wide open, horns blasting out into the damp air, tugboats pulling the lumbering liner into dock.

My father met us at immigration, and because of his diplomatic status, the process of allowing us into the US only took an hour. But having discerned that I had a bout of mumps we were escorted to a hotel for a period of quarantine. I have little memory of this event. What I do remember is arriving at the house in Great Neck, the night as black as pitch. Driving the car onto the drive of the rented weatherboard house with the veranda lit by a single bulb, my father pointed to what looked like smoke billowing out of the front door. 'Don't worry, it's just an infestation of Daddy Longlegs,' he said.

'You will have to get rid of them,' commanded Cécile.

On this matter alone, I could agree with my stepmother. Crane flies are the worst kind of insect: the flying kind, with spindly legs. They dropped into my hair and face as I clung to my father's trouser leg. Cécile cowered behind him as he marched through the swarm with military precision.

The house was plain and sparsely furnished. I had a single bed and there was a double bed in the main bedroom, each with feather down pillows, white plain linen and wool blankets.

That night, I slept in a strange room with nothing familiar around me except my birthday teddy from Walter. To avoid the cold bedding, I pulled up my legs inside my nightie.

In that first week, Cécile purchased wardrobes and furniture and china from a local store and put freshly cut flowers in tumblers around the house. I unpacked my vanity set and laid it out on a small dressing table, placing a photograph of my aunt and uncle by my bed.

78. HENRY

Tuesday 26 June 1990

Memoirs 1946/7

Because Wren had contracted mumps on board ship, we had to be escorted to a hotel in the city to quarantine together. It was one of the most tedious times of my life, with room service as the only distraction. I almost went mad with the boredom of it. After ten days, the doctor paid a visit and said Wren was as fit as a fiddle and we were able to leave.

The journey from the rented house on Long Island to my office took 25 minutes by car. The days were long, but it was all so rewarding. There was a great deal for me to do establishing systems and holding daily meetings in the big hall, budgeting the department, and meeting deadlines for research projects. I especially enjoyed being responsible for a team of five within Documents Control. It obviously made me feel hugely important, and I needed to feel important.

The winter of 1947 was one of the harshest in the USA and across Europe.

I enjoyed clearing the snowfall, with Wren, outside the house; Wren with her small green trowel, barely making a mark on the white wall that covered the path, higher than my waist. But even my dear little Wren couldn't reach me. Spending more and more time at the office I gave little thought for my fretting wife. Cécile accepted the status quo for a time, but one evening said, 'I want

Wren to go to boarding school. I can't be looking after her the whole time, especially, as you are never here much before nine o'clock.'

Cécile was so different from the person I had first encountered. During the war years, we seemed to have had so much in common. Now I felt distant from her. I was more interested in exploring New York and women, believing Cécile was distracted with her knitting and doing up the house.

79. SISTER CONSTANCE

Tuesday 26 June 1990

At our meeting today, Mr Walker described the winter of 1947 in New York. We had bad weather that year in Sydney with unprecedented hailstorms that made the headlines. At the age of twenty-four, I was fascinated with Jean Simmonds, an 18-year-old British Film star who was held up in Brisbane due to the flying boat being prevented from docking in Sydney because of bad weather. The day before she had been detained in Darwin because of a new quarantine regulation which stipulated that people entering Australia must possess cholera inoculation certificates endorsed by a Government Medical Officer. 'And although I have been vaccinated four times before, they made me have another,' she said. On 22 December, she flew to Figi to star in The Blue Lagoon.

It appears that Cécile got her way and poor Wren, at the age of six, was packed off to boarding school. The promised visits to Craigmore vanished. Mr Walker seemed to have no desire to go back to England and considering the flights were expensive, I suppose he had an excuse. It was never mentioned to Wren, and she instinctively knew not to press the matter, preferring to immerse herself in music, continuing to play the violin on the weekends, even when Cécile discouraged her. Occasionally, Wren received sheet music from Florence, and stayed up late practicing on the veranda. Mr Walker, proud of her efforts, was happy to listen to her performances.

As the years passed, Wren found love in the form of a floppy eared rabbit, and a tiny hamster that didn't do much to entertain except venture out onto its wheel at night. When Wren packed her bag on Sunday evenings, ready for her return trip to school, she didn't even have the comfort of conversations with her father. It seems Henry hardly spoke. Wren must have been so lonely most of the time.

80. WREN

Tuesday 26 June 1990

In March 1951, I turned eleven years old. My legs were long, and my hair remained bobbed. I learned to twirl a baton as a majorette, mainly because I loved the outfit of fashionable short skirt and bobby socks, making a change from Cécile's homemade creations. Cécile was a fanatical knitter, insisting that I wear her bonnets with long ties that looped in a bow under my chin, always brown in colour–brown to match the lace up shoes, brown corduroys, brown knitted jumpers, and socks–I was brown all over. Dull as mud.

During the summer holidays, I was left to my own devices. Cécile, gave me money to get supper from the drug store. After a cheese sandwich and a strawberry milk shake, I sometimes went to the cinema. One time it cost me a beating. After sitting through 'National Velvet' twice, I ran home in the dark to meet a furious Cécile waiting for me with leather strap in hand. 'I've told you before. You are to only stay for one showing of the film, not two! I'll teach you to disobey me young lady.' She proceeded to belt me across the backside. It made me only hate her more than I already did.

I didn't see my father that often as he was always returning late from work. Crouching on the stairs, I listened to the arguments, Cécile stressing about his infidelities. But I was lonely. In my bedroom I curled up and listened to the sound of 'Sparky and the Magic Piano' on the radio.

On one of those long summer evenings, when the sun was setting in a neat line of vermillion red, my father returned home and went to take a shower. I was sitting at the kitchen table, having just finished a late supper of scrambled eggs on toast, when Cécile said, 'I know there is someone else.'

'Who else is there?' I asked.

'I'll find out. I am not stupid. You'll see. Go to the car and bring back the ash tray.'

Reluctantly, I sidled up to the door of the Chrysler, looking around in case my father suddenly appeared. Taking out the ashtray, I ran back to the house. 'There it is,' I said, placing it down on the kitchen table, muttering under my breath.

Cécile took the ashtray and tipped the contents out onto the draining board. In amongst the debris, she picked out a lipstick-stained stub and holding it in front of my face said, 'I knew it! I knew it! That's not my colour!' There followed a huge argument upstairs. The screams and the rage were as unwelcome as a downpour on a sunny day. I returned to school the following day.

On the weekend, my father made me put on my tartan dress, the only dress in my wardrobe. He then took my photo in front of a budding magnolia tree. I held tightly onto Alice, my favourite doll, half my size. I sensed something was happening but had no idea of the change that was about to occur, except I was aware that he had written a letter addressed to Walter and Florence in Westcliff.

81. HENRY

Tuesday 3 July 1990

Memoirs 1951

The catalyst for the breakdown of my marriage happened one evening when I returned late from work.

I had established a relationship with my secretary, a beautiful woman whose raven hair parted on the side and bounced upwards at the ends. Ten years my junior, she wore bright red lipstick, a smart black pencil skirt and noticeably had a full bosom covered with a fitted cashmere jumper. Her legs were long, and her calves were slim and elegant, stretching on forever, due to four-inch heels. Her perfume, Chanel no 5, was intoxicating and must have cost her most of her wages, until I discovered that the men in her life, including me, kept her well stocked. I was besotted.

After an evening of passion, I went home and had a shower. Cécile greeted me at the bathroom door with a frying pan in hand, 'You! A priest once! You are a pig, an adulterer! How dare you! Quel cochon!'

Fortunately, my height was an advantage when faced with an angry woman wielding a cooking utensil, and as she took a swing, I swiftly ducked, spinning around, while she collapsed on the floor.

The house was silent for days, a dark cloud hovering, a cloud of misery blacking up the windows, with no escape, like a swarm of Daddy Longlegs.

Cécile stayed in bed for a week with her fragile nerves. Wren, went and came back from school, while I paced the floor, unsure of what to do next. My marriage was failing, and I knew it was primarily my fault. I was still in love with Queenie, and Cécile did not make the pain go away. It was true, I had accepted a few encouragements from women along the way, but only from women who had very few expectations. Cécile, meanwhile, hunched up, shoulders shortening her neck, was dressed in a permanent frown which travelled down the length of her body. She was no longer interested in me. She was only interested in the house and soft furnishings.

Suddenly, I realised the absurdity of trying to replace one wife with another. But I had made vows, hadn't I? Vows in front of people? Was I prepared to negate such promises? *Mere prose* I concluded. I was becoming tearful and given to weeping, and any ounce of joviality I may have had was now crushed in an unhappy marriage. To breathe deeply I was going to have to make some changes. I had grown very fond of Wren, my little companion, and I would miss her most of all. But there are times in life when one must instigate change. Pacing the floor, my feet scuffed the polish from the boards, and the perspiration gathered in droplets on my brow, and I knew the time had come.

That evening, I had a brief talk with Cécile, placating her until I was ready to make a move. I was fearful she might do something stupid.

That weekend, when Cécile was at the grocery store, I told Wren to go and smarten up and put on a dress. She insisted on keeping hold of Alice in Wonderland, her oversized rag doll, while I took her photograph in front of the Magnolia tree in the garden. I then took her to Macey's and bought her a blue cashmere cardigan. She held it to her face all the way home.

I wrote a letter to Walter and Florence. It was a bit of a begging letter as I was aware that I needed to take drastic action to make sure Wren was safe.

82. SISTER CONSTANCE

Tuesday 3 July 1990

I must confess to feeling angry at this point in the story.

Although I have empathy for Mr Walker's situation, his affairs and passivity about his marriage was bound to have such a huge impact on everyone concerned.

He told Cécile, that the marriage was a sham, and that he was leaving. 'I will give you money each month to pay the rent and have enough money for food.'

She shouted back, 'And you think that is enough?'

Mr Walker was rendered speechless for a moment, before saying that he wanted a divorce.

Cécile said, 'I will die first! I will never divorce you. You disgust me. You think you can make me break my vows because you want another woman. You will have a long wait before you can marry again.'

Mr Walker's face turned red, and his hands shook. He had never wanted to hit a woman before, but on that day, he had to use all his strength not to reach out and crush her. 'Whether you divorce me or not Cécile, I am leaving you,' he said.

Heading for the front room he opened a drawer in the bureau and took out a blue box with its silver clasp. From the study, he picked up a leather suitcase containing his typewriter and some of his personal writings and newspaper clippings from the war. He then left the house with Cécile crying and clinging to his trouser leg. It was pitiful, but his heart had hardened like shale. Opening the car door, he pushed her from his leg and drove off.

Corresponding with letters and money transfers, he made sure she was catered for but that was it.

Quite honestly, I am flabbergasted. Mr Walker is as disappointed with me as I am with him.

'I suppose you are going to tell me that I need to repent,' he said.

'Are you beyond repenting?'

'I'm not going to repent. Cécile was a dreadful woman.'

'Forgiveness then?'

'What do you know about relationships? You sit there in that habit covered from head to foot. You never tasted one in your life, and you tell me I need to repent.' Small drops of perspiration gathered on his forehead. Taking some tissues, he wiped the droplets away.

'You should never judge a book by its cover. You know that?' I said.

'Well, your cover is hardback,' he replied, giving a wry smile.

Breathing in deeply, I did something that even surprised me.

Removing the hairpins which held the white starched headpiece to the black veil, I placed both parts on the table, revealing my short, curled black hair laced with flashes of silver.

Mr Walker was a little dismayed.

'I'm not sure I should tell you this about me Mr Walker and I certainly wouldn't have been able to tell you a few weeks ago. But I have now reached a time in my life where I have dealt with the shame and guilt. I told you how my father was murdered by white men not long after my nineteenth birthday.'

'Yes, you did, and I'm sorry about that. But marriage and adult relationships are a whole other matter.'

'But that's not all, or the 'half of it' as you say. I didn't tell you that when I stayed with my father, my friend left me to go and get the police. She would never have gone if she had known that the men who killed my father would come back to the house to get rid of the evidence. They dragged me to the front room and assaulted me one at a time.'

The colour drained from Mr Walker's face.

'I was damaged internally and it meant I could never have children. Very few people escape pain in this life, Mr Walker. We are not living in paradise. We are on the earth, and it is fundamentally flawed, as are we. I was advised once to see confession as a way of voicing our pain, repentance as accepting our part in the events, and forgiveness to be free from it all.'

Mr Walker leant in towards me and took my hand. He looked genuinely shocked. 'I am so sorry. How dreadful for you. But you have no need to repent! You did nothing wrong. You were a victim of a horrendous crime. I hope those men were punished for what they did to you.'

'They were each sentenced to no less than thirty years in prison.'

'But how did you forgive those men for what they did to your father and to you?'

'I didn't for a very long time. I was damaged physically and mentally. I became wild and behaved badly towards my friends. I got drunk and had sex with anyone who would have sex with me. Believe me, I needed to repent for the hurt I caused. None of it made sense to me. In the end I went walk-about for three years, living like a nomad in the bush. The moon and the stars and the sun healed a big part of me, but it was when Jesus appeared to me in a dream that I felt reborn.'

'He appeared to Queenie in a dream when she was very young.'

'I remember reading about that. It was similar for me too. I dreamt I was lying at the water's edge and Jesus walked out of the ocean. He approached me and stretched out his hand. I realized he was inviting me into the water. I looked to my right and there was my father wrapped in a layer of fine white sand. He was dead.

I had to leave him and take the hand of Jesus who pulled me up. We walked into the sea together. I was at peace and able to live in the now rather than the past or the future, neither of which we can do anything about.'

'What happened then?' asked Mr Walker.

'I was renewed, and able to forgive for about six months, but the anger soon returned. It was only when I met the nuns at the convent that real peace enveloped me with their daily instruction of prayer and ritual. It was their ability to live in the present which helped me heal.'

'Is that enough for you?'

I smiled. 'It's all we have. The past has left us and the future is yet to arrive. We only have the day we are in... and a hope of heaven.'

Mr Walker sighed.

I continued, 'Yes... I mean absolution. I mean love... Heaven breaks into earth with every kind act, every moment of shared pain and shared tears, every moment of laughter and joy. Through Christ, God takes part, experiencing the pain for himself. I believe he suffers with us, and if we allow him to, he will hold our hands through it all until we embrace Him in our death.'

'I miss that certainty you have, Sister. I possessed it as a young man. I thought nothing would destroy what I had found. I ended up hurting so many people and behaving like Peter. I denied Christ before the cockcrow.'

Placing my hand on top of Mr Walker's hand I said, 'You know that Peter often gets a bad press for what he did, but just think about it. Peter was the only disciple that tried to defend Jesus in the garden when the Romans came to arrest him. And he stayed with Jesus when all the others had forsaken him. Peter was full of courage. I know he cracked under pressure and denied Jesus three times, but we are told that Christ forgave Peter's fear and reinstated him three times after the resurrection. In John's Gospel,

Jesus asked the disciples, "Do you want to leave too?" And it was Peter who replied, "Lord, to whom would we go? You have the words of eternal life."

'I would like it very much if you were to call me, Henry,' he said.

'And I would like you to call me, Constance,' I said, replacing my headdress. 'Do go on with your story.'

83. WREN

Tuesday 3 July 1990

Florence told me that when the postman arrived at Craigmore, she was leaning over the gate, chatting with a neighbour. Receiving the pile of letters from him with both hands, she gave a little curtsey. 'Thank you so much, postie.'

Realising the implications of the blue 'par avion' sticker and my father's unmistakable handwriting, she said goodbye to the neighbour and went quickly indoors for the reassurance of the comfortable velvet chair, calling Walter to come immediately.

'What is it, Florence? I'm rather busy. Couldn't you have opened it?'

She handed him the sealed letter. 'No, I'd rather you did.'

As Walter took the letter from the envelope, the photograph of me holding Alice slipped out. On picking it up and seeing me in my tartan dress she began to gush, 'Look at her shoes, they are worn out... she is so tall... bless her... her hair needs a brush... aren't they looking after her?' Anxiously she begged Walter to read the letter that she gave to me many years later.

His voice had a calm tone, one that Florence could not have managed. 'He posted it from the Grand Central Post Office, New York on 21 August 1951.'

Dear Walter and Florence,

Thank you for your recent correspondence. I am aware that we are many miles apart and have not been in regular contact. Maybe I had better explain the reason for my silence.

I do not get along well with Cécile, and I am sure that the atmosphere is not good for Wren, to whom I owe a heavy duty. There is now no alternative, but to decide that her future depends on her being surrounded with some greater affection than I believe she now has.

If it does not put too great a strain on you both, I would like to ask your help. I would like to know about Westcliff High School, the terms of entrance, as it maybe that I shall suddenly send Wren either by sea or air to you. If I were to cable you or phone you, would you be prepared to receive her at short notice?

I shall myself expect to go to Paris, to work with the UN, but also to have a break from Cécile. This, I do not have to say, is in all confidence.

Please correspond as soon as you have had time to digest.

Love from Henry.

Florence put her hand to her mouth to stop the excitement from bubbling over. 'Do you think he will really send her back to us?'

'He wouldn't have sent the letter, dear, if he didn't mean it. Things must be bad.' Walter went straight to the telephone in the hall. 'Wren is eleven, she will be just the right age to start at Westcliff High.'

When I left the house in Long Island, Cécile was as pale as the moon in a light sky and just as far away. On the drive to the airport, my thoughts were on my mother, Queenie. I asked my father what she was like. He didn't say much, just, 'You look so like her, except you have some of my height.' He was a little awkward with me at the airport, especially when I flung myself into his arms before I left.

Arriving at Heathrow in the early hours of a Saturday morning in late September, Florence and Walter embraced me but I was a little stiff, guarded, I expect.

Once at Craigmore, Florence opened the side gates, and Walter drove the car onto the front drive. Opening the front door, she signalled for me to follow.

Stepping onto the resin tiled floor in the hall, I recognised the familiar smell of polish mingling with the residue of a fried breakfast and fresh flowers. 'I remember this place,' I said, caressing the top of the bureau, the silver letter knife, the telephone, the very tips of my fingers connecting me with my past. 'Where are the boys, Auntie?' I said.

'They are no longer boys. Daniel is a dentist, married and living in Southend. Timothy is in the Airforce, and George, who is nearly eighteen, is still living at home. He is in his last year at school. You will see him at supper time.'

Florence showed me to my bedroom, situated at the front of the house, overlooking the road and an enormous oak tree. Sitting on the bed, I stroked the pale green eiderdown, once again allowing my fingers to generate the memory of having slept in the same bed when I was little. Unpacking my things, I adorned the dressing table with Queenie's vanity set, a few ribbons and some Kirby-grips. Looking in the mirror, I smiled.

'You look happy!' said Florence, surprising me.

'I am.'

'Shall I help you unpack?'

'I don't have much, and most of what I have is brown.'

'Brown? Oh, I see what you mean.' Looking through the case, Florence continued, 'I think we may have to take you shopping young lady. A trip to Southend will sort you out. Get a bit of colour into your wardrobe while the sea air will get some colour into those cheeks.'

Florence stroked my face and I spontaneously hugged her. Resting my head on her full bosom, I listened to the beating of my aunt's heart, my arms not quite managing to reach around her broad waist. Florence squeezed me and pulling away said, 'Come on my girl. You'll be all right. Uncle Walter and I are going to take good care of you.'

On opening the heavy door to the front room, I crept in. Sitting on the arm of the velvet chair I gazed at the clock. The mechanism kicked into action striking 1... 2... 3... times.

Walter appeared. 'Ah, there you are, dear.'

Quickly I rose to my feet. 'I wanted to hear the clock chime.'

'Do you know the clock was given to your mother and father when he became the Baptist minister at Burrowbridge Chapel? Your father left it with us when you came to live here.'

'I didn't know that. Why did my father give up being a minister?' I asked.

'Well, your father was shattered after your mother died. I don't think he could forgive God for her death.'

'But people die every day, and people still believe in God.'

'Yes, Wren, you are right, but when it touches you personally, that's when you can really struggle with your faith.'

'I understand that but she may not have agreed with what he did.'

'She may have understood.'

'I don't know much about my mother. What was she like?'

'Your mother was a strong and independent woman of great faith. She would have loved you, Wren. Don't ever doubt it.' Walter moved towards me, 'Try not to worry. It will just take time.'

I knew my uncle was right, and knowing I had time on my side made me feel safe at last: safe in that room with the green velvet chair, and the ticking clock, and Uncle Walter patting me on my head.

A trip to Southend took place the next day and when we returned, I went immediately to my room and unpacked the large paper bag which contained a bright red skirt and jumper, some short socks, and a rather snazzy pair of black shoes. I was delighted with one purchase in particular, a bra, the smallest they had. Changing into the new clothes, I walked downstairs as if I was Audrey Hepburn modeling for Gigi, my hips swinging from side to side. George was waiting for me at the bottom. He was tall and thin with soft brown hair, wearing round spectacles and a knitted argyle jumper and a light pair of trousers. 'Look at you!' he said. 'Jump.'

Leaping into the air, George caught me and swung me round and round before placing me down. 'You are all grown up,' he said. 'Goodness me, you are a knockout!' Laughing, he then ran upstairs. 'Have to dash, got homework to do. See you later.'

The Headmistress at Westcliff High School for Girls was surprised by my knowledge of American history and the Civil Rights Movement. Travel had broadened my mind, although I only knew decimal currency, which meant I failed the math test. However, I showed such confidence in general knowledge that the headmistress was happy to accept me.

The school day was long and demanding with choir, violin, and hockey practice, and despite the formality of the English school, I was able to make loyal friends. It didn't take long before things began to change and while my behaviour at home was impeccable, never openly defiant, at school it was another story. I enjoyed my new freedom, hitching up my school skirt, wearing long socks, exploiting the American accent, as girls surrounded me at break time saying, 'Go on say A...looom...inum!! Say, el...e...va...tor!'

Months went by and Florence assumed all was well, until one evening she attended a parents evening. My geography teacher, who delighted in telling the class about the fossilized sea creatures within the body of the White Cliffs of Dover, was also a violinist and played with Florence in the local orchestra.

'How is Wren doing with her studies?' asked Florence.

'Do you want the truth?'

'The truth and nothing but the truth, so help me God,' said Florence raising her right hand at the elbow.

'Well, I'm sorry to disappoint you, Florence, but Wren is the class clown.'

Florence learned that I spent much of the school day sitting under the clock outside the Head's office (the worst punishment available to a teacher). She was shocked.

'You have to talk to her,' Florence told Walter. 'She is always well behaved at home. I had no idea.'

Walter summoned me to the dining room. 'Wren, I hear that you are flouting authority at school?' my head hung low, pushing my chin into my chest. 'Look at me, Wren.' Walter was not smiling. I had never seen him so stern. I looked up and he continued. 'Do you realise how much you are upsetting your aunt? We have high hopes for you, that you will do well at school and get a profession of sorts.'

I heard the words, but they fell to the floor, not penetrating the screen I had erected – the screen that stopped people getting too close – the screen that said to the world, 'You won't hurt me, not now, not ever.'

I agreed to behave better, but I didn't, not until I turned sixteen years old and began to blush. I blushed when Florence confronted me, and when my cousins teased me, and when teachers reprimanded me. It was my age of course, but Florence put it down to my new-found interest in religion.

Freddy and Martha had invited me to attend their Methodist Church, which meant walking with them and cousin Eve, on the thirty-minute journey, each Sunday morning.

Betty, meanwhile, having moved in with Freddy and Martha showered me with affection whenever I stopped for Sunday lunch. On one such Sunday, Freddy asked me to help him sort the games cupboard out. 'Wren, it's wonderful that you spend time with us. You know your grandmother was heartbroken when your mother died and has never really recovered.'

'I love being with you too, Uncle Freddy, and my cousins, especially Eve.'

'Your grandmother always said you two would be good friends.'

Eve and I began cycling to church for the morning and evening service. Eve, was a good seven inches shorter than me, but despite the height difference we looked more like sisters than cousins, both delighting in the fact that we were born only one month apart. We helped run the Sunday school together, and in the late afternoon service we met up with friends our own age. The Methodist Hymnal provided many rousing songs, which had the effect of untangling my mind from the strains of growing up. At night, I often knelt by my bed saying my prayers, before lying motionless, inbetween the sheets, singing *Jesu, lover of my soul*, drifting off to sleep. Jesus was my comfort. He was safe. He was, to all intents and purposes, my first love.

In the summer, I wrote to my father with snippets of information about school and orchestra and my activities at the Methodist Church. He wrote back swiftly, 'In my opinion, the less you have to do with religion the better!'

This upset me and confused me but I was happy, at least, with the jars of boiled sweets he sent on a regular basis, along with the food parcels. Hiding the sweets under my pillow I sucked them in bed after cleaning my teeth.

'I haven't been christened yet!' I confessed to Eve. 'My father doesn't want me to go anywhere near a church!'

'In the Methodist church, you don't get christened. You become a member of the church,' she said.

'It's all so confusing. I know Florence and Walter belong to the Church of England, and you can get christened there.'

'When you are eighteen your father can't stop you,' Eve said. 'I don't remember him. He sounds horrible.'

'He's not horrible, he's just sad about something that's all.'

I did not want to have to explain to my cousin why my father had rejected the Church and God. She may have felt sorry for him, and I didn't want that. Of course, Eve knew the truth. Everyone in the family talked, from time to time, about my father's broken heart.

It was very likely that my experience as a Sunday school helper fashioned my decision to work with children. Florence advising me to, *aim for the best!* On such advice I sent for a prospectus for the Norland Nursery Training College in Chislehurst.

84. HENRY

Tuesday 10 July 1990

I had never thought of Constance as a beautiful woman, if anything I would have described her as plain. But having seen her with her veil off I considered her enthralling and it had caught me off guard. I was truly shocked by her confession and felt quite emotional about her experience for a good few days. How dreadful for a young woman to go through such abuse. So brutal. I wept for her in the silence of the night.

She is teaching me so much.

Memoirs 1950's
Breathing in the scent of summer, I walked, at a slow pace, through the Jardin des Tuileries, holding the hand of an attractive Chinese woman I had met on the Queen Mary passage. But that was not to last long.

My flat, secured by The United Nations for six months, was in the centre of Paris. The purpose of the trip was to complete a training course before moving to Geneva at the Palais des Nations, Switzerland. That six-month period was a wild time. Frequenting bars and drinking far too much alcohol, I was under no restrictions and proceeded to seduce several more women. My appetite was insatiable, and I began to put on weight. I think I was on a crazy mission to destroy myself and it was only the arrival of

Vivien into my life that secured my survival, lifting me out of the guddle I was making of everything.

Reluctantly, I had attended a mutual friend's cocktail party and fortunately for me we spotted each other over a crowded room. Corny, I know, but true. We became engrossed in conversation and that was it. I was in love. It was her intellect and immediate care for me that drew me to her. She was also stylish, witty, attractive and... divorced.

85. SISTER CONSTANCE

Tuesday 10 July 1990

I decided to do a little research.

The idea came to me in the early hours of the morning when I am often restless. I was singing It Is Well with My Soul by Horatio Spafford, surprising myself with how well I knew the words.

It is such a resounding hymn.

I cried.

I was wondering what happened to the Spafford couple after the drowning of their children.

Henry was very warm towards me today. He reached out and held my hand. 'I have been thinking about our meeting last week and I am truly sorry for being clumsy and rude. Please forgive me.'

'You are forgiven,' I said.

86. WREN

Tuesday 10 July 1990

It was a very hot summer's day when I went with Florence by train to Chislehurst, after which, we took a taxi to the beautiful grounds of the Norland College.

After a few minutes of waiting in a small room with no windows, the principal arrived and sat down behind a dark wooden desk, her frizzy hair pulled sharply off her low forehead and tied at the back. Once preliminary introductions were complete, she spoke with a highbrow English accent, 'Now Wren, you mention on your form that your father works for the United Nations. What exactly does he do?'

Florence started to speak, 'He....'

'I don't want to hear from you, Mrs Walker, I want Wren to speak.'

'He is the Head of Document Control,' I said.

'In Switzerland?'

Yes, I hope to visit him someday soon.'

'You must be proud of him?"

'Yes I am.'

'And do you play any instruments, Wren?'

'Yes, I play the piano and I play the violin in the school orchestra. I am also in the choir.'

'Ah good,' smiled the principle. 'What makes you think you would be able to care for young children?'

'I have recently become an assistant to the Sunday school teacher at the church I attend. I have also been babysitting for friends and family. My mother was a primary school teacher and later she ran the Sunday school at my father's chapel. I think I have inherited my passion for children from her.'

'You must understand that we expect a great deal from our students and many girls fail to complete the course.'

'I understand that, but I would appreciate the opportunity to show you what I am capable of,' I said.

The interview continued, and I managed to answer all the questions in a mature and sensible fashion. Florence looked on and was hugely proud of me. When we left the building, she put her arm around me and pulled me in close. 'You did well my dear, very well indeed.'

I was, however, concerned about something more pressing. I was in such pain, unable to chew my food properly and aware that I wouldn't be able to hide it for much longer.

87. HENRY

Tuesday 17 July 1990

Memoirs 1957

Looking out onto Lake Geneva, I made a phone call to Craigmore. Walter answered the telephone. 'Hello, Henry, how are you? We haven't heard from you for a while.'

'Walter, I received a letter from Florence this morning. I'm a little shocked to hear about Wren's teeth.'

'Yes, it was a shock to us too. When she arrived back from America. We took her to our dentist who unfortunately scared her. She then managed to dodge going to the dentist, always coming up with some excuse. It was only recently that Florence realised Wren was in pain as she refused to eat breakfast. Florence convinced her to go with her to the kindly Mr Cutler, and he was shocked when he looked in her mouth.'

'But five teeth removed Walter? That seems a ridiculous amount. She must be full of gaps!'

'Well, they are all at the back, mainly molars and the wisdom teeth may well fill in some of the spaces. The thing is, they were all rotten and she had abscesses, which is why she could no longer chew her food properly. I'm sorry Henry, but it was the only thing that could be done.'

'May I speak with her?' I said.

'Of course.'

'Hello, Dad,' she said, 'do you think my bad teeth may have been caused by my mother not eating enough cheese during pregnancy?'

'Your mother did all the right things and ate all the right things. Maybe it's more to do with you eating too many sweets.' I said, annoyed that she suggested Queenie had failed her in some way.

Quickly changing the subject, she said, 'What do you think about me becoming a Norland trained nanny?'

'I think becoming a nanny is a fine idea, Wren. You know your mother trained at Homerton College in Cambridge. She ran a Sunday school during the last five years of her life. But tell me what you know about the college?'

Wren having prepared her speech confidently answered, 'It was founded in 1892, and teaches young women to care for children, to meet their physical, emotional, psychological and educational needs from birth to seven years of age.'

'That's impressive, Wren. You will probably do very well as long as the college will accept you.'

'But that's the problem. They only accept seventy students each year and only half of them graduate.' Wren was bubbling over with excitement despite such harsh statistics.

'If you can get a place, I will pay the fees,' I said to reassure her.

Of course, she did get a place within ten days of the interview to start when she turned eighteen. I was pleased for her but knew the fees would be high, and the uniform would be costly as it could only be purchased from Harrods!

It was seventeen years after Queenie had died that I received a telegram concerning Queenie's mother. BETTY DIED TODAY STOP FUNERAL ON TWENTIETH STOP PLEASE COME STOP WALTER.

Betty dead?

That was a shock.

My initial thought was I must go to the funeral. I even liaised with Walter over the details. I was saddened by Betty's death, but not overly.

Betty was a kind woman and, of course, if I had been local, I would have attended the funeral but I think I felt guilty about not visiting her regularly after I buried my wife. Freddy and Martha looked after Betty, and I know they were a comfort to her. She even had my Wren who, to all accounts, spent many Sunday lunches with her after visiting the Methodist church.

I thought it better to stay put and let the past remain the past. Too much dredging up of history is no good for my soul.

If I still have a soul.

88. SISTER CONSTANCE

Tuesday 17 July 1990

When I entered room 7, Henry was busy typing away on his antiquated Remington. 'Have you never thought of buying a new one?' I asked.

'Why would I? This one is perfectly adequate. I am now jumping forward to 1976.'

'Why 1976?' I was intrigued. 'How old were you then?'

'I was sixty-eight years old, and living in Spain with Vivien.'

'How lovely for you. Whereabouts?'

'In a mountain house in Sierra Blanca.'

He pulled out the sheet from the typewriter and handed it to me.

Memoirs 1976

I was lying by the swimming pool in the heat of the morning sun when Vivien came clip clopping across the tiles. She was wearing her bright yellow kaftan which was shimmering in the sun. She handed me a letter on a silver platter. 'The stamp is from the US, so I think it must be from Cécile, probably asking for more money. I just wish she would allow the divorce as I want you to make an honest woman of me.'

'You are an honest woman in my eyes, my dear,' I said, realising that since the address was typed it was unlikely from Cécile.

'What does it say?'

After several moments rereading the information, I stammered. 'She's dead!'

'What?'

'It's from a lawyer. Apparently, she was found dead in her apartment two weeks ago.'

'What do you mean?'

I handed the letter to Vivien and began pacing the area around the pool. 'Look for yourself,' I said.

'Oh dear,' muttered Vivien, as she read the letter. 'She had a heart attack.'

I jumped into the pool, the water spraying out over Vivien. Under the water I wrestled with myself. *It wasn't my fault she was dead.* Struggling for air, I emerged. 'Oh God,' I said out loud, covering my face with my hands as the tears fused with the chlorinated water.

'Are you all right, Henry?' asked Vivien.

'No, I'm not. Just let me be!' I said, heaving myself out of the water and heading for the house. I was surprised with how upset I felt. I had no affection for Cécile but to think of her dying on her own was too much. It wasn't her fault that she met me when she had. I was not husband material at the time. But she was a torment to me. I was angry and frustrated with her failings and mine.

It was a few days later that I realised a weight had been lifted off my shoulders.

I married Vivien two months later. It was a simple affair at the local Registry Office in Malaga. Two friends attended: a re-run of my second marriage, but with more love on my part.

After the wedding, I was happy that Wren was coming on her own to see us for a few days. It seems that she was exhausted from work and had decided she could rest with us. We had spent time with Amy, my granddaughter, six years earlier and that was fine but it would be good to see my daughter. Or so I thought.

I picked Wren up from Malaga airport and drove her back to the villa which took an age as we lived high up in the White Mountains. That day, Vivien had prepared over 20 different Hor D'œuvres for a party inviting many of our neighbours. By the time Wren and I arrived she was stressed and had certainly been at the wine. That evening was slightly haphazard as Vivien danced drunkenly around the room flirting with all the men. I was embarrassed and so was Wren who seemed to get on very well with everyone. The next morning at breakfast she told me several things about our neighbours that I didn't know. 'Who are you? I said, 'Mata Hari?'

The next day I decided to drive her to Granada. It was a long drive and exceptionally hot. I got lost and she had to ask for directions. I'm really not too sure what went wrong but over the next couple of days everything I suggested she said no to. 'I just want to spend time with you and take it easy,' she said.

I think we fell out but I really don't think it was my fault. She has strong opinions and it was as if I had a stone in my mouth as I shied away from conversations with her. Vivien says I don't really listen. I find that hard if that is true. But maybe she is right because after that, I lost contact with Wren until 1986 when she came to the flat in Chelsea with Amy.

§

I was about to comment on Wren's visit but was interrupted by the receptionist who knocked on the door. 'Mr Walker, Vivien phoned. She said she still has that wretched headache and won't be able to visit until tomorrow.'

'Oh, right then,' Henry said, 'thank you for letting me know.' Turning to me, he added. 'She was coming to meet you. What a shame.'

'Don't worry, I'm sure to meet her soon,' I said.

An orderly, new to the care home, knocked on the door and entered. 'Would you both like a cup of tea?'

'I'd like something stronger,' said Henry.

'A strong tea?' said the orderly, smiling.

'A whisky?' replied Henry. 'I don't see why it can't be available. I am an adult you know.'

'It's a rule of this particular care home, Mr Walker. You were informed.'

Henry replied, 'I have my sources!' and winked at me. 'You are new here, aren't you?'

'Yes, sir, I am. My name is Peter, pleased to meet you.' He reached out his hand and Henry kept hold of it.

'Peter... you know what your name stands for?'

'No, sir, I don't.'

'It means stone or rock. Are you a reliable person, Peter?'

'Reliable enough to get you some tea.'

'Just hot water will do,' said Henry, as the orderly left the room. 'Please ask another member of staff to tell you what I require.'

'As you well know I like a whisky occasionally,' I said.

'Medicinal purposes?' he laughed.

I chuckled, 'Purely pleasure.'

Henry smiled, 'We have something in common.'

'I've been meaning to refresh these,' I said, picking up the vase of flowers on the chest of drawers and taking them to the sink.

'I wouldn't bother with them, they're on their way out.'

'They have a little life in them, and I need to stretch my legs.' I proceeded to tip the stale, pungent water out and fill the vase with fresh cold water from the tap. Placing them back on the chest of drawers the yellow flowers perked up during the course of our conversation.

Sitting back down on the chair, I filled the indent I had made in the grey upholstery and we talked for another hour.

89. WREN

Tuesday 17 July 1990

I had thought that spending four days, during the Whitsun break, with my father might be a good thing. David encouraged me to go because I had been having a difficult term at school, what with local inspections and several problematic pupils and their parents. David said he would look after Amy and Patrick, who were by this time twelve and thirteen years old respectively.

When I arrived at Malaga airport my father was waiting for me. The journey back to the villa was long and the car was hot due to aircon failure. He complained about the journey, saying he didn't like the airport run. I wasn't sure what he was saying. When we arrived, Vivien was clearly drunk. She had been preparing food for a party that evening. The last thing I wanted to do was attend a party but I made the best of it and was happy to chat to the neighbours. The next morning at breakfast, I let my dad and Vivien know snippets of information I had gathered. He seemed put out. 'Who do you think you are, Mata Hari?' he said. I thought it was a strange comparison as she had been an exotic dancer and courtesan during World War 1. She was tragically executed by firing squad in France for being a spy.

Over the next few days my father became distant and evasive. I don't know what triggered his behaviour, but it wasn't pleasant. Each morning he suggested a trip that would involve miles of driving in scorching hot June weather. I was exhausted but he didn't see it. By the end of the third day, I burst into tears. All Vivien could say was that my father wouldn't be leaving me any money in his will because they planned to spend their last days on cruise ships around the Mediterranean.

I left Spain, eager to get home to my life with my husband, my children and my work. I had lost any sense of duty to my father.

My life in the UK ran smoothly until Christmas day of 1977, when my world came tumbling down.

I arrived at Craigmore with David, Patrick and Amy. We were greeted by a friendly face at the door. Daniel, now in his fifties, was a large man with a big belly, who walked with a limp, the result of polio. His black hair had a few flecks of silver at the temples and his large, black-framed glasses suited his face. 'Hello Cousin,' he said, taking me in a bear hug, 'Happy Christmas.'

Timothy then appeared in the hall, as large as Daniel, with a handsome, distinguished face. 'How are you, Wren?' he said, embracing me with the right side of his body and taking some provisions from me with his left hand. His wife appeared, followed by their four children.

George and his wife greeted us all. George was in good shape, due to his cycling hobby.

Florence then pushed her way through the gathering. 'Is it my girl?' she said. 'Hello, darling. Did you have a good trip down?' Taking me in her more than ample bosom she hugged me.

'Hello, Mum,' I said. 'Yes, not bad, not too much traffic. Glad to be here.'

I went to look at the Christmas tree that filled much of the bay window, the strong smell of pine needles restoring early childhood memories. The tree was decorated in the same way as the trees had always been in previous years and I reached out to touch the wooden Father Christmas, a painted sleigh, a brightly coloured miniature present box. I liked the new additions, six metal musical instruments, a few inches in length and shimmering under the fairy lights. The granddaughter clock chimed twelve times entrancing everybody in the room. When it stopped, conversations were renewed.

Craigmore was a hive of activity. The adults set the table and the children organized the presents under the tree. Daniel, as barman, stood by the drink's cabinet, taking the orders, making gin and tonics, eggnogs, and lemonades. The men served drinks while the women laid the table in the dining room, chatting happily together about the events of that year.

I looked for Walter and found him sitting in his brown leather chair by the fire in the breakfast room, quieter than usual. He was wearing his dark brown suit, with a cream shirt and a tweed tie cut off by the V of a pale green sweater. He looked shorter than usual, but maybe it was because the chair had aged, and a hollow had formed absorbing ten percent of his body. He was quite bald, except for the familiar ridge of white hair that many men possess as they pass their seventy-fifth year. His spectacles, meanwhile, hung precariously from his nose and his rather full lower lip protruded as his mouth hung open slightly.

I bent down to be at his level. Taking his hand in mine I said, 'Pop, how are you?'

Peering over his newspaper, he said, 'I'm old and forgetful.'

'Not that old and not that forgetful!' I smiled, but I was shocked by his deterioration.

'Well at least I remember you, my girl.'

'Can I get you anything, Pop?'

'Yes... I'd like....' he paused. 'I can't remember what I wanted. Oh, never mind.'

Florence was surrounded by grandchildren. Taking her to one side I said, 'Pop doesn't look himself, Mum, what's wrong with him?'

Florence took me by the arm and led me into the hall. 'I wanted to tell you face to face, rather than on the phone. I am afraid he has Alzheimer's.'

'Oh, no! I'm so sorry!' I said, putting my arms around Florence's waist.

She pulled away. 'Yes, yes, I know you are, everyone is sorry, but there's not a lot anyone can do. Now we had better get on, there are many vegetables to prepare. I just didn't have time to get them all done.'

Working side-by-side, peeling sprouts, parsnips and potatoes, Florence softened, 'He has become more and more confused. The doctors say he will deteriorate and eventually he probably won't know who I am,' pausing, she held onto the wooden tabletop. 'Still,' she continued, 'we've had many happy years together, I mustn't grumble.'

'I don't know what to say, Mum. It's awful. He's always been such a bright man, so intelligent.'

'Old age never comes alone. I just hope he doesn't have to suffer too much. I couldn't bear it.'

Christmas lunch was a feast, with roast beef, a capon, and a huge ham, the table overflowing with copious amounts of food. Florence never liked to cook a turkey on Christmas day, saying roast beef was more traditional.

When it was time for presents to be given out, all the children, including Patrick and Amy, crowded around the tree. Darkness fell and wrapping paper was strewn around the front room as the younger children played with the toys and the adults caught up, over a sherry, a glass of wine and a box or two of jellies and chocolate covered ginger pieces.

Back in the kitchen, I was finishing the washing up when Florence turned to me and said, 'You can stop that now.' Drying my hands with some kitchen towel, she placed something into them. 'I want you to have this,' she said, closing my fingers over the gift.

Looking down, I unfurled my fingers, revealing a gold locket on a long gold box chain. 'This is lovely. Isn't it the one that you wear?'

'Yes, but I want you to have it now.'

'Is there anything in it?'

'Open it and see.'

It opened easily and I saw a girl of about three with bobbed hair and a big smile. 'Oh, it's me,' I laughed.

'Of course.'

I moved towards Florence and put my arms around her waist, holding her for a while. She stepped back and said, 'Don't be too kind to me, you'll make me cry.'

For the next two years Walter was cared for in a single bed in the breakfast room. It was easier for Florence not having to traipse up and down the stairs. His usual breakfast of two rashers of bacon and two fried eggs was replaced with spoonsfuls of porridge. Sleeping most of the day and diminished in form and with a memory as wispy as a cloud he said, 'Am I going to die?'

'You mustn't worry about that, dear. We are all going to die,' said Florence, staring at the net curtains which she could see needed a wash.

Writing to Henry, she informed him that he may like to pay a visit before the Alzheimer's devoured his brother completely. He replied, 'I prefer to remember Walter as a fit man, not as a dying man.'

In the middle of a warm night in July, Walter drew his last breath: Florence and Daniel by his side.

When I heard the news, I took a deep intake of breath to avoid passing out. An hour later I told my children the news and they burst into tears. For the next few weeks, I spent as much time as possible with Florence. There was a lot to organize.

The funeral was well attended. Over one hundred turned out. We all gathered for the wake at Craigmore. In the afternoon, many of us played cricket in honour of a husband, a father, an uncle, a good neighbour, a friend. In the sun-drenched garden, the balls were batted into beds of peonies which the grandchildren were tasked to find. Cake was in full supply and, of course, many teapots were passed around, overflowing.

90. HENRY

Tuesday 24 July 1990

'Henry,' the nun said, 'I did some research on Horatio Spafford and his wife.'

'Oh yes,' I replied, not imagining what for.

'Did you know that the two of them went on to have three more children and one of them established the *Spafford's Children Centre* in Jerusalem which still exists today? Their legacy has lived on for years having helped thousands of children and parents. Sometimes we don't understand a tragedy in our lifetime, but future generations can be inspired to create something out of it.'

'I never knew that,' I said, but I understood what she was saying. It rose over me like the icy water of the Atlantic when I was baptized at the age of fourteen. I shuddered.

The orderly obliged us with a white porcelain teapot, some bone china cups and two irregular shaped biscuits.

'Oh wonderful! Do tell the chef I love his shortbread,' I said, taking one of the triangles and breaking it in half. Pointing to the drawer in my bedside cabinet, Constance rose from her seat. 'In there. Just two will do.'

Pulling the drawer open she took out a box of Twining's tea bags. 'What do you feel like today? Assam? Darjeeling, English Breakfast?'

'I'm in an Assam mood. I decided it was the tea they served that I didn't like, and so Vivien found a box of the best in Brisbane. Paid a fortune for it.'

Constance pulled out two Assam sachets and gently ripped the tops off. Unravelling the thin cotton lines and holding the tags, she placed them in the teapot of boiling water.

For a few minutes we sat in silence.

'Shall I be mum?' said Constance.

'Yes, thank you, I'm quite parched.'

Taking a teaspoon, she stirred the tea. 'Strong enough?'

'Yes, fine, thank you.'

Handing me the cup and saucer, the steam rising from the freshly poured tea, she sat back down and poured herself a cup. More silence, except for the sound of me slurping the drink. 'Delicious,' I concurred.

There was a sudden commotion in the garden. The two of us leant forward to look at the event unfolding. Two nuns, in their habits, with arms outstretched, chasing the resident cat, a white macaw firmly locked in its mouth. There was a screeching and cawing and flapping of wings as the cat darted back and forth. Eventually one of the orderlies grabbed the cat and released the frightened bird, which flew up on to the roof. I looked at Constance and holding onto our stomachs we both roared with laughter.

Once we had composed ourselves Constance turned to me.

'What?' I said.

'Shall I pray for you?'

'I'm ready... if you are,' I said.

91. SISTER CONSTANCE

Wednesday 25 July 1990

I am sad to report the death of, Henry Walker.

Yesterday, I left my glasses in his room and so decided to pop in and retrieve them. When I knocked on the door there was no answer and so I pushed it open and immediately saw that he had collapsed in his chair. I responded quickly, pulled the chord for help and started CPR. But it was no use. He had gone.

I don't know what came over me but when the paramedics arrived, I sobbed. I prattled on while they tried to revive him. But I knew he was no longer there.

I picked up an unsealed envelope addressed to his daughter, Wren, and I have to confess to peaking inside. There was a sheet of paper, a letter he must have only just written, a cheque and a card. What I could see of the letter was moving and I was grateful to have seen it. I assume his wife will send it on to her.

Yesterday, we prayed together. I anointed his head with oil and he recited Psalm 23 from the King James Bible. 'The Lord is my shepherd; I shall not want. He maketh me to lie down in green pastures: he leadeth me beside the still waters.'

This was predictable as he had told me he loved the poetry of the King James, however, he decided to quote the last sentence from the Good News Bible. 'I know that your goodness and love will be with me all my life; and your house will be my home as long as I live.'

'Oh, Henry, you are full of surprises,' I said to him.

'You have surprised me too,' he replied. 'I am proud to call you, my friend. I can honestly say you have saved my life.'

'Not saved your life Henry, that is too much, just shown you something of the pearl you lost.'

'Thank you,' he said, and taking hold of my wooden cross from my garment, raised it to his lips and kissed it.

§

Rest in peace, Henry, I shall miss you.

EPILOGUE

WREN

Wednesday 25 July 2012

I am now seventy-two years old and still happily married to David. We ride our tandem on country roads and although we struggle with various ailments we support each other—our love as fresh as when David proposed to me in a red sailed Mirror—all those years ago.

As I grow old myself, I have been reminded of those I have lost, recently thinking of my father and when he died.

I was in the garden with David clearing out the shed. The sun was bright, and the garden desperately needed some rain. I had just asked David to get me a glass of water when I heard the telephone ring in the kitchen.

It was Vivien, and immediately I felt nauseous and dizzy sensing my father had died. Vivien said a nun had been with him that day and had tried to give him CPR but to no avail. The ambulance arrived promptly but it was too late. Vivien assured me that he hadn't suffered.

I rang Vivien back a week after the funeral had taken place. She wasn't keen to talk to me apart from tell me that the same nun who had been with my father when he died, had been visiting him every week for six months.

I was glad, hoping that maybe she had helped him in his last days.

I tried to cry for my father but failed.

I thought of Walter and the tears came easily.

I think of Florence, and what a long life she lived.

With both our children grown and flown, once a fortnight, David and I would spend the weekend with her at Craigmore. There was always a list of jobs to complete and we worked hard to make sure we got through it. Usually, David fixed things while I cooked and cleaned. We then sat with Florence and she told us all the family news. She was remarkable and there was hardly anything wrong with her until the last few months of her life in 2002. David and I drove to see her in Southend General Hospital. The nurses smiled at us and nodded towards the first bed, the smell of disinfectant hitting us while the noise of a floor cleaner hummed passed. As soon as Florence saw me, she pulled herself up in the bed and reached out. 'Hello dear,' she said, with a big smile on her face.

'Mum, how are you?' I said.

'I'm dead, but I won't lie down.'

'Mum, please stop saying that.'

'Oh, don't worry yourself so much my darling one.'

I re-organised her bedding while David listened to her chatting away enthusiastically. 'How did you sleep?' he asked.

'Not very well. All night there has been a baby at the bottom of my bed crying.'

'There are no babies in this ward,' he said.

'I was sure I heard a baby,' she told him.

'Maybe you were dreaming?'

'Yes, probably.'

Florence was frail and characteristically stubborn, refusing to use the nebulizer, which would have helped clear her lungs.

Later that evening, David and I went to Craigmore. A spread of purple Gladioli filled the vase in the hall, tall stems fanning out like a peacock's tail.

Craigmore had grown old, even older than Florence. It had many ailments, creaking floorboards, leaking windows, rusty pipes. David, with tool kit in hand, set about mending and repairing. I, meanwhile, cooked the supper. Afterwards, I went in and out of rooms picking up small items from around the house, holding them close to my chest: a jug covered in orange trees by Crown Ducal—a lace doily—a brooch, my eyes filling with tears.

David made some hot chocolate and lit the fire. The granddaughter clock chimed three times when it was meant to chime eight, missing out the quarter past and half past. It was unsettling but then the visits to Craigmore were unsettling. Walter, having been absent for over two decades was bad enough, but Florence not being present in the house was just unfathomable.

The next morning, I watered the garden and wound the clock even though the chimes rang out the wrong hour. I wanted to hear the familiar sound filling the house because then all would be well. Except it wasn't.

On the drive back to the hospital, I was deeply saddened. Florence's head was fixed to the pillow; she was breathless, and a little disorientated. 'I don't know where I am... but you know dear, don't you?'

'Yes, Mum, you are in Southend General.'

'I was here a lot during the war.'

'To visit Daniel?'

'My dear boy... I should never have written that letter.'

'What letter?'

'The one I sent to your father. He came and took you away.'

Stroking Florence's hair, I tried to reassure her, 'It doesn't matter now. He sent me back to you.'

'Yes, he did, but I missed you, all those years when I didn't see you grow up.'

'We have had so many more years together now. You have watched me grow old.'

Florence laughed. 'You have watched me grow even older. I'm ninety-eight you know.'

'You are quite a remarkable woman.'

'It's your birthday tomorrow, Wren,' she said. 'I would make you a cake if I could only get out of here.'

'You mustn't worry, David is taking me out for a meal. We will be back to see you in a few days.'

'The first ten years were the hardest, you know,' she said.

Removing a piece of stray hair caught in Florence's mouth I said, 'What do you mean?'

'Grow old with me, the best is yet to come, and then he died.' She was sad, reflective. 'I didn't want to live longer than Walter.'

'But you are so wise,' I said, 'such good company.'

'Wisdom doesn't necessarily come with age, but I am glad to be good company.' Reaching out, she put her arms around my shoulders and gently pulled me down onto the bed. 'The good Lord is keeping me here,' she whispered, 'I suppose he has his reasons, but I can't imagine what they are. I'm ready to go now.' Kissing my cheek, she released me. 'If you are going back to the house, please take the flowers in the hall.'

'We are driving straight back home as David has a couple of meetings. I'll phone your neighbour and she can collect the flowers. We will be back to see you in three days,' I said.

'All right, dear, tatty bye,' she said, waving as David and I left the ward.

On the morning after my birthday, the phone rang just as I placed my feet on the bedroom carpet, the soft pile resting in-between my toes. It was George, his voice was shaky, 'She's gone, Wren,' he said, 'she died in the early hours of this morning.'

'Oh, George, I am so sorry. Were you with her?'

'Yes. I am glad for that at least.'

'We will come now,' I said.

'There's no rush. You must be shattered with all the travelling. Come in a few days.'

Placing the phone down, the news of Florence's death rested on me like a murder of crows: solid, black, and menacing. David placed his hand on my back and like a cloak draped himself around me.

The funeral was well attended. People came from miles around. We held the wake at Craigmore. The house was bursting with Florence's grandchildren, great grandchildren, and numerous family friends.

When everyone had left, I sat in the front room with David, George, and his wife. The familiar green velvet chair looked expectant. 'You must take the clock with you tonight, Wren. It always belonged to you,' said George. 'Mum made it clear that you should have it. We mustn't leave valuables in the house as it might get burgled.'

'Really?' said David.

'It's a common occurrence. Burglars get wind of someone dying and they enter the house within a few days. Anything of any real value or sentimental worth should be removed tonight. We can do the rest later.'

'The clock has remained in the same place for the past sixty-two years,' I said.

'I know, but you have to take it now,' George said, placing his hand on my hand.

When we left the house, David and I put the clock on the back seat of the car, wrapped in a blanket. To my surprise, Amy married her soldier, William, in 1993 and in the summer Florence died, he was, in the most unlikely of transformations, to be priested at St Paul's Cathedral. I thought the clock a fitting present. I have grown fond of William, and despite my concerns, he was the best match for my daughter.

§

I miss Florence. I talk to her sometimes. I cry for no apparent reason. She lingers in my life, chatting to me about her day, her aches, and pains. I see her smiling or hear her cough in another room. She follows me around the garden, her voice brushing against the silence of an afternoon. She notices flowers in bud, and she comments on the tomatoes in the greenhouse.

I am not free of her memory.

I don't want to be.

It is comforting.

I just want to hold her once more, wrap my arms around her middle, cling to her as a four-year-old would. The loss is like toothache. However hard I pretend it's not there—it nags and nags—until I acknowledge it.

§

This year, twenty-two years after my father's death, Vivien sent me a large envelope containing my father's memoirs and a letter. 'I should have sent these to you years ago.' She wrote. 'I don't even know why I didn't. I hope you can forgive me.' Having read through them several times, I am astounded at my father's recollections. There are so many parallel stories that we have both documented but obviously I saw them differently from him. Still, I am happy to have his writings as they are a window into his love for my mother and his love for me. I found it cathartic reading them.

It was the letter that most surprised me. Inside was a postcard of *The light of the World* by Holman Hunt and a cheque.

Tuesday 24 July 1990
My darling Wren,

AMANDA COWLEY

Today I had a revelation and I wanted to tell you about it.

I have been having visits from a nun called Sister Constance and she has helped me see that grief destroyed my faith and I finally understand how I had mistreated those closest to me.

I am so sorry, Wren, for neglecting you. I should have taken you in my arms and held you tight. I should have said how proud I was of you for becoming a teacher and for raising Patrick and Amy. I may not be able to make it up to you now, and for that, I am truly sorry. I only hope you can find it in your heart to forgive me.

Sister Constance helped me see the bigger picture. When your mother died, I was distraught. I blamed myself, and ultimately, I blamed God. I now trust that God has restored your mother completely, and that I never lost my salvation, only my joy.

Today, when Sister Constance prayed for me, I felt the Holy Spirit. I do hope that you have found a lasting happiness as I have in returning to my first love.

The sun is flooding into my room, and I am no longer restless. All is well with my soul, although, I must confess to having an overwhelming tiredness. I do hope we can meet soon. I have missed you.

I love you.

Dad x

PS. I enclose some money for a return flight. Please try and come soon. I have so much to tell you.

§

297

The date on the letter was the day my father died. I was flabbergasted.

I began to cry and then I sobbed. Uncontrollable sobbing. It took me a while to recover.

It is the letter I had always wanted from my father, and now I have it, twenty-two years after his death. I am, at last, able to forgive him for his inadequacies and appreciate his struggles and I can move on.

Once a month, I take the train from Chichester and then the tube to St Paul's Cathedral, where I meet Amy. Walking up the steps, we pass through the revolving doors and proceed to the Northern Transept. In front of us is *The Light of The World*, in its splendid gold frame. We sit for twenty minutes and pray. Time and time again, I have looked into the face of Christ framed within the crown of thorns and a bright halo. The glow of a lamp highlights his tunic and gives life to his eyes set in a light varnish of Van Dyke brown. Inscribed on the bottom of the frame, in black, are the words from Revelation, *Behold I stand at the door and knock, if any man hear my voice, and open the door, I will come in to him, and will sup with him, and he with me.*

I was a young girl when I opened that door and invited Jesus in.

§

I have always missed, Queenie, my birth mother. Not knowing her scent. The normality of her.

What I experienced was the craziness of a life without her.

A father who couldn't cope, a father who was locked in grief, a father who I found impossible to access.

It was Florence and Walter who picked up the pieces of my fragmented life.

But as I hold Queenie and Henry close to my heart, I sense *faith* and *doubt* are telling the time like the hands on a clock face.

Faith is the hour hand, steady but moving slowly, whereas *Doubt* is the minute hand, trying to dislodge *faith* with every passing beat. They show me that within the hours of my life, there will be moments when I will be in working order and moments when I will be wound up or broken, but not irrevocably. There will be times when the chimes salute me, and times when they will mourn with me. But now I trust, that after the hollowing out of grief, there is, in the slow turning of time, a breathing in of *hope*.

There seems to be a perpetual sense of rhythm that is unstoppable, despite the cessation of a clock's tick tock, or the sudden halt of a loved one's beating heart. A rhythm that is independent of our whims and our frets, one that resonates deep within our very being: loving, steadfast—and timeless—the still small voice of God.

§

The Retreat by Henry Vaughan

1621–1695

Happy those early days! when I
Shined in my angel infancy.
Before I understood this place
Appointed for my second race,
Or taught my soul to fancy aught
But a white, celestial thought;
When yet I had not walked above
A mile or two from my first love,
And looking back, at that short space,
Could see a glimpse of His bright face;
When on some gilded cloud or flower
My gazing soul would dwell an hour,
And in those weaker glories spy
Some shadows of eternity;
Before I taught my tongue to wound
My conscience with a sinful sound,
Or had the black art to dispense
A several sin to every sense,
But felt through all this fleshly dress
Bright shoots of everlastingness.
O, how I long to travel back,
And tread again that ancient track!
That I might once more reach that plain
Where first I left my glorious train,
From whence th' enlightened spirit sees
That shady city of palm trees.
But, ah! my soul with too much stay
Is drunk, and staggers in the way.
Some men a forward motion love;
But I by backward steps would move,
And when this dust falls to the urn,
In that state I came, return.

After ten years in TV, from runner to Art Director, Amanda Cowley embarked on a writing career. She became an editor on numerous professional projects, co-wrote Paul Cowley's autobiography, Thief Prisoner Soldier Priest (Hodder & Stoughton 2020) and is in the process of writing her autobiography and a second novel, Normansfield.

Amanda is also a landscape painter and has exhibited in numerous galleries including: Cadogan Contemporary, South Kensington, and gallery@oxo, South Bank.

A Mile Or Two From My First Love is her first novel. Some names and places have been changed but it was inspired by the true story of her grandmother's death and the dislocation which followed between her grandfather and her mother. Amanda last saw her Grandfather in Chelsea in 1986, and the nun, a fictional character, was inspired by learning there was a convent attached to the care home where he died.

Cover illustration: Amanda Cowley
Author photo: Phoebe Cowley
Design: Ella Knight